PRAISE FOR THE AUTHOR

Praise for *My So-Called Bollywood Life*

Winner of the 2019 RITA award for YA romance of the year

NPR Best Books of 2018

"A strong, winsome heroine; a solid supporting cast, including family; and a romantic triangle that rivals any Bollywood plot."

—*Booklist*

"A delightful and humorous debut."

—*Kirkus Reviews* (starred review)

"Sweet, sassy, and totally swoon-worthy!"

—Ellen Oh, author of the Prophecy series

Praise for *Radha & Jai's Recipe for Romance*

NPR Best Books of 2021

"Sharma deftly crafts a sweet romance steeped in food, dance, and Desi culture."

—*Publishers Weekly*

"This novel offers up a charming, swoon-worthy rom-com with all the best ingredients. The real treat, though, is the emotional authenticity."

—*The Bulletin*

"A tasty treat! Nisha Sharma always delights."

—Meg Cabot, #1 *New York Times* bestselling author of
The Princess Diaries

"A delicious YA rom-com full of heart, flavor, and just enough heat."

—Julie Murphy, *New York Times* bestselling author of *Dumplin'*

"A sumptuous tale of dance, food, and culture. I savored every last page!"

—Pintip Dunn, *New York Times* bestselling author of the Forget
Tomorrow series

Praise for *The Legal Affair*

"An engaging love story peppered with intrigue and insight."

—*Kirkus Reviews*

"Sharma's sexy sequel to *The Takeover Effect* sizzles, and fans of workplace romances will be aching to find out what happens next in the Singh Family trilogy."

—*Booklist*

Praise for *The Takeover Effect*

"Sharma effortlessly blends the rituals of the culture she celebrates on the page."

—*Entertainment Weekly*

"Sharma's latest is highly recommended for lovers of romance involving big business and family drama."

—*Library Journal* (starred review)

Praise for *Dating Dr. Dil*

"With a light touch, Sharma immerses readers in a deeply emotional and witty story of love arranged and love inevitable."

—*Booklist* (starred review)

"Buoyant!"

—*New York Times Book Review*

"The character development is top notch, and readers will love seeing the protagonists realize that love can be a welcome surprise. Verdict: This first book in Sharma's 'If Shakespeare Was an Auntie' series is a recommended first-tier purchase."

—*Library Journal*

"The perfect addition to any rom-com lover's shelf."

—Emily Henry, #1 *New York Times* bestselling author of *People We Meet on Vacation*

"Bursting with character, spicy tension, and laughs, *Dating Dr. Dil* is the enemies-to-lovers dream book!"

—Tessa Bailey, *New York Times* bestselling author of *It Happened One Summer*

"What a joy! *Dating Dr. Dil* is further proof that Nisha Sharma is a megatalent who can do it all. Anything Nisha Sharma writes is an auto-buy for me."

—Meg Cabot, #1 *New York Times* bestselling author of *The Princess Diaries*

The Karma Map

ALSO BY NISHA SHARMA

Young Adult Romance

My So-Called Bollywood Life
Radha & Jai's Recipe for Romance

Adult Romance

The Singh Family Trilogy

The Takeover Effect
The Legal Affair

If Shakespeare Was an Auntie Trilogy

Dating Dr. Dil

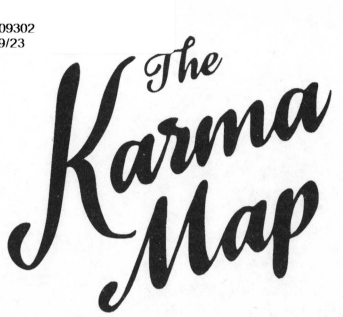

The Karma Map

a novel

NISHA SHARMA

SKYSCAPE

▥ SKYSCAPE

Text copyright © 2023 by Nisha Seesan

Published by Skyscape, New York

www.apub.com

Amazon, the Amazon logo, and Skyscape are trademarks of Amazon.com, Inc., or its affiliates.

ISBN-13: 9781662500770 (hardcover)
ISBN-13: 9781662500787 (paperback)
ISBN-13: 9781662500794 (digital)

Cover design by Lucy Kim

Cover image: © Jose Miguel Moya / Getty Images; © Tupungato / Shutterstock; © Cavan Images – Offset / Shutterstock; © Zhukovskyi / Shutterstock

Printed in the United States of America

First edition

In loving memory of Sushil and Mohani Punj

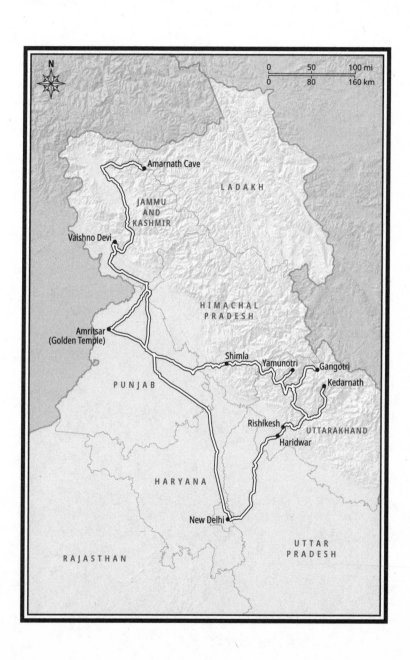

AUTHOR'S NOTE

I was born and raised in the US, but my identity has always been tethered to India because of my relationship with my immigrant parents and grandparents. However, in this book, my perspective is different from those who either live in India or have immigrated themselves. I want to respect and honor everyone's experiences, but it's important for me to share that this book is limited to my North Indian diasporic lens.

I was very young during my last religious pilgrimage in India. It was a transformative moment, but the memory is hazy with time. I leaned heavily on family, sensitivity readers, and fact checkers for this project, which is why I'm asking your forgiveness from page one: if you see something that is not accurate about the locations in the story, I take full responsibility.

I also want to stress that as a Hindu, I have profound appreciation for my faith, which is why I condemn all casteism, homophobia, and/or prejudiced ritual practices in Hinduism (applied as a blanket term for the various forms, sects, and interpretations of regional practice) and associated with religious pilgrimages.

There is so much I wanted to say with this book and so much I wanted to do. But the truest message is joy. This is my love story to India. To its beauty and complexity. Here's a story featuring second-generation South Asians. It's a rom-com with a grumpy girl and a sunshine boy who are running away and finding truth. This story explores identity and culture and how people sometimes aren't accepted by anyone other than those with the same experience.

Most importantly, it's about loving yourself and learning how to love someone else.

I hope you enjoy.

Trigger Warnings:

- Bullying (prologue on page and referenced in subsequent chapters off page)
- Addiction (off page)
- Homophobia (referenced in discussion)
- Casteism (referenced in discussion)

Prologue

New Jersey

Four Months to Departure: Flight AI102 Traveling JFK to DEL

Tara Bajaj knew the exact moment when her life began to fall apart.

Since her freshman year of high school, she'd worked diligently to hide her skeletons in the back of a very deep closet. In the front of the closet, she positioned racks of beautiful clothes, a social-media feed filled with parties, a spot on the Rutgers High Bollywood dance team, and an attitude so frigid no one questioned if her authority was insecurity.

But then she'd made a mistake. She'd said yes to a date with Jai Patel.

Thoughts of her ex flooded her mind as she left the dance director's office, chin held high even as bitterness clogged her throat.

Jai had always been good and kind even though he was on a rival dance team. He'd flirted with her at a community event and then asked her to dance. Their chemistry had been undeniable.

And he didn't run when he learned the truth about Tara and her family.

Instead, he wanted her to show those skeletons to everyone, which she couldn't do. So after two years together, they broke up, and Tara was left alone while she watched him fall in love with someone else.

She barely registered the hitch in her stride as she walked down the hallway on heeled boots, ignoring everyone's stares as she passed.

She had finally had enough.

Maybe it was seeing Jai and his new girlfriend's happiness that had her wanting that kind of honesty in her life. Or maybe it was realizing she'd been hiding for so long she was losing parts of herself. She was becoming something shameful.

And when her so-called best friend tried to get Jai's dance team disqualified from the regional competition by spreading a rumor about cheating, Tara knew she had to break character; otherwise, she'd never be the same.

She pushed open the door of her Bollywood dance team's rehearsal studio at the end of the hall. The team was sitting on the floor, legs spread out, stretching to a Bollywood song playing on the stereo. Laughter echoed around the room, bouncing off the mirrors and hard-wood floor.

In the middle of the circle sat Umma, with her short, curly hair pulled back, accentuating her high cheekbones and perfectly winged eyeliner. Her smile fell when she saw Tara at the door.

Someone shut off the music.

"What are you doing here?" Umma said, getting to her feet. "This is a private rehearsal. You're not on the team anymore."

Obviously, Tara thought bitterly. They'd kicked her out via text message two days ago after she admitted to everyone that she'd been the one who warned Jai Patel about the rumors. The Princeton Academy of the Arts and Sciences team had been able to stop the train wreck before it cost them a spot in the competition, because she gave them the heads-up.

Umma viewed it as an act of betrayal, so much so that she couldn't even tell Tara to her face that she'd been ousted.

"I'm not here to dance," Tara said. She knew her cheeks were probably tearstained, but she couldn't give a shit right now. "I wanted to let you know that I went to the director. I told her that you're the one who spread lies and rumors about the Bollywood Beats dance team because you wanted them disqualified just so you'd have a shot at winning."

Umma's jaw dropped.

She straightened, recovering from the shock within two bats of her long lashes. "Our rivals—and *your* ex—are still in the competition, so obviously whatever information you shared isn't true. I'll just go talk to the director and clear this up. I can't believe you'd try to sabotage your own team—"

"I showed her," Tara said. She took her phone out of her jeans pocket and held it up. "I showed her all the texts from the group chat. The ones where you admit to finding out some gossip about Jai's girlfriend. I showed her that you started the rumors, what you said and who you said it to. You may have kicked me off this team, but there is no way I'm going to sit back and let you try to cheat again."

The dance room was pin-drop silent now. "There's nothing the director can do," Umma said with a shaky laugh. She turned to the dance group. "So what? A few rumors never hurt—"

"It's bullying," Tara said, cutting Umma off. "Rutgers High has a zero-tolerance policy for bullying. And because I happened to have the group chat up, I showed her some of the other stuff you've done. My only regret is I didn't come forward sooner. You, all of you, are disqualified from all competitions from this moment forward. The director is calling your parents right now, and there's a chance you'll be on academic probation during the investigation. The director will tell you herself, but I couldn't let her have all the fun."

Her humorless smile felt wrong, but it happened before she could stop herself.

This time, the team reacted en masse. People started talking all at once. Umma—the friend with whom Tara had spent so much time, taken so many selfies, sneaked out to party, and spent countless hours dancing—began to cry.

"You were part of this team! No—you're going down with us. I'll make it happen. Why would you do that and jeopardize your high school record? Or your Berkeley college admission?"

Tara hated the small bit of pleasure that she felt in this moment. "I'm not on the team anymore, remember? I won't be investigated."

"Get out," Umma snapped, pointing a finger at the door. "I should've known that Sunny was right when he told me not to trust you. I thought I knew you; we all knew you. But he called it. You're a backstabber after all."

Sunny.

Tara's heart began to pound. Umma's on-and-off boyfriend of the last four years knew about Tara's skeletons. He was the only one at the school who had proof of them, too. She'd made a critical error by forgetting about him. It had been so long she never thought he'd open up about Tara's past and their history.

"What," Tara said slowly, "did Sunny say about me, exactly?"

Umma brushed away her tears angrily. "That you didn't want us to date. That you liked him and made yourself look like a total fool over a boy. That you lied about me so he wouldn't be interested. I have receipts, and I sure as hell will be posting about it. You can't ruin all our lives and then not expect karma to kick you in the ass, Tara."

"Whatever you think you know about me isn't even half the truth," Tara said. She could hear her breath growing shallower. "Sunny doesn't know anything."

Umma whipped out her phone and tapped her screen a few times, then held it up like she'd just won an award. "Go ahead. See if I'm fooling around now."

Tara snatched Umma's phone out of her hand and swallowed the metallic taste in the back of her throat as she read the messages between Umma and Sunny.

She tried to break us up.

She's really manipulative. I don't think you guys should be friends.

I've known her family forever because our parents go to the same temple. Trust me, I've seen how she can be.

No, she thought. No, there was no way she was going to put up with lies like this, either. She'd come so far; she would not stay quiet now.

"What do you have to say?" Umma said, taking her phone back. The team stood behind her, quietly watching. "Now everyone is going to know what kind of person you really are. Even those text messages you shared with the director won't—"

"What did I tell you about fucking with me?" Tara said evenly. She dropped her bag to the floor. "Hold, please."

Tara quickly located the text chain that she hadn't used in years, scrolled to the beginning of the conversation, and took two screenshots. She heard the team whisper as she worked her magic.

"She's got nothing."

"She's all talk. There is no way the director thinks we're bullies. That's insane."

After tagging Umma, with the press of a button, she posted the conversation she'd had with Sunny before the start of their freshman year. An echo of buzzing phones was the sound of her victory.

"I have screenshots, too. It's been nice knowing you, Umma." Tara then turned and strode out the door. Shocked faces stared back at her in the semi-empty hallway. People with phones in their hands and mouths ajar.

For the first time in a long while, Tara thought of her sister. Her brave, smart, sharp older sister, who would know exactly what to say to make her feel better. She hadn't seen her in four years. *I wish you were here, Didi.*

Tara held herself together until she reached her car in the student lot and slipped behind the wheel. Then the tears began to fall in earnest.

1

New Jersey

Five Hours to Departure: Flight AI102 Traveling JFK to DEL

Postcard dated July 1—two years ago:

You were only eight when Mom lectured you on karma. You used to walk around parroting her textbook, saying, "It's commonly known as a universal principle of actions following an accumulation of good or bad deeds in the cycle of life." I learned the same lesson, and I thought I understood, but it wasn't until I was much older that I felt like I finally got it, thanks to a meme I found online. Karma is only a bitch if you are.

Miss you, munchkin.

Love,

Didi

Tara's finger hovered over the big red delete button for a short, shallow breath before she pressed it.

A pop-up flashed across the screen, asking her to type the word *DELETE*.

"Seriously? You can't make this easy for me?"

She rage-typed the letters and clicked okay.

Your profile has been deleted.

Done. All 1,605 pictures, videos, and memories. All nine thousand-plus followers who'd first loved her, then shamed her.

Before she could second-guess her decision, she went to her other social-media platforms and quickly completed the same process.

When the last one disappeared, she let out a ragged breath.

She'd done it. She'd finally cut the cord. She was no longer connected to Before-Tara.

Before-Tara would've wanted to know what everyone was doing and where they were hanging out. Before-Tara stayed on social media so she could keep tabs on what people were saying about her. Before-Tara had become a doom scroller who lurked in comments sections and read every vile, hateful, snarky message until her eyes were bloodshot from lack of sleep.

Most importantly, Before-Tara knew that she had to stay plugged in because her friends were no longer her friends. Her friends used to love her, used to confide in her, but now those same people spread rumors about her, even though she'd done everything right for the first time in years.

They were the reason the entire school had turned on her. She used to walk down the hallway and random kids would say hi to her. People that she didn't even know. When she became public enemy number one, those same strangers would whisper names or block lunch tables or shove things in her locker because Umma told them something malicious.

Tara's parents and her therapist urged her to delete her profiles months ago, but she just couldn't do it. Not when she had to face those people every single day at Rutgers High. If she didn't know what they were saying about her, then she couldn't brace herself for the number of times she was called bitch, backstabber, or traitor in a day. She was essentially walking onto a battlefield without understanding what her opponents were bringing to the war.

But graduation was officially over, and she'd never have to talk to anyone at Rutgers High again. Now she was After-Tara. After-Tara had no social-media presence. After-Tara didn't have to be afraid of the skeletons in her closet.

Finally.

Her heart felt lighter. She was free.

Sort of.

Now she had a summer job that reminded her of everything she was before high school. She had to get reacquainted with her secrets.

But would anyone care?

She giggled, then slapped a hand over her mouth. No. No one would care or even know where she was. She would be completely off the grid and, within weeks, a distant memory. Especially since everyone's social-media feed was about to be filled with senior-week celebrations at the beach while she would embark on her holy-girl summer volume 2.0.

"Tara!" her mother called from downstairs. "It's time to go to the airport. Are you ready?"

Was she ready to revisit a part of her life she never thought she'd voluntarily have to experience again? Sure.

She stood from behind her desk and shoved her laptop, cords, and notebook inside her backpack. Her writing prompts—the colorful stack of her favorite world-travel postcards her older sister, Savitri, had sent her over the years—were safely tucked in her notebook. After her parents and Savitri's explosive fight years ago, the postcards were the only piece of her sister she had left. They were her most prized possession.

Tara slung the backpack over her shoulder and checked her desk to make sure she had gotten everything she needed. The printout of the letter from Berkeley stood out like a sore thumb from its place next to her mouse pad. The school had accepted her formal withdrawal better than her parents had when she decided that she wanted nothing to do with her old dance community.

Folded neatly underneath was a basic acceptance letter to a small liberal-arts college in Pennsylvania. It had been her safety school, and she'd only applied to it because its custom creative-writing major had caught her eye for some reason. She'd never intended to go since it was so isolated, but now she realized that the safety school was a blessing in disguise. More importantly, she was lucky the college was still willing to offer her a partial scholarship; otherwise, she would've been stuck going to the same university where her mother taught religious studies.

"Tara!" her mother yelled again.

"I'm coming," she shouted back.

She checked her suitcase she'd left next to the door, everything that would accompany her during her two months in India. Sure, she would've preferred to spend her time on the beach instead of reliving childhood memories, but she needed the money. Tara was just going to have to get through the trip as best as she could.

Her father stepped into her bedroom doorway, crossing his arms over his chest as he sized up her things. He wore one of the dozens of free merch shirts featuring cartoon characters that he'd received from his marketing department. It contrasted with the long streak of white and red powder on his forehead from his morning trip to the local temple.

"Do you need help with your bag?"

Tara stiffened, her muscles tight with irritation. "I'd prefer if you could help get me out of this trip, but if you want to carry my stuff, that's fine, too."

"Tara, this is going to be a stroll in the park for you." Her father gave her suitcase a little spin, then tested the weight. "You've been taking these pilgrimages since you were barely old enough to walk. Not to mention the fact that you were a student on this exact tour four years ago. Think of it as easy money. Which, might I remind you, you need to pay us back for all the expenses we accrued for admission fees, application fees, and college tours."

"I still don't understand why I can't get a job at your office. I bet all the other executives hired their kids. I'm not like Savitri Didi—"

"I told you already. It has nothing to do with your sister's history at the company. My office made their hires for the summer, and I can't be showing favoritism. Now, if you want to work in the theme parks . . ."

Tara made a gagging sound. "Wasn't it torture enough that you dragged us to those hot, crowded parks for years?" To this day, she still wanted to throw up at the smell of buttered popcorn.

Her father raised his brow. "You loved it when you were a kid."

"I'm not a kid anymore, and I haven't been for a long time. Between the parks and the temple tours, I don't know how people never figured out that I was a total weirdo with culty religious parents and a dad who is obsessed with roller coasters."

He held up his hands in surrender. "You're a weirdo with life skills. Now, this summer is an opportunity for you to reflect on what you want in your future."

"The only reflecting I'm going to do is on how much money I'll be making to pay my debt and to cover book expenses for college. India in the summer is literally a hellscape, Dad. Even if we'll be in the mountains for most of the trip."

"Be respectful!" her mother shouted from downstairs.

Tara rolled her eyes just as her father's narrowed, as if to tell her to stop it.

"I'm just surprised Mom isn't insisting on going with me," Tara said, motioning to the door.

"You're lucky she has those theology summer sessions," her father replied with a grin. "Since you're on your own, maybe you can look at this trip as an opportunity to cultivate your art."

"Is that what you told Savitri?"

Tara regretted saying the words as soon as they were out of her mouth. Two references to her sister in the span of five minutes was a lot. Her father still kept in touch with Savitri without her mother's knowledge, but it hurt him not to have seen his oldest in years. She could see the sadness reflected in the sheen in his eyes.

"Dad, I'm sorry, I—"

"I'm telling you now," he said softly, straightening from his relaxed position against the doorjamb. "You can work on your short stories. You used to write all the time. And you'll have great pictures for your social media. Those temples are gorgeous."

She shifted the strap of her backpack, reveling in that light, floating feeling in her gut. "I deleted them."

"Deleted what?"

"All of my social-media accounts. Every single one of them. Finally."

Her father's jaw dropped. "What? When?"

"Just now."

There was pounding on the staircase. Her mother appeared in the doorway next to her father. The bright-red streak of sindoor in her hairline stood out like a beacon, and her gold nose ring glinted.

Usually, Tara's mother looked at her with horror, but this time, she had hope in her eyes. "Do you feel okay? You were so against doing it for a long time."

"I'm turning over a new leaf," Tara said, motioning to her bookshelves crammed with romance and fantasy novels, dance trophies, and pictures of her former friends. There was even one of Jai, which she kept around to remind her how badly she'd screwed things up with such a great guy. "And I don't want people who've already made assumptions about me to find me."

Her parents shared a look, the same sort of silent communication that used to drive her absolutely bonkers.

"Beta," her father said, "we've been supportive of whatever you want to do online for a while now, because frankly, we don't understand it. Getting rid of something that no longer gives you peace is a good thing, but you shouldn't be doing it because you want to hide."

Her mother nodded. "We talked about you disconnecting gradually, one platform at a time. Otherwise, it's going to create a withdrawal-like reaction, and you may go back to—"

"I've been disconnecting for the last few weeks," Tara said. Which was true. Sort of. Automatically, she checked her phone, her thumb hovering over where one of her apps used to be. She almost cursed out loud. "Oh, look at the time," she said, and slipped her phone in her back pocket.

"I think I need to see your cell," her mother said, holding out her hand, palm up. "I don't know if I trust—"

"Mom!"

"Tara, you've been so difficult all through high school," her mother said shrilly. Her open hand closed into a fist. "You stopped coming to temple with us these last months, you withdrew from a perfectly good school, you started Western science–based therapy. Look at this from our perspective."

"Yeah, and all I see is that you started all of this!"

"How *dare* you—"

Her father clapped as if he were trying to get the attention of a boardroom full of executives instead of his wife and his eighteen-year-old daughter. "Let's not ruin the last few hours we have together. This is still progress, Tara. We can manage withdrawal if we have to. Now you have all this free time to—"

"Think about my future?" she said, cutting him off. "You sound like a broken record." Tara grabbed the handle of her suitcase and pushed it between her parents and into the hallway. "I just want to make my money and come home. Then when I get to college, I can figure out who I want to be and what I want to do." Bending at the knees, she lifted her bag and headed downstairs.

Her parents started whispering behind her until her father's voice carried over the sound of her struggling with the weight of her bag.

Their argument grew louder as she made it to the landing until she heard her father say, "You tell her!"

Great, what now? She turned around and waited.

"Uh, Tara?" her mother said.

"Yeah?"

"Hahn Ji," her mother corrected.

"Hahn Ji," Tara parroted back, a reflex she'd learned as a child from her mother's language lessons.

"I know that you've done temple trips with your father and me plenty of times," her mother said, coming down the staircase one hesitant step after another. "And your sister . . . well, she responded in an extreme way—"

"If you're going to go on another rant about Didi, please save it."

Her parents shared that unspoken communication again as they all stood in the foyer, staring at each other.

"I want to tell you about my first pilgrimage," her mother started. "As someone with experience, I think you should know a few things. I remember when I was your age—"

"Nope! No, thank you." Tara opened the front door. This was exactly why she'd decided to say yes to being a junior guide after she swore she'd never go back on another temple tour. Because anything was better than dealing with her pushy, invasive mother, who refused to take time to understand her daughters. "I am not interested in a journey down memory lane. Whenever you compare your experience to mine, we end up arguing. I'm just trying to get through this summer."

"No, I feel like we need to discuss this," her mother replied. "Now that you're a woman of a certain age, and by yourself without parental authority, you may experience certain desires—"

"Oh my god, I'm going to throw up," Tara said. She rushed out the door and called out over her shoulder. "I'll wait in the car for you two. With earplugs."

2

JFK Airport

Three Hours to Departure: Flight AI102 Traveling JFK to DEL

"Do you have everything you need?" Mama asked. She adjusted the straps on Silas's day pack for the hundredth time. "Snacks, copies of all of your identification, some bills tucked in a safe place?"

"Yes, I'm ready to go." Silas scanned the JFK terminal. It was bursting with large families pushing bag carts, employees hauling oversized luggage, and harried couples rushing from kiosk to ticket counter and back. On the other side of the glass windows, cars moved at a snail's pace, dropping off passengers at the curb. Some goodbyes were quick waves; others were long, teary farewells. Silas should've done the speedy drop-off with his mothers, but they insisted on coming inside.

Now, the three of them had been standing in front of security for ten minutes. If they had to wait any longer, Mom and Mama would both start crying.

"Mala, we raised him in New York," Mom said. "He's smart enough to take care of himself. Yes, India is different, but he'll be safe."

Silas looked down at the two women who were his whole world, and when he saw tears in both Mama's and Mom's eyes, he gave in and looped an arm around both of their shoulders. The waterworks had apparently already begun. "I love you both. I promise I'll be fine."

"I just don't understand why you're determined to work as a junior guide on a youth group temple tour," Mom said. "When we asked you if you were interested in this same trip right before high school started, you said no."

Silas rolled his eyes. "I wanted my first time in India to be with you two. Now that I've gone to Goa and I've explored the place where I was born, I can do this tour by myself without any regrets. And as a tour guide, I get to understand the whole process from a unique perspective."

Mama squeezed his waist. "You could've worked with us doing wedding photography and made the same amount of money. This season is going to be very busy now that people are hosting big weddings again."

Silas had been hearing the same complaints since he signed his contract with the temple's cultural society a month ago. "Both of you loved this trip."

"Not at first," they said in unison.

"Okay, but you both *met* on this temple trip. That's incredible. I get to experience your history."

He also wanted to do anything *but* wedding photography for the next few months, and he refused to hurt his moms' feelings by telling them that. This was a chance for him to try to expand the family business away from grueling weekend hours and the constant grind of drumming up more business. His moms never complained, but Silas knew that there was something different out there for all of them. There was something different for *him*.

Silas's parents hugged him harder, which only made him wonder if they were scared for him because they were reminded of how their über-religious families condemned their queer identities right before they left on their tour. Everyone had made amends now, and his moms had good relationships with their families, but Silas was familiar with the demons from the past. His moms had taught him the importance of honoring those memories and demons. His stomach fluttered at the thought of going into this trip unprepared to face his own.

"Silas D'Souza-Gupta?"

Silas turned, his jaw dropping. This man was beautiful. A Ranveer Singh doppelgänger. His mustache was enviable, and he wore a white kurta top stretched across broad shoulders, jeans, and flip-flops. A streak of red powder formed a line between his brows up to his hairline. He had a large backpack strapped to his wide shoulders and a tablet in one hand.

"Y-yes?" Silas croaked. He cleared his throat. "Yes?"

His mothers choked on their laughter next to him, and he shot them a dirty look.

The man stepped forward and held out a hand to shake. Silas swallowed and gripped it, hoping the Ranveer Singh look-alike wouldn't notice how sweaty his palm was. "I'm Neil. One of the tour guides. My wife, Chaya, will meet us in India. She is the one you interviewed with. I have our students gathered over there."

He motioned to a group of teenagers standing at a distance near the glass wall. They stared at their phones, either in the process of taking selfies or reading something. They looked like the most bored group of kids in the entire airport.

"Do you have your instructions?" Neil asked.

Silas looked at the kids and then back to his tour guide. "Yes. I got the info package. I'm ready to go."

"Wonderful," he said in a crisp accent that reminded Silas of Mama's mother. Her Delhi English had always seemed so cosmopolitan.

Neil turned to Silas's moms. "I heard you were former tour members, Mrs. D'Souza-Gupta, and, uh, Mrs. D'Souza-Gupta."

"I'm the only D'Souza-Gupta," Silas said. "I decided to hyphenate my last name when I was ten with my birth name and adopted name. I was adopted in Goa." The explanation rolled off his tongue after years of telling others why he had two South Asian last names that came from different parts of the Indian subcontinent.

Mom stepped forward. "Madhu Gupta. My wife, Mala. Please take care of our son. I know he's one of the junior guides, but I'm expecting you to bring him back safely."

"Mom!"

Neil laughed, and the sound was straight from the throat of a Bollywood action hero. "Don't worry, Mrs. Gupta. You've been on this trip yourself. You know how safe it is. We will be visiting some of the holiest places in India. And although Silas will be working, I can promise you he'll be blessed and protected."

"We were blessed and protected, too, and now we're married," Mama said.

Mom snorted.

Neil looked between the two women and then nodded. "Fair enough."

"Now, our baby is probably too innocent to fall in love just yet—" Mama started.

"Oh my god, will you stop?"

The moms both began chuckling.

"You two are the cause of my childhood trauma," Silas said flatly. And he hated that they were right. Not about his innocence, but about falling in love. It was highly unlikely that he'd find a soulmate-caliber match while hiking and busing to pilgrimage sites in the Himalayas.

Neil glanced at his watch again. "If you've said your goodbyes, let's get our students through security. Our second junior guide is waiting for us at the terminal. I sent her ahead to hold seats if possible."

"Okay." Silas let out a deep breath and faced his moms. He opened his arms so they could share another group hug. As soon as his parents started sniffling again, his own eyes dampened. "It's only for two months," Silas said, kissing the crown of both of his mothers' heads.

"We'll watch your social media for your videos," Mama said, brushing a tear from her eye.

"I packed you an extra camera battery in case you need it," Mom added, patting his backpack. "Along with print copies of our temple tour to go with your digital ones. I still don't understand why you want them."

"It's easier for me to lay them out side by side to see how much things have changed. I'll re-create some of the pictures for you." He hoped that would be enough of an explanation for why he was so adamant about getting all their tour pictures. He'd tell them about the competition later.

Mom squeezed his arm. "Call us when you get there."

"I will," he said. "Hey, think about taking some time off while I'm away."

They shifted, rolling their eyes at him. As if the very thought of a vacation during wedding season was preposterous.

"Ready?" Neil said, motioning to his tablet. The man was apparently a fan of punctuality.

"I'm ready," Silas said after one last hug from his family.

He waved at his moms. As they turned and walked away, panic fluttered in his chest. Their retreating backs became smaller and smaller, their linked hands swinging gently as they headed to the parking lot.

"You have a lot of things," Neil said at his side.

Silas turned to face his Ranveer Singh tour guide. "Excuse me?"

Neil motioned to his giant camera bag. A tripod stuck out of the corner. "You brought a lot of things. And you checked your bag?"

"Yeah, this is a bunch of camera stuff. I plan on taking pictures along the way. While I'm chaperoning, of course."

They started walking toward the group of kids. "We have ten students that are thirteen and fourteen years old," Neil said. "That's two students per junior guide, including myself and my wife, Chaya. You'll have to get their parents' permission for any photos that you use and post online, but I'm sure that Chaya and the other junior guides won't mind." He paused, then stroked a hand down his cheek. "I prefer if you only shot my left side."

"Sure. And I won't post pictures of the kids." Silas held up three fingers. "I promise."

Neil looked at his fingers with puzzlement.

Okay then. Silas put his hand down. "You know what? Never mind. Just know I'm more into the scenery than the group." He had a vision of doing a climate-change and population angle for his photos, where he'd compare the older pictures to the ones he'd take of himself standing where his moms had in their pictures decades ago. It was the perfect theme for a nature magazine photojournalism competition.

"The temples are beautiful," Neil replied. He paused again before they reached the group. "Do you have any questions for me before I introduce you to the students?"

Silas thought about the hours he'd spent poring over the tour guides, itinerary, rules, and training manual. His biggest concern was the language. He didn't speak anything other than English and high school Spanish.

"Just ah, nervous about being able to communicate, I guess." Not knowing Hindi or a regional language had always been a sore spot for Silas. He hated that it made him feel like he wasn't Indian enough. It was a stupid thought, and absolutely not true, but he couldn't help harboring some doubt.

Neil's mustache twitched. "Right. You'll be worrying more about the heat once we come down from the mountains than you'll worry about being able to communicate."

"Heat I can handle," he said. "Most weather, actually. I don't mind roughing it. I once spent a winter break at a camp in Alaska. Now that was rough."

Neil looked him up and down, one dark brow winging up in surprise. "Mm-hmm," he grunted. "We'll get along fine." With a nod, he motioned toward the group.

As they stopped in front of the students, Silas's concern mounted. Was he ready for this trip? The students looked like children. He knew nothing about children. Was he the same way right before he entered high school?

Neil stuck two fingers in his mouth and let out a sharp whistle. The sound was commanding enough to make every single student straighten their shoulders.

"This is your second junior guide, Silas D'Souza-Gupta."

Silas saw three girls in the back lean in and whisper to each other. One of them raised a hand, her sparkly nail polish glittering.

"Yes?" Neil said.

She turned to Silas. "Did you volunteer for this trip because you have no friends?"

Ouch, third-degree burns. "I'm on this trip because I want to be?"

"It seems pretty lame to me—"

He grinned. "Then I guess we're all going to be lame together, right?"

There was a resounding groan. A few guys snickered.

Neil snapped his fingers in the air. "Please make sure your passports and your tickets are in hand. We'll all be making our way through security now. Is everyone ready?"

After semicoherent mumbling from the group, Neil led the way as Silas stayed near the end of the group to make sure everyone was accounted for. He waited until the last student passed him before he let out a deep breath.

Holy shit.

Emphasis on the holy part.

He might not be ready, but he'd have to figure out a way to fake it until he was.

3

JFK Airport

Two Hours to Departure: Flight AI102 Traveling JFK to DEL

The group walked single file through the serpentine security line, passing police dogs and checkpoints until they reached the bag and body scanners. When one of the last students was pulled aside for a pat-down, he began lecturing the older TSA agent about systemic racism against Asian and Middle Eastern travelers.

"Do you even try to pretend it's random selection, or has our last administration made you feel safe enough to corner me out of a lineup just because of the color of my skin?" he said, his voice cracking with puberty and indignation.

"I'm just doing my job, kid," the older man said. Wand in hand, he motioned toward the large metal Spider-Man buckle. "Go on now."

"I have a few more things to say—"

"Which we'll talk about on the plane," Silas interjected, stepping between the agent and the student. "Dude, if he holds you up, we're all going to miss our flight," he whispered. "This is not one of those screw-around-and-find-out moments."

"I can't believe you interrupted my speech, you coward," the kid replied. He dragged his feet as they made their way to the end of the conveyor belt to get their backpacks. "I'd been working on that for weeks."

"Weird, but okay. I'm sorry. If you get stopped on the way back, you can try it again."

"No, I have a different speech about corruption and bribery for when we travel back from India."

"Oh yeah, coming from a US-born diaspora kid that lives with privilege? That's going to go over well," Silas muttered. He made a mental note to tell Neil to watch out for the dude in the classic nineties vintage T-shirt and Spider-Man buckle when they got to the airport on the return flight.

The group walked together down two corridors before they finally reached gate B41. Rows of chairs faced each other, the long tables along the center corridor filling with passengers trying to charge their accessories.

The gate was relatively full except for an empty row near the windows, where two people stood, getting into what looked like a heated argument.

The one on the left was a South Asian girl around his age, her long hair tied back in a ponytail. Her arms were crossed tightly over her chest. She looked so rigid he wouldn't be surprised if one jerky move cracked a bone. Silas shifted closer.

"Do you want me to call the airline manager?" the man who stood across from her boomed. He had to be twice her height and three times her age. His salt-and-pepper hair stuck straight out, and a purple inflatable pillow collared his neck.

"Why don't you go ahead and do that? I'll wait right here."

Silas grinned. There wasn't a representative in sight.

"Oh no," he heard Neil say behind him. "I did not expect her to fight people for chairs."

Silas looked at him over his shoulder. "She's part of our group?"

"Yes. Stay here. I'll go—"

"Actually, I can help her," Silas said. He didn't wait for Neil to respond as he crossed the waiting area and almost tripped on a Mickey Mouse carry-on. As an only child, he knew what it was like to fight your own battles without any support. Not that Silas knew anything about this person or whether they wanted help.

The closer he got, the more clearly he was able to make out her sharp features, which added to the edge in her voice. What was it with this temple youth group? Why was everyone his age or older so freaking attractive?

"We have a group of students heading to India, and that's who I'm holding the seats for."

"And I want to sit next to the windows," the man said. "I don't see your students, so I'm going to move your bag to do it."

"You touch my bag and we're going to have a problem," she responded.

"Oh hey! We're here!" Silas said, sliding up next to her.

She looked at him like he'd just lost his mind.

"The temple tour." He motioned to Neil and the students wrestling with carry-ons as they headed toward them. "Sir?" Silas said to the man. "Thank you so much for being so patient while we got all of our students through security. Are you headed to India for business or pleasure?"

His brows furrowed, as if he was contemplating whether to respond or walk away. "Family. And I would like to sit next to the—"

"Family you're traveling with!" Silas cut him off. "Good for you. We're going on this pilgrimage tour to find ourselves. Mostly Hindu sites, all in North India. It's sponsored by the Durga temple cultural society in Central New Jersey. Have you heard of it? It's great. Neil, that tall, good-looking guy coming toward us, is the tour leader. You'll want to talk to him. We're really, uh, changing the world. Hey, you can join our . . . uh, prayer group?"

"No. Look, have the seats," the man said. With a huff, he turned and walked away.

"Thank you!" Silas called after him.

"Changing the world? Prayer group?"

Silas turned to the other junior guide now, taking in her full mouth, slightly downturned, and dark lashes barely lined with makeup. "It's the best I could come up with on the fly. You were determined to hold these seats, huh?"

"Neil told me to." She looked at him up and down, then raised a brow. "Did he think I needed you to rescue me?"

"Thanks, Tara," Neil said, finally reaching their side. "Good work. Silas, appreciate the help here."

Neil was already gone when Tara said, "I didn't need help."

"But?" Silas added.

Her frown deepened. "But what?"

"Oh, this is the part where people say, 'But I'm thankful for your help.'"

Her lips parted. He braced himself for a sharp retort, but it never came.

"*But* I'm thankful for your help," she parroted.

Silas winced and rubbed a hand against his chest. "Wow, that looked like it hurt."

This time, he saw the barest hint of a smile. "I'm batting zero, and karma is kicking my ass. Anything helps to balance the scales. You don't look like a high school student."

"Not anymore," Silas said. He held out a hand. "Silas D'Souza-Gupta, junior guide. You must be the other junior guide. Nice to meet ya."

She eyed his hand and then shook it like it was against her better judgment. "Tara Bajaj," she finally said. "Are you always this perky?"

He bowed slightly. "Guilty. Does the cactus personality work for you?"

This time she laughed. Her face lit up like a moonbeam. "Yeah. It used to, anyway."

Their eyes met. She held his stare, even after pulling her hand back.

"What? Do I have something on my face?" he asked.

"No. Do you have any relatives in New Jersey by any chance?"

"Nope," Silas replied. He rubbed the back of his neck, thinking about the last time he saw his cousins a few years ago. "Just some extended fam in Toronto and Fresno, California. Why?"

"You remind me of someone."

"Someone good, I hope."

"The best, actually," she said quietly.

Her words surprised him. They sounded earnest. "I'm a bit competitive," he said with a grin as he tried to lighten the mood. "Does this person I remind you of have any weaknesses? Strengths? I bet you I can be better."

"You two have your ticket numbers, right?" Neil said, sidling up to them again. "I'm checking to make sure we don't have any unassigned tickets."

Tara pulled hers out of her back pocket. Silas did the same. Their seats were in the same row.

"Hey, seatmate," he said with a grin. "I guess we'll have more time to figure out who my competition is."

Tara rolled her eyes before she turned her back on him, walking to the last chair closest to the terminal wall. She put on a set of headphones, ignoring the buzz of rising high schoolers around her.

Silas figured that was probably how his next fourteen hours would be, too.

He turned to Neil. "I think she's warming up to me."

Nisha Sharma

"Absolutely." Neil patted him on the shoulder. "At least I don't have to worry about you two and funny business. Now—excuse me. I am going to get myself a pizza. Don't tell my wife when you meet her. She's worried about my blood sugar. Please watch the kids."

"Great," Silas said after Neil walked away. Before he could sit down in the nearest chair, two of the guys from their group approached him.

"I wouldn't even waste my time," one of them said, motioning toward Tara. "She's supposed to be super toxic."

"Toxic?" Were these kids thirteen or eighteen?

The other student nodded. "Ina and Gina said that their older sister was in her class at Rutgers High. Their sister told them about how Tara Bajaj used to be on the dance team but betrayed her best friend and co-captain by, like, leaking something to the competition. No one really knows what it was, but it had to be serious because the dance team got disqualified from everything."

"And then Ina and Gina's sister said that everyone was talking about how she cheated with her best friend's boyfriend," the second kid said.

"And you got all of this from someone whose sister went to school with Tara?" Silas asked skeptically. "How do you know it's the same person?"

The first kid pointed to the twins. "They said that when they saw her for the first time in front of security, they sneaked a picture and sent it to their sister. The sister confirmed it."

Silas retrieved his phone. "I need to see this for myself. Maybe Tara posted something on her social media about the rumors. What's her handle?"

Both boys looked back and forth at each other, until finally one said, "Most of her online life is gone. Deleted. Everything. Apparently, it was recent. And now she's here."

Silas looked over at Tara, who was engrossed in her phone, her chunky headphones huge on her head. "Okay, wow. That's a lot . . . of absolute garbage. Do you guys hear yourselves? I mean, there is no way

28

that's true. None of it can be verified." As someone who spent most of his high school life behind a camera, he was fortunate enough to be in the room when people shared their secrets.

The relationships he'd had also put him in the middle of a lot of drama. Vinny in freshman year, Damien in sophomore and junior, and Michelle the summer before senior year. He learned very fast that almost every rumor was an inflated version of a very boring truth.

But then again . . . what part of Tara's story was true?

"Don't say we didn't try to warn you," one of them said.

"Fair. Hey, did either of you bring games?"

They nodded.

"Cool. Let's play."

He sat down next to them but remained aware of Tara, in his peripheral vision, away from the rest of the students. His curiosity was definitely piqued. If she was treated like crap in high school, then Silas knew it would take a lot to get close to her. But if he did, would she be willing to share her secrets with him?

4

DAY 1: DELHI, INDIA

Postcard dated June 12—two years ago:

I've traveled all over the world now, but there is something about India that makes me feel like every part of me is accepted and loved. I am a foreigner in a foreign land with a celebrated common ancestry. When I step out of the airport and onto the dusty soil, it's a warm welcome. "Hello. We've been waiting for you. We love you." I don't even feel that way in New Jersey, where we were raised. Where we learned how to be human. This feeling just happens in India.

Miss you, munchkin.

Love,

Didi

When Tara accepted the position as a junior guide on the tour, she'd braced herself for the worst travel experience of her life.

Until she met Silas.

She watched him out of the corner of her eye as they boarded the plane and waited for takeoff. He laughed openly with the kids across the aisle and twisted his hat around backward so that his curly hair peeked out over his ears and at the nape of his neck. He was tall and lean, reminding her of Bollywood dancers.

Of Jai.

No, that wasn't fair to Jai. Her ex was so serious because family obligations and work demanded him to be. Silas just seemed like a fun guy.

He kept talking to the group in front of and behind them before and after the flight attendant's safety speech, but when the cabin lights dimmed and the engines came to life, she stopped paying attention to the conversation. She was too distracted by her circumstances, which finally hit her.

Holy shit, she was going to India. She was finally separating herself from everything that had haunted her over the last few months. From the name calling, the locker pranks, and the horrendous bathroom encounters. Even graduation was atrocious. The sound of a crowd of students booing would echo in her ears for years to come.

She deserved all of it. The bullying was nothing that she wouldn't have laughed at as Before-Tara.

When the jumbo jet lifted off the ground and into the sky, she let out a deep breath. The seat belt sign dinged as people began pulling down their window shutters.

Tara was sure Silas would start talking to her, which would probably be another welcome distraction from her thoughts. But he surprised her yet again by shifting so he could grab the bag he'd stuffed between his sneakered feet. He caught her staring and winked.

"I hope you're not a chatterbox," he said wryly. "I'll be a bit busy here."

He started his laptop and pulled up a streaming platform playlist that included a downloaded *Lord of the Rings* marathon. Without another word, he plugged in a headphone splitter on one side of his laptop and angled the screen toward her.

He wanted her to watch with him?

She debated the open port for a second and, with a sigh, took her wire out of her phone, which she'd intended to use to listen to audiobooks, before plugging it into the splitter. The iconic soundtrack of the first hobbit movie began to play.

She was instantly sucked into the story. She hadn't watched all of them through before, and for some reason it just made so much more sense together. They reminded her of the folktales and mythology her sister used to tell her when she was young. The watered-down versions of ancient texts about underdogs who scaled mountains, slayed demons and warriors, and fought for good with wit and faith.

Fourteen hours passed, with momentary interruptions for food and bathroom breaks.

The three hobbit movies, then *The Fellowship of the Ring* and *The Two Towers*.

The wheels bounced once, and then the brakes had Tara straining against her belt.

"Flight AI102, welcome to New Delhi, where the local time is twelve o'clock in the afternoon."

"I guess we're here," Silas said after he paused their last film. Those were the first words he'd spoken to her the whole flight. Even during meal service when he had to shift the computer to rest between their trays.

"Yeah," she replied, her voice husky from disuse. "That was . . . fast." She hadn't even had the urge to reach for her notebook or her phone, because she'd been so preoccupied with the movies.

Tara looked out the window at the New Delhi airport outer buildings in the distance. The creeping electricity she used to feel as a child traveling to India began to sizzle through her.

She was in India. The unfamiliar familiar. No matter how miserable she was on all the long treks to remote religious sites, joy bloomed in her heart whenever she landed in the dusty, smoggy city where her parents had been born. Her sister had written her a postcard about it once.

33

I've traveled all over the world now, but there is
something about India that makes me feel like every part
of me is accepted and loved. I am a foreigner in a foreign
land with a celebrated common ancestry.

Savitri would've loved having this moment with her.

The buzz of the students added a spring to her step, even in the slog of passengers getting their carry-ons and disembarking from the plane.

Almost an hour and a half later, through customs and baggage claim, Tara stepped outside the gates and into the noisy heat and bustle of New Delhi. Her spirit weightless—however briefly—at the feeling of home.

Didi was right. Even though Tara had been born and raised in the US, there was something magical about being in a place where everyone looked like you and spoke the same languages.

The rickshaws and cars crowded the roadways, ignoring any semblance of lanes. Handcarts pushed along the outskirts of the terminal exits, piled high with burlap bags of produce. The smell of diesel and dust was a familiar welcome.

"Holy shit," Silas said as he rolled his bag next to hers. "Neil wasn't kidding. It's a sauna here. I hope we have air conditioning."

Despite the soft breeze, sweat was beginning to trickle down her back. "Maybe."

Silas's mouth dropped. "Maybe? What do you mean, *maybe*?"

Before Tara could respond, a bus pulled up in front of the curb with red letters painted on the side: "NC Pilgrimages." The paint looked new, and it had large tinted windows.

The accordion doors opened with a hiss, and a blast of cool air spilled out. Behind the wide, flat wheel sat a small woman with a long black braid, red sindoor streaked down her center hairline, and a small gold nose ring that matched her tiny gold hoops.

"Welcome to India!" the woman said, her voice soft but filled with excitement.

"Chaya!" Neil shouted over the crowd. "Everyone, this is the second tour lead, Chaya. Chaya is my wife and will be driving us."

"Thank god."

"I'm dying."

"My hair!"

"Is it going to be like this for the next two months?"

"Okay, I'm not that bad, right?" Silas murmured, nudging Tara.

"Oh, you absolutely are, Mr. Air Conditioning."

He laughed. The sound made a few students turn to look at them with curiosity.

She waited for Silas and Neil to open the luggage bays and began ushering kids to drop off their bags and get on the bus, as requested.

When the kids gave her a wide berth, her gut twisted. Did they know about her past? About her reputation? Especially if they were connected to the same temple and lived in the same area in New Jersey. Or was it just because she hadn't talked to any of them and they didn't want to get to know her? She had become so paranoid over the last few months.

After the group boarded, Tara rolled her suitcase past Silas and Neil, who had been filling the luggage bay, and lifted her bag before sliding it neatly in the last remaining spot. She stepped back and dusted off her hands.

The guys looked at her with strange expressions.

"What? Is there more luggage?"

"I wondered if you meant what you said in your interview about not being afraid of some heavy lifting," Neil responded.

She figured she'd give him the benefit of the doubt and chalk up his comment to generalized misogyny. Tara had encountered a lot of generalized misogyny in her very short lifetime. "How long is it to the hotel?" she asked in Hindi.

Neil checked his watch and wobbled his head back and forth as if debating. "It will take at least forty-five minutes."

"Thank you." She boarded the bus, welcoming the cooler air. The cloth seats looked new, with overhead storage for their backpacks. Everyone had piled in the rear of the bus, leaving a few empty spots up front. Tara ignored the curious looks, even though they felt like pressure on a bruise, and took a seat closest to the window on the left.

Her headphones were already blasting Taylor's *Reputation* album when Silas sat next to her. She scooted over to give his long legs more space. He said something, but she couldn't hear him.

She needed a moment. Just a few minutes to remember why she was here and why no one's opinion of her mattered.

The shifting city outside her window grabbed her attention.

It had been almost two years since her last trip to India, and it was comforting to see the colors and chaos again. Despite their disagreements, Tara's parents created a deep love for being Desi, nourishing and caring for it in their home, in their community, and in their souls. But in the US, it was like houseplants: vibrant and alive in pockets of rooms. Here, under the bright sun, their culture was as free and immersive as a jungle. It didn't need constant work and attention, because it surrounded her, growing and breathing on its own.

When the bus stopped in front of a large white building sandwiched between shops, she let out another sigh of relief. Unlike the temple visits with her parents and the one she was forced to go on as a rising freshman four years before, she wouldn't have to stay in shared living spaces or hostels. The pandemic, and an influx of donations to the temple cultural society, had changed that.

More importantly, junior guides got to stay in their own rooms now.

After they exited the bus and unloaded all the luggage, Tara followed the group into the foyer of the hotel.

Chaya, the badass bus driver that she was, managed to park quickly and meet them near the reception desk, where they handed over their passports to get checked in.

Her smile was sweet and welcoming, as were her warm, deep-brown eyes lined with black kajal. "Are you all ready to embark on your spiritual journey?"

Neil was the only one who cheered and clapped in response.

Tara looked around at the small lobby. There were pots of marigolds in the corners, a beautiful marble wall behind the reception desk, and plush low-backed chairs in conversation sets around the center space. A few other hotel guests, mostly European, walked through with purses and sneakers, as if heading out for an early dinner.

"Now I'm sure all of you are exhausted from traveling," Chaya said once they were huddled closer together.

A resounding groan spread throughout the group.

"That's why the rest of the day is for relaxing."

Everyone cheered.

"After we check in, there will be two to four students to each room, depending on the hotel we stay at, throughout the trip," she continued.

There were more cheers.

Chaya held up a hand. "Not so fast," she said. "Even though there will not be an adult staying with you in your room, you must abide by the code of conduct you were given prior to this trip."

"No hanky-panky," Neil said, wagging his finger. "We will periodically knock on your doors for room checks to make sure you are where you should be."

"Otherwise," Chaya continued, "your parents will have to come and personally pick you up, and you will be removed from the tour. I'm sure they would love to spend the money on a ticket to do that."

Tara watched as the group hushed until there was absolute silence.

Chaya smiled, her sunny disposition never wavering. "In a few hours, we will have our first dinner together as a group in the hotel dining hall. When you first arrived at the airport in New York, you were given name tags. You must all wear name tags to dinner so we can get to know one another. A few of you with food allergies will have to wear a wristband throughout the meal in addition to your name tag. Keep your wristbands with you after you're done, because you'll be using them again throughout the trip."

The desk clerk slid a stack of key cards across the counter. Chaya picked them up, and like a synchronized dance, Neil took out his tablet and began reading names and room numbers.

The students lined up and took their key cards as each group was called. After all the students received individual keys, two remained in Neil's hand. He gave one to Silas and one to Tara, both of whom had stood in the back throughout the room-delegation process.

Tara glanced down at her key card. The very idea of privacy and a shower sounded like heaven right about now.

"Okay, everyone," Neil called out. "I'll be leading students upstairs. Let's get going."

They all followed in a single-file line toward the elevator bank. Chaya held out a hand to stop Silas and Tara from trailing behind the group.

"I just want to go over a few things with you," she said.

"Sure," Silas said. "This is going to be great. I'm excited." He turned to Tara. "What about you?"

She didn't say anything. When Chaya smiled, Tara could practically see little hearts floating in Silas's eyes.

"We have rules for our junior guides as well," Chaya said when all the students were finally in the elevators and out of earshot. "I know you received information packages, but I want to go over some of the details with you."

Tara wanted to tell her that she was more than capable enough of reading, but she bit her tongue. That was the old Tara. Before-Tara.

The new Tara made a promise to herself that she wouldn't say anything at all if she had nothing nice to say.

"Some of these children are bitter about being here, and rightfully so. They were forced to come on this trip because of their parents, who believe their children are either taking a path of self-destruction or are not devoted enough to succeed in their futures. Other students are just grateful to be away for the summer. Either way, every child in this group will test boundaries."

Tara rocked back on her heels. That was not the opening she expected to hear.

Chaya was right. There were a lot of exceptions, but many parents didn't send their kids to India on a religious excursion just for fun. Tara had the same experience.

Chaya held up a finger, her voice going hard and militant. "Rule number one. Neil, myself, and the junior guides will have rooms between each student quarters. You are able to have your evenings to yourself after dinner, unless there is a problem, in which case you must be available. Over the course of the trip, you'll have two nights off where you don't have to dine with the students and can leave after the excursion. Okay?"

Tara shifted her backpack, eager for this whole process to finish. Meanwhile, Silas grinned, standing at attention like a golden retriever.

"Rule number two," Chaya continued. A second finger went up. "You will share responsibility for all ten students, but you will sit with the same three to four every night at dinner. We ask that you keep the conversation focused on their spiritual journey. Feel free to talk about history, mythology, and folklore after each pilgrimage. If there is a problem or a concern, we will have a discussion and address it together."

"Sounds great," Silas said. After a beat, he elbowed Tara.

She had to bite back a laugh. "Yes. Sounds *great*."

"I'm here!"

Tara's breath caught at the sound of the familiar voice.

No.

This could *not* be happening. She turned slowly to face the hotel entrance, dread pooling in her stomach.

This was not real life. It couldn't be. The gods could not hate her so much that they would do this to her.

Across the lobby, Sunny Deol strode toward them, his Louis Vuitton suitcase in tow and his leather backpack slung over one shoulder. His hair was longer and spikier than when Tara had first met him all those years ago, and he'd filled out his lankiness, thanks to hours on the varsity tennis and golf teams. He had the barest hint of scruff on his face.

His mouth set in a thin line when he saw Tara.

"Hi," he said when he reached their group. He stuck out his hand to Chaya. "Sunny Deol. Not the Bollywood actor, obviously," he said, chuckling at his own joke. "Chaya Auntie, it's nice to finally meet you in person. Thank you for being so understanding when I called earlier this morning."

Chaya looked down at his hand with an expression of distaste. Tara instantly appreciated her for it.

"I'm not your auntie."

"Oh." He dropped his hand. "I've never missed a flight before, but my masi lives pretty far from the Mumbai airport. Mumbai traffic. In hindsight, visiting family for a week before the tour probably wasn't the best idea. What did I miss?"

Chaya looked down at her tablet and then back up at him. "I have emailed you the details. We didn't know if you'd arrive before dinner, so your key card is at the front desk."

"Oh, great." He turned to Silas and held out a hand for him to shake as well. "Sunny Deol. Nice to meet you."

"Silas D'Souza-Gupta," Silas responded. "That's some expensive luggage, dude. Don't know how you're going to manage not banging it up on this trip. We're hiking in the Himalayas for most of it, right?"

Sunny laughed, the sound easy and charming. "That's what I told my parents, but they've always had obnoxious style. I didn't have the time to go out and get something a little less loud. Hey, Tara."

For a moment, she forgot where she was and whom she was with. It was just Sunny and Tara, sharing secrets like they did the first time they took the youth group temple tour.

Together.

"What are you doing here?" Her tone was so frigid she wouldn't have been surprised if a puff of cold air came out with each breath.

"I'm a junior guide on this temple tour, just like you. Didn't your parents tell you I was coming along? Or were they too busy trying to do damage control with their reputation after your blowup?" His voice was light and cheerful, despite the hard glint in his eye.

"Holy shit," Silas murmured.

"You know each other?" Chaya asked slowly.

"Unfortunately," Tara replied.

"We went on this same tour together four years ago," Sunny said lightly. "Before you and Neil Unc—ah, Neil took over."

"I see," Chaya said. "I don't know what's going on between the two of you, but please don't let it affect the way you are with the students. Now, you have a few hours before dinner. I am going to go spend some time with Neil."

She turned on her heel and left them.

Tara felt Silas's hand on her bicep. "Do you want me to walk you upstairs?" he said quietly.

She softened before shaking her head. She didn't know what she did to earn Silas's thoughtfulness, but she appreciated it. It felt different to have someone care about her.

It was . . . nice.

"I'm okay," she said. "I'll head up in a bit."

Silas nodded, then did the same toward Sunny before he left, following Chaya to the elevator bank. Tara waited until they were both out of sight.

"Why are you doing this?" she asked.

"What, you think I'm hiking through the damn Himalayas with a bunch of idiots because I *want* to?" Sunny snorted. "I hated when I had to do this four years ago. But now that I'm the villain in everyone's story, there are zero places that would hire me."

Was this guy for real? She took a step back, hands up. "*You're* the villain? I spent months being laughed at and ostracized by everyone in school. You got winks, nudges, and pats on the back because the whole student body thought you were juggling two girls. Don't you dare play the victim here."

"You shared my private text messages with everyone!" Sunny said, his voice climbing an octave. "I sent those to you after we both agreed we'd never tell people we knew each other."

This was the Sunny she knew—the Sunny no one else believed her about. Beneath the charm, he always wanted everything to be about himself.

"Why would I keep my promise after you broke yours?" she said evenly. "You told Umma we knew each other! Then you lied about me and said I tried to hook up with you! Then after she posted your messages online, and I posted mine to prove her wrong, you convinced everyone that it was all made up, making things with Umma and me so much worse."

"What else was I supposed to do?" he snapped. "Ignoring things is your style, not mine. I had to deal with the fallout. And Umma was never your friend. None of that fake bullshit you had at Rutgers High was real. I know what a weirdo you really are, with your fanatical father, your obsessed mother, and the fantasy fan fiction you used to write in your notebooks. And your sister, looking for any yoga retreat she could find, constantly doing whatever drug she—"

"Don't you dare talk about my sister," Tara said, her voice rising an octave.

The receptionists were practically leaning across the front desk to listen in on the conversation now.

Tara backed up, creating space between them. "How about you and I just keep our distance?" she said. "Because how shitty would it be if I texted your parents about what really happened over the last few months? How their precious baby boy was the asshole in this whole mess?"

She saw the look of panic on his face and knew that was the upper hand she needed. For all his flaws, he was still scared of his parents.

"You better not say anything—"

"Later, Sunny Deol, not the actor. I can't believe you still introduce yourself like that."

She spun on her heels and strode toward the elevators. Thankfully one came quickly. She stepped inside, the door closing before Sunny could follow her.

Finally by herself, she leaned back against the wall and let out a deep breath. For a second, she was the old Tara again.

She'd had to be the old Tara. That was the only version of herself strong enough to push back against someone like Sunny Deol. The new Tara was still lost. She needed more time.

She needed a lot more time.

5

Day 1: Delhi, India

Silas loved a good mystery, and Tara was a mystery. First, the kids had told him some wild rumors, but he doubted they were all true. He found it hard to believe that someone like Tara, who had been incredibly direct since the moment they met, would resort to subterfuge to get what she wanted. Second, there was the third junior guide. Tara obviously had a past with Sunny Deol—god, what a name—even though it didn't seem like it had been a romantic one. Her so-called "reputation" and the frigid response to Sunny contradicted what he'd felt from her in the fourteen hours they'd shared an armrest and watched *Lord of the Rings* movies in silence.

He paused in the process of unpacking his bag for a shower. Okay, he was probably an idiot to feel a connection to a person based on how silent they were for fourteen hours, but it made sense in his head.

Silas walked into the tiny adjacent bath and began the process of scrubbing almost twenty-four hours' worth of travel off his skin. While squeezing shampoo onto his head, he thought about trying to find old pictures of Tara online. To corroborate his gut feeling about who she was versus what people said about her.

But if her social media were gone, he wouldn't really have much to work with.

Instead, he put thoughts of the intriguing Tara aside and got ready for dinner. He needed to focus on his reason for taking part in this trip.

The photojournalism competition.

Thirty-two years ago, his homebody moms were part of the first cohort to take the temple tour through the local New Jersey temple's cultural society. His grandparents sensed that their daughters were not exactly the way they wanted them to be, and in an effort to dictate his moms' futures, they turned to god.

The tour was considered wildly successful, and the temple decided to host the same trip every year. His moms, on the other hand, rarely traveled after that.

Once Silas got dressed, he spread out the copies of memories from his parents' temple tour on his bed and began categorizing them by location. They'd started with a bus trip to Punjab. In Punjab, there were shots in front of the Golden Temple and the Durgiana Temple. Similarly, there were photos in Jammu and Kashmir, a yoga retreat in Shimla, and the four religious pilgrimage sites in Uttarakhand known as Chota Char Dham, followed by Haridwar and Rishikesh, and back to Delhi.

In each picture, his moms grew closer and closer together, until the final shot was of them laughing with their arms slung around each other's shoulders. He smiled at the image, tracing a finger over the edges of the four-by-six capture.

This was his favorite picture of his parents' childhood.

After a moment, he set it down and looked at the neatly organized stacks on his bed. He'd compared trips a dozen times, but he wanted to make sure that he'd have an opportunity to mirror as many images as he possibly could. He'd change the lighting and take wider shots; then he'd build his submission around the shifting landscape, climate change, and the increased number of pilgrims. The winning photographs and essay would get to participate on field expeditions with a world-renowned nature magazine. He'd be set as a photojournalist for life with that kind of credit in his portfolio. Hopefully.

It would also mean no more family photography.

Not that family photography didn't have merit. But Silas wanted more. He wanted to understand people beyond the microcosm of a single joyous moment. And his mothers, as incredible as they were, didn't understand that. They preferred safety, which family photography gave them.

Silas made a few notes about lenses, flagged the pictures that were the most striking, and started to pack them up in the protective sleeve when he heard a knock. He skirted the small bed frame and opened the door to Chaya and Neil standing in the hallway.

"Ready?" they asked.

He saw Tara standing behind them, her arms crossed over her chest. She also looked like she'd showered. Her long hair was in two French braids tightly wrapped against the sides of her head. He could see the AirPods clearly over her earlobes.

"Yeah, I'm ready," he said. "Let's do this."

He trailed behind the tour leads, with Tara a few paces behind him. They walked in silence. Surprisingly, most of the students were already downstairs in the dining hall, along with Sunny Deol, who looked like he was holding court over a few enamored kids.

"At least he's here," Neil whispered to Chaya. "Is that a fanny pack?"

"Maybe it's an American thing," Chaya whispered back.

"Or maybe it's a douche thing," Tara replied.

Neil and Chaya turned to her, their mouths gaping. Silas had to cover his chuckle.

"You heard that?" Neil asked.

"I'm wearing the AirPods so other people don't talk to me. I'm not actually listening to anything."

Silas was delighted with her. "I wonder how long you can keep that up with everyone."

"A long time, as long as you stay quiet."

Neil turned his back to them, then let out another piercing whistle. The dining hall grew silent, and even the few patrons who weren't part of their group turned to stare.

"We're so excited to share a meal together with all of you on our first night of the tour," he said in a baritone voice. "First, it's important that you build a relationship with your junior team leads, so we're going to split you all up at random. Make sure you ask questions and get to know each other. Silas? I'd like to have you sit at that table. Okay?"

Silas looked at the kids staring back at him, as if expecting him to do or say something entertaining. Anything to save them from boredom. He swallowed hard. "Yeah, sure. That sounds perfect."

It did not sound perfect.

As Neil and Chaya separated the rest of the students, Silas sat at his group's table, grateful to finally put faces to the names in his tour packet.

Beth, Chetna, Dax, and Amit. All rising high school freshmen.

Silas had spoken to Dax and Amit at the terminal and on the plane. Dax's hair was gelled straight up like a garden hedge, and Amit had his signature Spider-Man buckle. Then there was Beth with her sweet smile and large glasses. Chetna stared at her cell phone like it had all the answers in the universe.

"Hey, guys. Welcome to team Silas! Should we have a group name?"

They looked at him like he'd grown two heads.

"Okay. Team Silas it is." *Tough crowd.*

Everyone took their seats, and Chaya called for attention again.

"Every night, we will have dinner together," she said. She stood with her hands folded. "It may be communal style like this, or you may order from a menu. When we reach the yoga retreat center, we will be cooking our own meals. Everything will be vegetarian, and we will all be gracious to our hosts." Her voice was as sharp as a knife's blade.

Well, that sounded like a threat, Silas thought. But he knew it was hard to feed a large group. He'd worked in restaurants himself for a while, before his photos started getting traction and he could sell some of his work.

"Tomorrow, we are on the road to Punjab," Chaya continued. "Breakfast will be early, and we'll leave first thing in the morning."

Silas clapped and let out a whoop. "Thanks so much, Chaya Didi!"

Everyone turned to stare at him.

"Oh god, we're in trouble," Dax said.

Before he had the opportunity to embarrass himself even more, an army of waitstaff exited the kitchen with large serving trays towering with bowls and plates. Within seconds, they set down place settings and, in the center of their tables, platters of rice, roti, daal, and sautéed seasoned vegetables. There was hardly any room for cups and mugs.

Silas looked over his shoulder at Tara, who was already passing bowls to her left so that her group could start eating. He turned to his kids, and they all stared back at him expectantly.

"Why don't you guys dive in?"

"Do you like her?" Amit asked.

Silas did a double take. "Uh . . . what?"

Beth let out the most auntie-like sigh. "The other junior guide. Tara. Duh. Do you like her? You just met her, right?"

"You sure stare at her a lot," Chetna said. She delivered the blunt remark all while looking at her phone in one hand and ladling rice on her plate with the other.

"We told you she's toxic, man," Dax said, shaking his head.

"No, there are rumors that *say* she's toxic," Chetna corrected. "But we really don't know if that's true. Right, Silas?"

"Jesus, can't a guy look?" Silas blurted out.

They all shook their heads.

He was fighting a losing battle here. "Fine, then let's just eat, please?"

By the time they finished divvying up the food, Silas's plate was heaped with white rice covered with yellow daal, okra, potatoes, and paneer.

"This trip is going to be exactly like I knew it would," Dax grumbled, dropping his fork with a clatter and slouching in his chair. "It blows."

"Because of dinner?"

Beth was also pushing vegetables around on her plate. "It's the same food we get at home. They told us that the best part about this trip was dinner every night, and this is . . . my grandmother's cooking."

"I say try it first before you assume," Silas said. "That's my plan." He made a show of scooping up a mix of everything onto his fork and taking a big bite.

The explosion of flavor was unlike anything he'd ever had at home. His moms were great cooks, but as the rich, creamy, spicy heat sat on his tongue, he let out a groan. Maybe the path from farm to table was a lot shorter here, or the way that it was prepared was uniquely for palates like his. The food was made for every part of him to enjoy.

"I don't know about you," he said after swallowing, "but I plan on eating all of this. Indian food in India is next level."

They looked like they didn't trust him, but one by one, his table took a bite.

And then another.

And finally, they were eating, mostly in silence.

"Did you know," Amit started after a few minutes, "that the largest population of South Asians in America immigrated in the nineties and two thousands? That's why there are so many kids of immigrant parents running around. My guess is that our parents all wanted us to connect with our culture because they have no other way of giving it to us in the education system in the US."

"I don't want to believe everything my parents do, so that's why I'm here," Dax said.

"Yeah, I'm with him, Encyclopedia Brown," Chetna added. "My parents think I'm *too American*. That I'm not their brand of Indian enough."

"I can't tell if you're being racist with that Encyclopedia Brown comment," Amit replied smoothly. "All I'm saying is that whatever we know about our culture, we all understand Indian food. And we all think that our food at home is the same food that we'll get here. But if it's not . . . what kind of food have we been eating?"

"I haven't slept enough to think about that, Amit," Beth groaned.

The group nodded again, including Chetna, who was still looking at her phone next to her plate.

"Silas, can I ask you a question?" Dax started. "We're here because of our parents. But you had to *volunteer* to be a part of this trip without anyone forcing you. Why did you want to come to India with all of us?"

Silas thought about telling them that he wanted a job that traveled. Then he debated telling them honestly that he wanted to do something that was just for him, that would help him do photography the way that he always envisioned for himself, and opted for a half truth. "Because my parents took this trip thirty-two years ago. And they fell in love over the eight weeks they spent together. They're still married to this day."

Heads whipped up. Eyes widened. It was as if he'd dropped a bomb in the middle of his table.

"Your parents," Chetna said in a hushed voice, "met on this trip? And they had a romance?"

Silas nodded. "Maybe tomorrow on the bus to Punjab, I'll show you some of the pictures they took. I brought a lot of camera equipment with me because I want to be able to re-create a few of them. The tour spots are identical. Instead of my moms in the pictures, it'll be me."

"Moms?" Dax asked.

Silas braced himself, the way he always did when he was talking to South Asians about his upbringing. "Moms. I'm adopted."

Amit reached across the table to refill his plate with rice. "That's pretty cool. You have two moms who took the same religious tour in a country that still criminalizes homosexuality in a lot of places. You could write the best memoir ever."

"I'm good with taking pictures," Silas said with a laugh. "And did your parents have you memorize the dictionary or something?"

"I'm a National Spelling Bee Champion."

"Of course you are."

"How can we help?" Beth asked. "This has to be a group effort to get your pictures."

He had never thought of it that way, but considering how much setup he would probably need, it wasn't a bad idea to get a few extra hands involved. Especially if it would take their minds off everything they'd said about their parents' desires for the trip.

"Okay," he said. "This is what I was thinking."

They leaned in, food forgotten.

6

Day 1: Delhi

Postcard dated December 25—four years ago:

> *The hardest part of traveling alone is not being able to share the simplest pleasures with someone else. Sometimes all I want to do is have a conversation with a person who is willing to listen to me. Don't ever take that for granted. No matter where you go or what you do, always be grateful for the people around you and the people who understand you.*
>
> *Miss you, munchkin.*
>
> *Love,*
>
> *Didi*

Tara hated the silence at dinner.

She'd completely lost her appetite within the first few minutes when she realized that the students at her table didn't want to talk with her or to each other in front of her. She spent the rest of the meal staring at her plate like everyone else.

Then when they were ready to go back to their rooms, Gina, the girl sitting to her left, told her that her older sibling graduated with Tara.

She then asked whether Tara missed dancing since she'd been kicked off the team. Apparently, Gina had wanted to join the Rutgers High Bollywood dance team, too, after seeing Tara win last year's regional competition.

Tara had shaken her head, wishing she could say something more encouraging. All that popped into her mind was *make friends that you can trust.*

Out of the corner of her eye, she saw Sunny having a low conversation, huddled over his table, his students glancing in her direction periodically.

That son of a bitch.

She wouldn't be surprised if Sunny or one of his new student friends took a picture of her and posted it online.

But luckily, she didn't have a way of finding out what people were saying anymore. Even though the urge to reach for her phone was like a constant itch she couldn't scratch. After they left JFK, she'd been working hard to replace her social-media-scrolling addiction with audio-books and writing.

The stories were coming back.

Ever since she'd packed her secrets away at the beginning of freshman year, she'd suppressed the writer side of her as well. But now that her secrets were exposed, it was as if her dreaming had been unlocked.

Fantasy. Gods, goddesses, and locations where magic shrouded thick like the clouds circling the Himalayas.

Technically, she'd been researching to write an epic fantasy her entire life. All the theme parks her father had dragged her to for his job and the painful hours when she had been forced to read mythology texts with her mother were, oddly enough, the perfect breeding ground for awesome stories.

The thought of writing kept her occupied through most of dinner. She was grateful when she was able to go back to her room to work on a new story, but the moment she walked in the door, her phone rang with an incoming FaceTime call. She answered.

As usual, her mother's hair was perfectly styled, graying at the temples. Tara's father stood behind her, wearing one of his dad-joke cartoon shirts. The morning sunlight filtered through her family's familiar kitchen windows, brightening the screen.

"Hi, beta," her mother said. "You arrived safely?"

"Yeah, I'm at the hotel now."

"Ah, you leave for Punjab tomorrow," she said.

The woman had probably memorized her itinerary so she could validate Tara's response to make sure she was telling the truth. "We leave first thing in the morning, Mom."

"Do you have everything you need?"

"Yes."

"Show me your room. Tell me what you've done so far."

Tara had to fight the urge to simply hang up the phone. But she'd done that countless times before over the last four years, and it had only made the relationship with her mother worse. Instead, the easiest way to get her off her back was to just comply and deal with the questions.

If Didi were still around, the two of them would be able to deflect and distract Mom. After Didi left, Tara bore the brunt of her mother's inquisition.

She quickly turned the camera and scanned the room. "It's late here, and I should get going."

There was a stretch of silence. Her mother's mouth thinned. "Maybe you're not in the right place in your life to take this trip without me and Dad, Tara. Are you sure you're up for something this strenuous for this long?"

And there was the gaslighting.

She sat against the edge of the bed, hunched over, and rubbed at the space between her eyebrows to try to ease the ache. "I've taken the pilgrimage to Punjab, Jammu and Kashmir, Chota Char Dham, Haridwar, and Rishikesh a dozen times with you and Dad. Remember, I was the one who helped you develop your four-hundred-level syllabus on North Indian regional religions and customs the last time we were here."

"But you're by yourself. God knows what influences are out there."

"Oh yeah, who knows? I might become even *more* religious."

"Stop pestering the girl," her father said from the background. He took the phone from her mother, his bright, happy face filling the screen. "Hi, Tara."

"Hi, Dad," she said with a sigh.

"How was your flight?"

She thought of Silas and almost smiled. "The flight was okay. The hotel here is pretty nice, too. Way nicer than what Mom made us stay at growing up."

"So many people can't afford anything better than that, Tara," her mother yelled from the background.

"But we can," she said in a singsong voice. She shook her head at her father. "Seriously, I'm fine. I would tell you to go look at my social for pictures, but of course, I haven't taken any. I don't plan on it, either."

Her father began pacing back and forth through their kitchen, as he often did when he was taking a call. "How is the great digital detox going? You know, now that you've deleted your social media."

"Fine, I guess," she said. "I'm in the dark, though. Like, if I was still online, I would've probably found out that Sunny Deol was another junior guide on this trip."

Her father winced but said nothing. Her mother remained quiet.

The truth dawned on Tara. She had an inkling when Sunny had mentioned her parents. "You both knew? I can't believe you didn't tell me!"

Should she have been surprised, though? This was the parent–child communication that they were so terrible at.

"Now, Tara," her father started.

She checked her watch. "I am going to get some food."

Her mother's face appeared again on the screen. "What happened to the food in the hotel? It's supposed to come with the perks! Where are you going? Who are you going with?"

"I'm probably going to McDonald's. I'll be about thirty minutes. I'm going by myself. It's one block away. And no, I'm not turning on location services."

"Please be careful and let someone know where you're going." There was still tension in her mother's voice.

"Of course," she said, even though the only people who'd care were Neil and Chaya, and she didn't want to wake up the tour leads because of the late hour. "Mom, I'd like to point out that you were the one who thought this job was a good idea."

"But only if you stay with the tour the whole time," her mother said, breathing more heavily now, working herself up. How could she forget all the family outings to McDonald's when Tara and her sister came with her to India? Apparently, Tara was the only one who remembered the few moments in their history where they laughed together over tikki burgers and, for a brief moment, weren't grilled on religion or mythology.

"I'll take a picture of my food just for the two of you," Tara added. "Bye, Ma. Bye, Dad."

Her parents waved, wariness etched on their faces. The screen went black. Tara got off the small, squeaking bed and stood in front of the air conditioning unit for a moment before she slid her feet into sandals. The minute she'd said the word *McDonald's*, her mouth began to water.

She scanned the room and checked to make sure she had what she needed. The clothes she'd tossed aside after her shower, along with her melanin-specific skincare supplies, were all over the place.

Her folder, the one that included all of the rules for junior guides, sat on top of her open suitcase. What was she supposed to do again?

She had to be available every night for "on-call" emergencies. But could something really go wrong over the course of thirty minutes on their first night? No, she didn't even want to think that into existence.

She pressed her ear to the door. After making sure she didn't hear anything, she opened it carefully to peek outside.

The hallway was quiet with no one in sight. She grabbed her wallet, then slipped through the small opening and, as quietly as she could, locked the door behind her.

She made it three steps before she heard another door open.

Silas stepped outside in board shorts, and leaned against his door-jamb. "Hey, stranger," he said.

Tara held a finger to her lips and shushed him. Her burger was so close. Within reach. "What is wrong with you? There are *children*."

Silas shrugged. "Why are you in the hallway at eleven at night?"

She turned to leave. Maybe if she just walked away, he'd disappear. But then he knocked on his door frame. She froze.

"Tara, I *will* yell 'fire.' Or the name of a K-pop band. Either way, our entire group is going to wake up."

Damn it. If that happened, the likelihood of her getting an aloo tikki burger was nil. She pivoted to look at him. "I am going to get some food."

"Great," he replied in the same soft tone. He stepped back inside his room and re-emerged with flip-flops and a key that he tucked into the front pocket of his shorts. "Dinner was pretty great, but I'm still starving. Let's go."

"I plan on going by myself," Tara said as he closed his door behind him.

"Amit, one of the kids in my group, told me about how dangerous Delhi is at night for women. Especially in this area. I don't know how true that is, but it wouldn't hurt to have someone come with you. And besides, I'm starving."

She weighed her options. She could go back in her room, wait until he was asleep, and then try again, or she could go with him and deal with his company. When she saw one sharp eyebrow raise until it was covered by a flop of curl, Tara sighed. His company hadn't been terrible so far, and he didn't treat her like she was garbage.

"Let's just go."

He followed her down the hallway into the dark stairwell. She didn't want to alert anyone with the ding of the elevator. The receptionist behind the desk didn't even look up when Silas and Tara passed her and exited through the gated front door.

"Wow, I thought sneaking out would be a lot more exciting than it was," Silas said blandly.

"Not going to lie, I did, too," she said. Damn, there wasn't even a little thrill in the moment.

When they stepped out onto the street, they were immediately encased in darkness. There were no building lights or streetlamp posts. She could make out the shape of people in the distance, but they looked more like shadows. The sidewalks were narrow, snaking between building overhangs and hugging small parking lots. Cable and electric wires looped over the walkways, crisscrossing in a haphazard mess. The sound of laughter echoed in the distance, and the smell of diesel from the rickshaws gunning down the main road filtered through the air.

And then there was a quiet, a softness that only happened at night in India, when people were settled down at home with their meals. Together.

It was wonderful.

Tara fanned herself. It was still hot, but thankfully, the humidity had subsided.

"Do you know where you want to go?" Silas asked. "And should I have packed a flashlight?"

Tara looked at the maps app on her phone, the glow from her screen illuminating their pathway. "The main street is a block down."

"Great. I'll follow your lead."

They walked in silence for a few minutes before Tara's curiosity got the best of her. "Have you been to India before?"

"Once. I went to Goa with my moms when I turned sixteen. They adopted me from a center there, and they helped me retrace some family roots."

"Goa is definitely a different experience than the temple pilgrimages we're about to do."

Silas jumped over a large crack in the sidewalk, then turned with hand outstretched to help her. She looked at it, then simply stepped over the gap. He shrugged.

"Goa was a great experience, but you're right," he continued. "Definitely different. We met more Europeans than local Desis. Which honestly freaks me out about this trip."

She paused. "Wait, are you saying the lack of white people freaks you out?"

"God no," he said, laughing. "I'm saying that I didn't have to worry about the language when we were in Goa. But now I do. Places like Delhi and Amritsar? I'm sure I'll be fine. But the remote places are going to be hard for me to communicate. But you speak multiple languages, right? I heard you talking to Neil and Chaya."

"Yes. Hindi, Urdu, and Punjabi."

"Wow, all I have is high school Spanish."

"You can always learn," she said.

Silas laughed, his voice deep and warm. "Senor Fernando would say that my language skills are not the best. But yeah, I could always try to learn."

They turned the corner onto the main road, which was livelier than the side street they'd just come from. Noisy cabs and passenger vehicles raced by, and the diesel smell was stronger here. A strip mall lined the opposite side of the street. In the distance were the iconic golden arches.

"I don't know what it is, but something about seeing McDonald's feels like a safety beacon," Silas said.

"The menu is way better here, though." Tara led the way across the intersection, snorting when Silas let out a high-pitched eek as she ignored the traffic light. But she felt a tingle at the base of her spine when he extended a hand out in front of her as a bicyclist zoomed by.

That was . . . nice.

A few minutes later, they pushed through the open door and passed the brightly colored walls to stand in a short line at the register.

"I don't think I've ever seen a McDonald's like this before," Silas said. He scanned the sparse crowd of friends and families.

Tara tried to remember the first time she'd walked into a McDonald's in India. She'd been so young. Even then, the tables were modern and full of families having a night out together. The walls had neon signs and abstract murals.

"In India, McDonald's is like going to a restaurant. A casual date or a dinner with family. The culture is different."

If she was being honest with herself, India McDonald's had ruined American fast food for her. Here in North India, there were masala fries. The McSpicy paneer. Then her favorite: the McSpicy aloo burger, the most delicious fried potato tikki ever.

"Okay, this is unreal," Silas said, looking up at the menu screens. "What do I even get?"

She smiled despite herself. "Whatever you want."

When it was their turn, Tara ordered her McSpicy paneer, McSpicy aloo, a side of masala fries, and a Fanta soda, then waited for Silas—she didn't want to be an asshole and leave him in case he had questions. He pretty much repeated her order, then swiped his credit card instead of pulling out American dollars, which was a good move considering conversion rates.

A few minutes later, they grabbed their trays and moved to the closest open table. Silas sat, and their knees knocked together.

"Sorry," he said with a laugh, adjusting his legs to bracket hers. "They don't make tables for two tall people, do they? You're what, five seven, five eight?"

"Barely," she said. "And that's not tall. Wait until we get to Punjab. What you mean to say is that they don't make these tables for people your height. Over six two. But does anyone make tables for people over six two?"

"Not in my experience," he said.

He patted her knee companionably, and his fingers left a warm imprint on her leg.

Even though they'd brushed against each other a few times between their plane ride and their walk, it was still surprising to feel something with someone she just met. Although, if she was being completely honest with herself, not unwelcome.

Tara decided she'd figure it out later when she had hours to over-analyze and unwrapped her McSpicy aloo burger first. The mix of fried potato and spices smelled indescribable. After taking a bite, Tara closed her eyes and sighed, mouth full of deliciousness. She almost groaned out loud at the taste. Some of the tension in her shoulders eased.

When she returned to planet Earth, she realized that Silas still hadn't unwrapped his first burger. Instead, he was staring off into space with a look of complete bafflement.

"Do you have a problem?"

"I just realized something," he said, eyes wide.

"What?"

"It keeps hitting me. It's so strange to be in a place where everyone looks sort of like me."

Had the same realization ever hit her like that? Or had she always known as a diaspora kid that India was awe inspiring?

She followed his line of sight to the families at the neighboring tables, who were laughing and holding rapid conversations in Hindi.

"You know how other Indians stare at you in the States?" she finally asked. "Like, they aren't sure if you're Indian, so they give you the piercing 'Are you Desi?' glare until you acknowledge the gesture with a nod?"

"Yes!" Silas said. "It's like I don't have to do that here."

"Right. Because even though there might be moments where we feel like we don't belong because we're American, too, we usually look like we do."

"That's so . . . nice," he said.

She laughed. "It's better if you don't actually do the Desi stare here, though. It's weird."

"Yeah, I should eat." He picked up his McSpicy aloo and unwrapped it before taking a monster bite. His eyes popped open wide. After he chewed and swallowed, he exclaimed, "What the hell? McDonald's India, what is this sorcery?"

"Welcome to the secret of India's fast-food industry. It's better here than anywhere else." Tara took a sip of her drink and then bit into her sandwich again.

They chewed in silence for a few more minutes before Silas spoke. "I bet this isn't Sunny Deol's scene, huh?"

She choked.

"Hey now." He reached across the table to pat her on the shoulder. Tara coughed into a napkin, her eyes watering as she struggled to clear her airway.

"Damn it, Silas," she said.

"That's the first time you've said my name! We're making progress."

"But not enough progress that you get to know about my history yet." She waved his hand away, then blurted, "Sunny Deol isn't my ex. He's my ex–best friend's ex."

Shit, she hadn't meant for that information to come out.

He held up a hand. "I picked up the animosity between you two. Sorry, I was just trying to make a joke. We don't have to talk about it if you don't—"

"Everyone is talking about it," she cut in.

God, she was still irritated. With her mother, with dinner, and, now, with this conversation. "Everyone is gossiping about what happened a few months ago, and how I'm the evil villain who tried to seduce my bestie's boy away from her."

Silas bit into his burger and watched her through the disheveled curl that flopped over his brow. He took his sweet time swallowing.

"Well?" she said, impatience grating her nerves.

"Growing up, my moms used to say to me: Do you want to vent, or do you want advice? I'll ask you the same question."

As Tara thought about his offer, she wondered if Silas had heard something about her history. If he had, why was he here now?

"Just tell me," she finally said, "what are people saying about me?"

"Does it matter?"

Yes, she thought. Yes, because now that she was disconnected from social media, all she had was paranoia to keep her company. There was no way of keeping track of the rumors about her. But would knowing really change . . . anything?

She shoved the rest of her sandwich in her mouth. When swallowing, the lump slid down thick into her chest. "I guess it doesn't. Do you believe the rumors?"

"I think you already know the answer to that one."

She did. Who would want to spend time with her if they believed she was such a bitch? Tara had a feeling that Silas made his own opinions about people.

"I don't want to vent, and I don't want advice. All I want to do is start over. Be the person I was before high school but smarter, less insecure, and with better eyebrows." She paused. "You know what? I don't even know why I'm telling you all of this."

He held a fry in one hand and his burger in the other. "It's always easier telling someone you don't know all your secrets."

Secrets. Could she share them that easily after keeping them locked away for so long? It had taken her over a year of dating to tell Jai about her life.

"You look like you're trying to solve all of your problems with one fast-food meal," he said, nudging her knee with his.

"I wish it was that easy."

"It never is." Silas held a masala fry out to her. "We have two months. If you want to tell me later, I'm here. Literally every day."

Tara took it like a peace offering. "Thanks."

"So. Do you know anything about the Golden Temple in Punjab?"

Tara snorted. "I do. More than I want to."

"Can you tell me?"

Did he sense that she'd had enough? Or was he just really good at conversation? Either way, she was grateful for this surprising moment of respite during their late-night McDonald's run. "Yeah. Yeah, I guess I could."

7

DAY 2: ROAD TO PUNJAB

The tour bus left after an early breakfast. Most of the kids were rubbing sleep from their eyes because they were up half the night, but after they climbed aboard, they put in AirPods and dozed off again.

There was too much for Silas to see for him to snooze through their entire seven-and-a-half-hour drive. He sat next to Tara, despite the irritated scowl she gave him, and proceeded to ask Neil, who sat right in front of them, as many questions as he could. Where did he and Chaya grow up? How did they meet? When did they decide to be tour guides for this temple youth group tour?

"You like your questions, Silas," Chaya said, head leaned back, eyes meeting his in the large overhead mirror, and loud enough so that the motor didn't drown her out.

Tara muffled a snort next to him. In retaliation, he pulled out one of her AirPods and dropped it in her lap.

"Hey!"

"If you're going to eavesdrop, have some dignity and do it out in the open," he said.

This time, she didn't hide her snort. The earbuds disappeared.

As they drove out of the city, the scenery changed, and so did the frequency of Silas's questions. When they passed their first stretch of green, he felt his world shift.

The road to Punjab was punctuated with towns and small cities, with acres of farmland in between. Lush vegetation lined the thruway, interspersed with thick trees that grew wide and curved to create a canopy of branches. The fog had dissipated by late morning, and in the far distance, Silas could see lookout points in bright colors in the center of the fields. The whole scene was a postcard.

He took out his camera, ignoring Tara's grunt of irritation at being jostled, and tried to get what he could through the front and side windows.

Halfway through the trip, when they were far enough outside of Delhi that the air coming through Chaya's open window smelled fresh and sweet, they stopped in Murthal where dozens of roadside dhabas lined the road. The bus pulled into a large lot with space for parking. Green plastic lawn chairs and small white tables spread out in front of a brick stand. There was a grill station and huge signs that read, "Chaa" and "Parantha." On the left side of the open kitchen hung a billboard with an arrow that said, "Toilet," pointing to the side of the building. Considering they'd been on the road for almost four hours, pretty much everyone on the bus had to pee, including Silas.

What sucked was that as a junior guide, he had no choice but to wait until at least half the students had their turn in the communal bathrooms first.

"Does anyone have any wipes?" Amit asked. "I think I touched something gross."

"Here," Beth said, handing him a wet wipe from her pink backpack.

"Is this antibacterial?"

Beth rolled her eyes. "What, did you wipe your butt with your bare hand after pooping?"

"Ew, no!"

"Then take the wipe."

Chetna wiped down her phone, then continued scrolling. "Public restrooms are usually icky, but my mom took me to Europe last year, and we had to go use a London restroom—now that's luxury."

"Well, they did take India's money and resources to build their infrastructure," Amit said. "So you can actually thank India for that."

"I wonder if *she* is complaining about public restroom use," Dax said. He nodded at Tara, who stood separate from her group, looking at her phone. "When we were talking in the back of the bus, Sunny said that she's the worst to travel with."

"First of all, that's uncalled for and mean." Silas adjusted his backpack. "I think y'all underestimate her."

"You're only saying that because you have *ulterior motives*," Dax said.

Beth, Chetna, and Amit giggled.

Why did Silas have to deal with the smartasses? "If you're done roasting me, let's get back to the bus. I think we're supposed to meet there."

They walked over to the group. Tara stood to the side by herself while the rest of the students surrounded Sunny, who sounded like he was telling some story about the first time he was in India. Before Silas could approach Tara, Neil let out his annoying piercing whistle again.

"We're going to have lunch here! Sit with your groups you sat with last night, please. If you need help ordering, we'll come around and assist, but your junior guides can help you."

Silas spotted the small chalkboard next to the counter. Most of it was in Hindi or Punjabi. He couldn't tell. He sure as hell wouldn't be able to guide his kids in picking pretty much anything at this rate. As usual, a part of him wished that he'd grown up speaking the language, but his moms and he had always communicated just fine in English with Hindish words thrown in.

Hopefully the students were self-sufficient—and they could help him.

As he pulled out a chair to sit, Tara passed behind him and leaned in so only he could hear. "Just tell everyone to get the parantha thali."

"What?"

"The parantha thali," she said again. "You know. Paranthas? Stuffed bread? Everyone in Murthal gets the paranthas. It comes with a huge lump of white butter. Just don't eat the raw salad or yogurt; otherwise, you'll get Delhi belly since you're not used to the food."

Thank the gods for that. He winked at her. "Thanks. You're a lifesaver."

"It's payback for letting me vent a little."

"I'm here if you ever need to do it again."

Silas could tell she was trying to hide a smile as she walked away.

He watched her for a moment longer and knew that there was no way she was as cutthroat as people made her out to be. Tara had been brutally straightforward with him so far, and he couldn't imagine someone like that changing so drastically over four months.

He took his seat, then realized his entire group was staring at him. "What?"

"Pathetic," Chetna said, scrolling on her phone.

He didn't bother responding.

When a boy came around to ask what they wanted to eat, Silas asked for the parantha thali and chai like he was a pro. A natural. Still, his group continued to roast him and slow-clapped at his efforts.

While they were waiting for food, two large open-bed trucks pulled up to the stop, filled with Sikh men at varying ages dressed in white kurtas. They had been driving in the opposite direction and had done a U-turn through the opening in the median to eat at the dhaba. That meant they were coming *from* Punjab, Silas realized.

"Whoa," he heard someone from one of the neighboring tables say. Whoa was right. These dudes *worked*. They had broad shoulders and thick hands and beards. Their skin was weathered from the sun, and wide pagdis were expertly tied around their heads. Even the ones well into old age looked stronger than Silas could ever be.

They made such an impression at first sight that Silas itched for his camera, to capture their image of resiliency, but he was sure that would be rude as hell.

A few of them began chatting with the men in the open kitchen in rapid Punjabi.

"Does anyone know what they're saying?" Beth asked.

"They're going to Delhi to join the ongoing rallying for the farmers' protest," Tara said, looking over at his table.

"I thought that ended a while ago," one of her group members replied, a girl named Jhumpa with a mass of curly black hair and large oval glasses. "Didn't the government say yes to everything they asked for? They repealed a bunch of stuff, right?"

"A lot of farmers died during COVID," Tara explained. "The government tried to seize their land, but as a result of the protests, the government promised to give it back to the families. There are ongoing talks about delivering on those promises. Chances are, with the state of the government, talks will last years."

Now Silas really wanted to reach for his camera. This was a memory he should freeze in time. The fight for preserving farmland was so important, and it fit in perfectly with his photojournalism project about conservation and climate crises.

"Those laws would've been great for farmers, if you ask me," Sunny Deol said, walking over to them. "I read in BBC that some could've made so much money if they would've let the three little laws go through. No big deal, but Punjabis are always trying to pick a fight. It's in our nature, I guess."

The whole group stared at Sunny Deol like he'd lost his mind. Thankfully, none of the other dhaba patrons seemed to notice what was going on with the American kids.

But then Tara slowly stood.

She looked *pissed*.

It would only be a matter of time before things got heated if she confronted Sunny the way she was about to do. Silas gripped the arms of his chair, waiting in case Tara needed backup.

"You're in Punjab, wearing thousands of dollars of designer shit, commenting on the livelihood of people you know nothing about," she said evenly. "The least you can do is shut the hell up and be respectful in front of them."

Sunny Deol smirked, crossing his arms over his chest. "Oh, did I hit a nerve, princess? You, with your daddy's money, have no right to talk. Or are you defending them because your mom is a religious cultist and she guilted you into having a bleeding heart?"

"That sounds better than spending my entire life trying and failing to live up to the success of four older brothers," Tara shot back. "You just sound like an asshole. Saw your oldest in *Forbes* last month, by the way. He's looking fine."

"Sunny didn't tell us that," one of the kids at Tara's table whispered.

Sunny's face mottled with rage. "I wouldn't be comparing siblings if I were you. Considering *your* sister's history."

"Literally every nasty comment that comes out of your mouth is a joke," she said, inspecting her nails, then buffing them against her shoulder. "You want to bring up my sister again? Fine. But just as a reminder, your parents named you *Sunny Deol*, the least talented Punjabi actor in the history of India. That's how much faith they had in you to succeed. How can anyone take you seriously?"

Silas winced, and Tara must've seen his expression. "Too much?"

"Just a bit," Silas said.

"If I'm the least talented person here," Sunny said, "then why am I the one headed to Berkeley and you're off to some no-name liberal-arts school in the middle of nowhere?"

"Because your parents paid for you to get in?"

The students collectively oohed.

The accusation didn't faze Sunny in the slightest. "Money gets people places, and I'm not ashamed of mine like you and your mother are. It comes in handy when I need something from someone, and I'm smart enough to use it in my favor."

What a douche, Silas thought.

"Oh, so you're completely okay with using money for people to like you?" Tara asked.

"Of course," he replied. "It's the only way to get ahead."

"Someone's been listening to dude bro finance podcasts, but fine. Let's put it to the test."

Sunny's cocky expression disappeared. "Wait, what?"

"I want to see if your theory works." Tara pushed past him.

Silas watched as she first approached Neil and Chaya and said something in low tones. When they nodded vigorously, she crossed the dhaba, approaching the group of farmers settling down with their chai. She began calling out something in Punjabi to get their attention. The crowd quieted.

Tara's voice carried across the seating area as she spoke in Punjabi as crisp and clear as if it were her native language—at least, that's what it sounded like to Silas. Then, she turned and pointed at Sunny Deol.

The group of Punjabi farmers began cheering. A few got out of their seats and approached Sunny, who stood frozen in confusion as they clapped him on his back, shook his hand, and spoke to him in a mix of heavily accented English and Punjabi.

"That's badass," Chetna said. She had finally put down her phone and was watching the show along with everyone else.

"What did she say?" Amit asked. "I didn't understand."

Tara came back to her seat, sparing Sunny one last glance over her shoulder. "I told them he's paying for their meals and chai to honor their hard work in protesting for agricultural rights in India."

"You did *what*?"

"You heard me," Tara said to Sunny. "And look at that; your theory is right. People who should hate you for your political beliefs seem pretty happy with you right now."

As Sunny tried to tell people that Tara was mistaken, that there was no way he was paying for everyone, strangers kept approaching him, talking over his quivering voice, and shaking his hand in their large grips.

Silas couldn't wait anymore. He retrieved his camera from his bag, adjusted the lens, and began taking pictures. Of Sunny Deol's face. Of Tara's smirk. Of the dhaba patrons who had obviously figured out what had happened. Frame after frame after frame, he tried to get as much as he could.

When the chai arrived in melamine cups, Neil demonstrated how to cool the drink with the empty glass included with the carrier. He poured the steaming liquid back and forth, creating a long arch of rich golden-brown liquid. A perfect chai stream.

Sunny's voice faded into the background as Silas gripped the empty cup in one hand and his hot drink in the other so he could try for himself. Over the dirt ground, he began pouring back and forth, watching the chai make a perfect arc like Neil's demonstration. Then he took his first sip of the complex, rich milk tea at the roadside dhaba.

He didn't know what kind of tea they used, or anything about the recipe at all. All he knew was that what he got in the US and during his one trip to Goa was not real chai. This Punjabi chai was sweet and spicy, with hints of cardamom, ginger, and cinnamon. It was the most perfect beverage he'd ever had.

"Neil, this isn't cool," Sunny said, interrupting Silas's chai moment.

"You can clear this up by telling the owners they'll have to resume billing everyone," Neil said to Sunny.

"Make Tara pay for it," Sunny whined. "She started this."

"Technically, you started it," Neil replied. "And you can end it, too."

"They could literally beat me up."

"No, but they won't like you."

There was a long pause before Sunny let out a sigh. "I guess I'm paying for everyone's meal." He looked at Tara, who toasted him with her chai cup. "This means war."

"I look forward to it."

Silas glanced back and forth between the two of them, then down at his chai. "I love my India."

His table booed him and threw their napkins.

8

DAY 5: AMRITSAR, PUNJAB

GOLDEN TEMPLE

Postcard dated January 19—one year ago:

Did Mom give you the genealogy lecture? If not, here's the quick version. Our grandmother was born in Lahore before the partition, then moved with her parents to Amritsar as a child, and finally settled in the hill station Shimla high in the mountains. Our grandfather found work in Delhi, and that's where they lived until Mom was born. When she was fifteen, Dada had a research opportunity at Rutgers University, and moved to the States. Then Mom met Dad when they were in their twenties, a story I still don't really know. I tell you all of this to say, give yourself grace. The ink of our immigration story is not dry yet.

Miss you, munchkin.

Love,

Didi

Tara woke to her phone buzzing under her pillow. She answered without opening her eyes.

"Hello?"

"Tara? It's Chaya."

"Yeah?"

"I just wanted to remind you to bring something to cover your head today at the Golden Temple."

"Yeah, I've been there before. I know."

There was silence on the other end. Her sleepiness cleared just enough for her to realize what she'd said sounded mean. When had it become an automatic knee-jerk reaction for her to be rude to people? At some point in her life, she'd realized that the meaner she was, the more people thought she was cool, but she'd had to work at it at first—unlike Umma, for whom being mean came naturally. Now, it was like second nature to Tara, too.

One of her family friends, Shakti, had told her at last year's Diwali party that she made a terrible first impression. Tara was beginning to think she made a terrible third impression, too. No wonder her relationships and friendships had failed. Even in her sleepy state, she could see that she'd screwed up.

"Sorry," she said, her voice clearing. "I didn't mean to snap. I just woke up. Thanks for the reminder."

"No problem," Chaya replied, her voice more cheerful. "Breakfast is in fifteen minutes. Will you be ready by then?"

Biting back a groan, Tara grunted a yes and said something she hoped sounded like a goodbye before hanging up.

Jet lag was finally catching up with her. She usually had a foolproof method of getting through it, but she'd been too busy trying to avoid Sunny Deol. After the little stunt she'd pulled at the dhaba—which was freaking hilarious, in her opinion—she figured he was probably going to carry through with his threat of getting back at her. She didn't know what she'd done to gain Silas's support, but he'd been running interference between them, thankfully.

She grabbed her phone to check the time, her thumb automatically pressing on the same spot as the social-media apps she'd used the most. She had thought it would be easier to cleanse and detox from social media once she'd officially cut herself off, but every day, she felt the desire to redownload them and plug back in to her old world. Thankfully, the urges were growing further and further apart.

After another moment of scrolling through her phone, with zero new emails, zero text messages, and zero notifications, she got up and got ready for the first temple trip of the day. Her laptop was open to research and notes she'd started to pull together for a story she was thinking about, so she quickly saved her work and locked it in the safe.

She wished she had more time to spend researching that day, but the good news was they were at least going to the Golden Temple. It was huge, filled with a reverent silence that was expected of patrons.

After brushing her teeth with bottled water and taking a quick shower, she braided her hair tightly. If there was something she had to pray for, it was the lack of frizz. Luckily, there was an abundance of deliciously fragrant coconut oil at her disposal to keep her hair healthy while she was here.

The sound of the air conditioning kicked on in the bath, a pleasant reminder that the tour group was staying at a hotel in Amritsar near the Golden Temple that was a hell of a lot nicer than the accommodations she and her parents usually stayed in. There was even a swan towel animal on her bed when she walked in. The lobby was encased in marble from floor to ceiling, yet according to the website, it was forty US dollars a night. Her parents could spend more than that, and still she'd taken bucket baths in a communal living space for years.

Tara remembered once that a high school friend said that she loved camping, and it was now a *thing*. Bucket baths were her mother's version of camping. Glamorous if done by choice, frowned upon if done by necessity.

That's when Tara had learned about guilt. She was taught to feel shame for what she had, the life she went back to, and according to her mother, living without means for a few months to conduct research was enough penance for privilege.

Her sister was the only person who ever called her mother out for that bullshit behavior.

After applying sunblock, Tara dressed in a pair of linen pants and a short kurta kameez cut at midthigh. She pleated her long cotton chunni, which matched her kurta top, then decided to go full Punjabi and draped it across the front of her neck. That way, she would have better luck fitting in at the temple and blending into the background. Otherwise, she'd get quite a number of odd looks as part of a group of South Asian diaspora teens.

After checking the mirror to make sure the back ends of her chunni were even, Tara grabbed her small day pack, which was compact enough to get through temple security, and went downstairs for breakfast.

When she entered the small restaurant off the main lobby, she saw that most of the tour was already eating. She approached the group she'd sat with a few times now, who all stopped to stare at her as she pulled out an empty chair.

"What?" she said at their shocked faces. Low-level anxiety buzzed within her whenever she was around them. She already knew her presence made them feel uncomfortable, but this was more than usual.

"You're dressed in *Indian* clothes," Faruk said, adjusting their glasses. "Was that part of our assignment?"

Tara motioned to the rest of the group. "Obviously not."

Their cheeks reddened. "Right. Yeah. Uh, you look nice."

This was awkward.

"Thanks," she said, then remembered Chaya's phone call that morning. "Do all of you have something to cover your hair with for when we go inside?"

Three heads nodded.

"Oh, I forgot," Happy said, one of the younger girls in the group. She had a riot of thick curls that she'd pushed through a hair tie on the top of her head. "What do I do?"

"Do you have something in your room?"

She shook her head. "I have money to buy stuff if I need it, but will we have time to stop somewhere? Are they going to let me in?"

Tara reached into her day pack and pulled out a small shawl that she always carried for emergencies on holy trips. She handed the shawl to Happy. "You can use this if you want. Or you can wait until we get inside the gate. They offer head coverings at all the gurdwaras in India for people who leave theirs at home."

Happy's eyes widened, but she nodded and took the shawl. "Thank you."

"Sure."

When everyone at the table continued to stare at Tara, she decided that her best option at this point was to ignore them. She plugged in her AirPods and ordered breakfast. She was halfway through her book and bhature chole, systematically demolishing the puffy, yeasty bread and chickpea curry, when someone tapped her on the shoulder.

After wiping her hands, she took out her AirPods and looked up at Silas's smiling face.

"Hi," he said, his voice cheerful. "You look great."

"Hi." She glanced at him up and down. He was wearing a fitted T-shirt and jeans with a thin corded belt that had a subtle pride flag on the buckle, as well as an orange bandana tied around his head. Curls popped out at his temples and at the nape of his neck. She'd always been into the artistic types, and Silas had artist painted all over him. "Do we have to go now?"

"Yeah. Neil and Chaya asked me to come over here and tell you that we're getting on the bus in ten minutes. If you guys have to use the bathroom or record one of your dance videos in the parking lot, now is the time to do it."

Her tablemates climbed out of their seats and dispersed like ants.

Silas collapsed in one of the vacated chairs. "Man, middle school kids are intense. They just stared at you for, like, fifteen minutes while you ate."

Tara tore off another piece of her bhatura and folded it into a triangle to scoop her chole. "I would say that you could've come over and helped a girl out, but you've done enough already."

Silas grinned. "You mean keeping enemy number one away? I don't mind that. Besides, it's fun watching you be completely unbothered by how hard he's trying to get your attention. You are the coolest cucumber ever, Tara Bajaj."

She thought about his assessment as she scooped up more chole. It was so much harder than she realized to take the compliment. "Would you believe me if I told you that a month ago, my doctor prescribed medication for my anxiety because I was losing sleep, spending every night reading comments about me on social media?"

He tilted his head to the side. "Nothing wrong with getting help. Did the medicine work?"

She shrugged. Her mother had taken the script and tossed it, fearing that Tara would develop a substance-abuse problem like her sister.

"I'm fine."

"I think you're better than fine."

She raised a brow, delighting in the fact that his cheeks darkened in color.

"That's not what I meant," he said, rubbing the back of his neck. "And you know it."

That made her laugh. "I'm offended that that's not what you meant. But yes, I'm better than fine. I think my saving grace is that I still have one or two friends left despite the fact that I haven't talked to them in a long time." She still considered Jai a friend. There was also Swati, a family friend from the community culture events. And then

Jai's new girlfriend, who was kind to her, even when their first meeting was atrocious.

Tara had stopped responding to their texts a while back. She deserved what happened to her after her falling-out with Umma, and she didn't want them to get caught in the crossfire.

Hopefully when she returned to the States she could reconnect with them.

"Well, now you have me," Silas said. "We junior guides gotta stick together. Or rather, you and I do. After Sunny shelled out a few hundred USDs for that stunt you pulled, I doubt he'd hold out a hand if you were falling off a cliff."

"Thanks for the reminder," Tara said dryly. She wiped her hands on a napkin. "I'm pretty sure he's telling all the kids every dirty thing he could think about to get back at me." That was what she was assuming was happening, anyway.

"I think his story is the only one they've heard," Silas said. "And it's up to you to either show them you're not what they think you are or tell them. Either way, the ball is in your court. You don't have to do anything you don't want to."

"You're giving me advice this time," Tara mused.

He smiled at her, bright and carefree. "I am. Come on, sunshine. Let's go see a temple!"

He picked up a clean spoon from the utensil holder and dipped it into her chole bowl before she could stop him.

"Oh man," he said, after slipping the spoon in his mouth. "I should've gotten that."

He placed the spoon back on the table and walked out the exit.

Tara was left alone in the dining room with half a plate of food.

~

Even though the religious pilgrimages of her childhood were exhausting, Tara was always struck speechless when she visited the Golden Temple. She loved its majestic architecture, the long causeway stretching from the complex walls to the gold structure in the middle of the Amrit Sarovar, the sacred pool where some worshippers dipped in the waters. Most of the rectangular building in the center of the Amrit Sarovar was overlaid in gold leaf, a central dome shining brightly in the hot morning sun. She was standing in the epicenter of Sikhism, a place founded on the premise that everyone is welcome regardless of faith and background.

Not that she would ever admit her love for the Golden Temple to her mother.

Tara followed behind her group as they attended the religious service. Neil was the tour guide, sharing history and philosophy as they walked through the outer complex and saw the clock tower, the Central Sikh Museum, the tree where it was rumored that Buddha sat to meditate, and the memorials. As time ticked on, the crowds became a mix of international and domestic tourists, mostly Sikh Punjabis with their pagdis tied with artistry or long guttis on women, decorated with a parandi dangling in a colorful display at the end of their braid.

Happy, one of the quietest people in Tara's group and one of the few who was Sikh, tapped her on the arm halfway through their tour.

"When was this built again?" she asked, adjusting the borrowed shawl draped over her head.

"1604," Tara answered automatically.

"Wow, and this is the original architecture?"

"Original architecture with a few modifications. The temple was destroyed multiple times over the centuries by invaders. What you see now is the rebuild from the early nineteenth century."

"Holy cow. How do you know all this?"

For the first time since she was a kid, she didn't hesitate or feel any shame at telling Happy the truth. "My mom is a religious studies scholar. I've been reading about religious history and structures built to commemorate ritual practices since I was a kid."

Happy cocked her head. "Did she make you go on this trip, too?"

"This trip and, like, a dozen others."

Happy nodded. "My mother sent me because she and my dad said it would be good for my college applications and also a way for me to become more spiritual."

"As long as that's what you want," Tara said.

Silas turned to look over his shoulder from where he was walking with a few of the guys. He glanced at Happy, at Tara, then winked before turning around.

Now what was she supposed to make of that?

When they reached a quiet corner in the quickly crowding complex, Neil asked everyone to huddle in. "One of the most important ways that Sikhs uphold the golden principles of their faith is through sewa, or selfless service," Neil said at the head of the group. "This afternoon, during the lunch hours, we'll be supporting the langar here in serving meals to those in need."

"You've done this before, right, Tara?" Sunny asked casually. "Oh wait—no, I remember. Didn't you disappear the last time you were supposed to do langar?"

She *had* disappeared when they were on the tour together, but that was only because the volunteer leads had recognized her. Her mother had dragged Tara and her sister to the Golden Temple to observe and assist in langar for months the year before so that her mother could work on a paper about the largest volunteer food kitchen in the world. Tara had gotten very familiar with the massive roti machine, which made over twenty-five thousand rotis an hour, and had been asked to help with the machine again. She wasn't exactly in a position to say no since she was so young.

"It was disturbing then and it's disturbing now the way you are constantly trying to figure out where I was going and what I was doing," Tara said calmly.

Irritation crossed his face, and maybe hurt. That was a low blow.

Okay, now she regretted throwing that in his face. It wasn't fair to use his feelings against him. He *had* genuinely liked her, and mocking him for it was what she'd done in front of Umma all those months ago, too.

Before she could say something else, anything to lessen the retort, Chaya began issuing directions.

Silas inched closer to Tara. "This volunteer thing sounds intense, huh?"

"You have to be . . . fast," she murmured back, still distracted by what she'd said to Sunny.

"If you could do it, then I'm hoping I can do it, too."

Tara snorted. "My mother trained me for langar like the Olympics."

"What about your dad?"

"My dad trained me to eat three veggie burgers and then go on the same roller coaster six times in a row before finishing with dessert and not even feeling nauseous."

Silas's eyes widened. "You are way scarier than you let people believe, aren't you?"

"Probably."

"Right now, you all have about two hours to yourself," Neil said, cutting through the conversation. "You cannot leave the temple gates, and you must stay with a junior guide or one of us. Absolutely no one is allowed to be left alone. We'll meet right back here." He pointed to a white sign above his head, which was written in three languages. "Have fun!"

The twins, Ina and Gina, and quiet Ravi followed Sunny to one of the museums, where paltry puffs of air conditioning blasted from the entrance. Jhumpa and Happy trailed after Chaya toward the gift shop to get more head coverings for themselves. The rest of the five students stayed back, looking expectantly at Tara and Silas.

"It's so hot I'm going to drown in my own sweat," Faruk complained. "Where should we go that won't kill us?"

"My mother says I'm a delicate wildflower," Amit added. "Wildflowers die in this heat, Silas. Save us."

Silas smiled at Tara, then tilted his head toward Amit and Faruk as if to say, *Look at these two.* "You guys want to help me with my pictures? This is my moment to re-create my moms' photo."

"Maybe Tara can help you find the spot where the picture was taken," Chetna said, looking as bored as Tara felt.

"You know, that's actually a great suggestion," Silas said.

Tara had no idea what they were talking about. Before she could ask, Silas took his cell phone out of his pocket and scrolled across the screen. "Here," he said, holding out the phone.

Tara took it and squinted at the old photo. Two young women in their teens stood at least ten feet apart at the left side of the Amrit Sarovar, facing the causeway that connected to the sanctum in the center. The water was brilliant blue under the sun, exactly how it was today.

Although blurry with age, the photo was beautiful.

Tara remembered Silas mentioning the pictures and a contest, but he hadn't gotten into it. They'd been too busy eating McDonald's.

She squinted in the light, and then pointed to the end of the Amrit Sarovar, where she was pretty sure the picture was taken. "Based on the angle, it's around the corner over there to the left."

Silas's face broke out in a grin. "Seriously? I thought it would take forever to figure out where some of these locations are. Come on! Let's go."

He took his phone back, and then, in a move that shocked Tara down to her bare feet, he grabbed her hand and pulled her toward the pool. His fingertips were calloused, and his palm was sweaty with warmth, but it was . . . nice. It had been a long time since she held hands with someone.

And this hand, Tara thought, was steady. That meant a lot to her after being so unsure of everything for the last few months.

All five kids followed in a close huddle, weaving through the crowd of visitors. They chattered away as Silas sprinted to the location, dragging her along.

"He's trying to re-create all these old photos of his moms. They met on this trip, and he wants to do a whole photo series of past and present pictures."

"Isn't he supposed to be here for us? As our junior guide?"

"Do you have any better ideas? This is probably the best entertainment we're going to have for the rest of the day."

"We're literally in India, at the Golden Temple. There are lots of things to do."

"Oh, shut up."

When they reached the correct corner of the Sarovar, Tara slipped her hand out of Silas's, knowing it was for the best, and pointed to the spot. "There, I think? If not, then maybe farther down, but based on the angle, I think that's it."

Silas walked in a circle that led right back to her. He took a deep breath. "Wow, I think you're right. This is where my moms took their first picture together."

"That's the moment you're choosing to re-create?"

"Yup." He slid his shoulder pack around to the front so he could pull out a compact tripod. With speed and efficiency, he unfolded the tripod, hooked up the camera, and began adjusting the lens.

Tara stepped back, watching him work quickly. The students did the same. He was in his element. He knew exactly what he was doing, and he was obviously enjoying every minute of it.

When his camera was set up and positioned at the right angle, he motioned for his group to come forward. "Amit, I set the camera and the timer. I just need you to press this button here when I say the word. Chetna? I need you to try to make some space for me on the left side.

Dax on the right." Silas pointed to one of the quietest kids at Tara's dinner table. "Sorry, I didn't catch your name."

"I'm Faruk," they said. "My pronouns are they-them."

"Faruk," Silas said. "Do you think you can help block the right side so that we don't get anyone crossing the shot when we take it?"

"Yeah, sure."

"Great. We'll probably only have a few moments to get a shot because of the people walking by. Let's move into position now."

The students spread out. Tara stood next to Amit, watching as Chetna, Beth, Dax, and Faruk directed Silas into the right position. He stood to the left of the frame, and five minutes later, there was an opening. Amit took the shot.

"Got it!"

Silas ran over to look at the picture on the small display screen.

"I guess it's okay," Beth said. "But it's weird that it's just you."

Dax smirked. "Maybe *Tara* can stand in the spot where your other mom is in the picture. You know, to balance it out."

All the kids groaned at him, shoving him in the arm.

"No, he's got a point," Silas said. "Tara, will you be in this picture with me? I want to submit it for a competition, and it might end up on display."

She looked down at her linen pants, her bare feet, and the ends of her chunni, which she'd draped over her head and across her neck. "I'm good."

"No, you totally should!" Beth said. She snatched Tara's pack and nudged her forward.

"Come on, it'll be fine," Silas said. He gently cupped her shoulders and began shifting her into place, positioning her at one end of the camera frame and angling her body after checking the picture. He then asked her to bend a knee, slide her foot forward, and tuck her hands behind her back. His fingertips, the calloused ones that she didn't mind so much, angled her chin ever so slightly. "There," he said quietly, then moved into his position and assumed the same pose as before.

"What's this for again?" she asked, her heart beating just a tad bit faster than normal at his close proximity.

"A photojournalism competition," he said. "I'm starting by using my moms' photos as a frame to re-create an image, but I'm hoping to build a story around the differences in the setting."

She scanned the slowly moving crowd around them. "What kind of differences?"

He moved away, giving them distance to match the photo. "I think I want to focus on how India's attempt at keeping up with Western worlds in industry is costing the country in history and ecology. Pilgrimage sites like these are now moneymakers, and it's coming at a cost."

The words that came out of his mouth were so jarring that she almost stepped backward into the pool. "*Excuse* me?"

She didn't even notice the students calling out to them about the shots.

"What?" he asked, his attention divided between her and his camera.

"I'm sorry, but there is no way I can be a part of that project," she said. The very idea of it made her cringe.

Everyone stopped to stare at her.

"Wait, why not?"

The kids were whispering. She began to step down and separate herself from them when Silas stopped her with a touch on her arm.

"Please," he said. "Tell me. Because if you have a problem with it, someone else might, too. I want to be able to fix it if I can."

She hesitated before saying, "You're raised in the US with more privilege than more than half the people here." She motioned around them. "India has become so powerful, but like the US there is a different type of oppression here that we're looking at as outsiders. You're coming to India, on a religious youth group trip that is supposed to be a *job*, with the intention of taking pictures to win a contest. On top of that, your submission is solely about how shitty India is."

Silas's face went ashen, his eyes widening. "That wasn't—I mean, I just wanted to show—"

"We don't have the same rights over places like these as our parents do," she said. "There are a lot of shades of gray to how temples and religious pilgrimages support communities. Yeah, not all of it is great, especially since so many are casteist to this day, but you're not acknowledging nuance. I can't support that."

"Tara, we *belong* here. We're from the same ancestry. That's why this is so important to me. Because I feel like I *can* speak on this and create change."

Tara took another step away, increasing the space between them. "I don't make it a habit of agreeing with my mother, but I do on this. These people here can talk about what's happening to them and their communities. You're a kid of immigrant parents in America. The India your parents own is not the same India that belongs to you. What change can you make if what you say lacks truth?"

She hopped off the ledge and began walking toward the gift shops.

9

Day 8: Punjab

Silas couldn't sleep for days. Tara had deflated his entire project with one quick prick of a needle. He should be grateful that she'd saved him from embarrassment, but that still left him with absolutely nothing for his submission.

He'd felt an itch of desperation when he graduated with no foreseeable way out of the wedding-photography business, but now that desperation was all consuming. What was he supposed to do? Here he was in India with so much creative opportunity in front of him, and absolutely zero direction.

No, that wasn't true. He had direction. He was there for the kids, as Tara had reminded him. He was being paid to be a junior tour guide. He wasn't there for himself. The pictures were supposed to come secondary to the experience.

They'd visited the Durgiana Temple that day, a near replica of the Golden Temple except on a much smaller scale, and helped with langar again, dishing out food to rows of people seated side by side on the floor. The monotony of it had helped him focus his thoughts.

By the time he got back to his room after dinner, he was tired of pretending to be invested in the conversations around him. He showered the sweat of the day off and slipped into a pair of shorts. It was almost eleven when there was a soft knock on his door.

He opened it a crack. Before he could greet the person on the other side, Tara had slipped inside his room and closed the door behind her.

"Hey, what—"

"Shh," she hissed. "I think I saw Chaya in the hallway when I came up here."

"Okay," he said softly, acutely aware of how close she was standing to him. "What's going on?"

"I, uh . . . came to check on you."

Her eyes dropped to his naked chest. Silas had to admit he enjoyed the way they widened at the realization that he was in only shorts. But he didn't want to scare her off, so he walked over to the bed and slipped on a T-shirt he'd discarded that morning.

"As you can see, I am completely fine."

"You looked like hell at dinner." She paused, her arms crossed tightly over her chest. "Are you mad at me? You haven't spoken to me all day, and if you don't know this about yourself, you're a bit of a chatterbox."

Her question had him shaking his head. "What? No, not at all. I'm mad at *me*. I wish I saw how problematic my project was sooner. And I'm glad you said something at the very first picture. I can't imagine what I would've done if we'd gone through Jammu and Kashmir." He cringed. "Well, I guess it doesn't matter either way. I have no idea what I'm supposed to do."

She turned to open his door a fraction to peek outside. After a few seconds, she shut it again. "The coast looks clear. Meet me out front in a couple minutes."

"Yes—wait. I mean, why? Where are we going?"

"To get food, of course. Hurry up, please."

With that, she was gone, leaving the scent of jasmine and coconut in her wake. He'd noticed she always seemed to gravitate to the flowers whenever they walked through a temple tour. She was beginning to smell just as sweet.

It took him less than five minutes to switch into board shorts and flip-flops. He sneaked down the stairs, which were closer to his room than the elevator bank, and stepped into the muggy night air moments later.

"You ready?"

He turned to see Tara leaning against the side of the hotel building. Now that he wasn't consumed with the thought that she was in his room, he noticed how effortlessly beautiful she looked. Her hair was in those braids again, her face devoid of makeup, and her T-shirt was knotted at her waist. As always, she wore simple black sandals that matched all her outfits. They showed off freshly painted toes.

"I'm always ready," he replied.

They followed the map on her phone, much like they'd done the first night they were together. He wasn't exactly sure where she was taking him, so he relied on faith and relaxed into the quiet.

"It should be right . . . there," she said, pointing across the street at what looked like an outdoor bazaar. "I knew there had to be one close by."

"I think the food we've been eating in the hotel has been pretty awesome," Silas said. "That will be hard to beat." He was definitely up for the challenge, though. He'd never say no to eating.

"When my mother would take us on these research trips, my sister would sneak me out at night, and we'd go explore the food markets. To this day, I think the best food in India is the street food. Especially in the outdoor bazaars. They are so fun, and vibrant."

"We'll have to test it out."

They turned into a small alley lined with carts. The string lights made a web of twinkly stars over their heads, brightening the way. Couples and families strolled at an easy pace, enjoying late-night walks. The sound of metal dishes against portable grates mixed with conversation. A rainbow of colored canopies created the perfect snapshot that Silas would remember for years to come. This was a part of India he never knew and was always desperate to meet.

The first cart they came across had tiny little boats made out of dried banana leaves, which were filled with yeasty bread, brushed with hot ghee, and stuffed with vegetables. Black sesame seeds were sprinkled across the top.

"Amritsari kulcha," she said. "Want to try one?"

"I'm down."

She rattled off the order in Punjabi, handed over a few rupees, and accepted the kulcha. They stepped to the side, away from the trickle of passersby enjoying the late night, and hovered over the hot, spicy kulcha, which Tara held out between them.

"Vent or advice?" she asked.

Silas tore off a corner of the kulcha, his mouth watering as tendrils of steam escaped the white, fluffy triangle, before he took a bite. He moaned at the salty, spicy flavors exploding across his tongue. "Holy shit, how is bread that good? It's just bread!"

"No, it's kulcha." Tara laughed. "You're stalling."

"I'm enjoying kulcha," he said, then sighed. "Okay, I'm stalling. God, I feel like such an idiot for not seeing it before. Like the minute I would've submitted my essay to the contest, I would've gotten *roasted* for that view. But I was so determined to take advantage of my opportunity to be a part of this trip that I didn't even think about how it might look to everyone else. Or how shitty it was to misrepresent where I was born. And that makes me feel even more like an idiot. I'm jealous of you."

"Of *me*?"

"Yeah," he said, nudging her in the arm. "Of how well you know the brown side of who you are. I still feel so disconnected sometimes. And this contest . . . well, I thought it would both help me connect more with being Desi, and help me get the opportunities I need."

"What's the purpose of this whole contest thing?"

"It's for a huge media company, kind of like *National Geographic*. They want thirty photos in an order that tells a story, and a two-thousand-word article that goes with it. A commentary on our world and the shifting cultures, communities, environment, you name it. Nothing is off limits. The person who wins gets to be on the cover, and they'll have a chance to intern with one of their travel groups. There's a *job* attached to this."

Tara nodded, chewing on a small piece of kulcha. "What do your moms think about it?"

He let out a frustrated huff. "I'm a chicken. I still haven't told them."

"What? Why?"

"Because they have this incredible studio they've worked so hard to build. They do weddings, graduations, bar and bat mitzvahs, quinceañeras, and sweet sixteens. Which is great—"

Tara shook her head. "It's okay. You can say it's not for you."

She got it, he thought. She understood. "It's not for me. I see how hard they work and how small their world has become." He motioned to the Juliet balconies lining the buildings. The food carts sputtering with fresh deliciousness. The people speaking in quiet conversation in a mix of languages. The pagdis, both muted and colorful, passing by. "I want to understand this. I want to be a part of all of this instead of a spectator."

Tara nodded, polishing off her half of the kulcha. "My sister is one of the smartest people I know. She said to me once that sometimes, it really sucks being a diaspora kid. We're not fully accepted in the US, but we're not fully embraced in India, either. We are our own people. We belong to each other. That means understanding that you can be marginalized in one place and privileged in another. Or marginalized and privileged at the same time and the same space."

He nodded, digesting her words. "I think I'm following." He liked seeing this part of her, with her flushed skin and fire in her eyes.

"All I'm saying," she continued, "is that you don't have to give up on this contest. You just have to . . . do something different."

He took the empty carton from her and tossed it in a nearby trash receptacle. "That's a lot harder than it seems."

They rejoined the flow of people and moved through more food carts.

"I've been thinking about this contest forever," he finally added. "And when the opportunity to be a junior guide came up, I was, like, great. I can work, learn about all these amazing places that my moms visited, and take pictures for this contest, too. I don't have money to do it on my own, and it's the same itinerary, so why not do it this way? It was selfish of me to think that."

"We're glorified babysitters," Tara admitted. "That part isn't really that big of a deal. As long as you're not, like, ignoring the kids. Kind of like we're doing now, I guess. You know what? I feel like if we do this again, we should just come clean and text Chaya and Neil."

"Probably," Silas said. He still wanted to sneak out even if Chaya and Neil said no. It was as if he was sharing a special secret with Tara. "God, now I feel guilty about eating delicious food!"

Tara stopped in front of a stall that sold crispy Amritsari fish pakoras. The coolers next to the fry station looked suspiciously like some of the sketchy hot dog carts in New York, so much so that Tara motioned him forward to the samosa cart across the walkway.

"I feel like we're all trying to find out if we're Desi enough through our parents' experience because we have no other connection," Tara said, taking the offered samosa and waiting while Silas handed over a couple of rupees.

"Yeah, I mean, my parents met on this trip," he said. "They fell in love, then decided to come back and adopt me. They are the sole connection I have to this country. Also, why wouldn't I want to understand my connection to India through them? Have you seen their pictures? They're so adorable it hurts my face. I keep smiling at them."

Tara laughed; the sound was still so new to Silas that he smiled in spite of his worries. Then her fingers gripped his arm.

"Wait—Silas, that's your key." Her eyes went wide. "You're thinking conservation, but you should be thinking cultural education. The contest covers culture shifts, right?"

He popped a piece of samosa in his mouth to distract himself from her touch. And then he was distracted by the samosa, which was hot and rich, the potatoes inside fluffy and light. He barely registered her words.

"Silas!"

"What? Yes, I'm listening."

Tara tore off a corner of the triangle and said, "If you want to explore India, explore your history."

"History. Got it."

She raised a brow.

"Okay, don't got it. How?"

"How many states in India criminalized homosexuality when your parents came here and fell in love?"

"All of them," he said automatically. "Moms were scared as hell since they were thirteen in a time and place that didn't let them process their emotions." He still felt a trickle of fear at the base of his neck every time he thought of what could've happened if they hadn't made the choices they had to protect themselves.

Tara's eyebrows wiggled. "And how are you, their adopted son, thriving on the very spots they stood?"

He thought about it. "I get where you're going, but what would the article even say? My moms were lesbians, and I'm their bisexual son? I don't think that will fly."

"No, of course not." She shook her head, her braids sliding over her shoulder. "It could be more like 'my moms were lesbians, and here I am, thirty-some years later, free to express my queer identity because they thrived, and India is the same in some respects yet different in others, just like the diaspora.'"

He stood frozen in place, processing her idea.

It was . . . complicated, but if he could pull it off, it was genius. He thought about all the pictures—the distance between his moms, the moment at the end where they looped arms around each other's shoulders.

"I did some research before the start of this trip, just because I was curious," he admitted. "Did you know some of the temples celebrated gender diversity and sexuality?"

"Yup," she replied, and began rattling off facts like she was a college professor, repeating words from a textbook she'd written herself. "You can't ignore the casteism, homophobia, and the treatment of women that are layered into belief systems, but there are beautiful celebrations in aspects of Hinduism that champion queer identities. Kind of makes you connected to India in more ways than just your moms, right? It could be worth exploring."

He nodded as he tried to process some of the ideas that began rolling through his head. "Do you think I have a chance if I change my submission to this new idea?"

"You can," she said. "And maybe you'll figure out what India and a pan-Desi identity means to you in the process. What your connection to Hinduism means to you."

"Pan-Desi?"

"Oh boy," she said, shaking her head. "You have a lot of research to do."

Pan-Desi. Maybe it was the word, or the confidence on Tara's face, but it was starting to gel in his head. The article, the photos, and the concept. Maybe he could salvage this after all. In one fluid motion, he tossed the empty samosa container away, wrapped his arms around Tara's waist, and spun her in a circle.

She let out a little shriek. "Put me down!"

"Sorry," he said, grinning. He released her and turned to look at all the people staring in front of the food carts. "Sorry," he repeated.

Tara pushed her braids off her shoulder, her cheeks pink in the dim glow cast by the lights that stretched from cart to cart. "Idiot," she mumbled, a smile tugging at the corner of her mouth.

No, he thought. He was an idiot with a *plan*. His mind raced with possibilities, his heart full of hope.

"You're a genius. You've saved my butt. I bet that liberal-arts college gave you a scholarship because of that big brain of yours."

"So did Berkeley."

He paused. "I'm sorry, what? I swear I thought you said, 'So did Berkeley.'"

Tara nodded, the smile coming easier now. "I was supposed to go, but after everything that happened with Umma, Sunny, and the Bollywood dance team, I didn't want to attend the same school. Or be a part of the same dance team circuit. That liberal-arts school in Pennsylvania has no Bollywood dance team, which is perfect for me."

"But dance was a big part of your high school career," Silas said. "It must've been really shitty to lose that."

Tara shrugged, and she shifted from one sandaled foot to the next. "I joined the team because my mom enrolled me in classical dance classes as a kid, and I knew the high school team was the best way to fit in. I was tired of being the religious parent's kid. Or the kid with the Disney dad. I just wanted . . . normalcy."

"Disney dad?" They started walking again, slower this time, their knuckles brushing against each other.

"My father is an executive for . . . well, he's a bigwig that moon-lights as a Hindu pandit. I think he would rather work full time as a pandit, but his day job funds all these religious pilgrimages and temple donations. In addition to my mom's research pilgrimages, we would travel with him on work trips. When I was a kid, I used to think that the theme parks we'd visit were the reward for what my mother put us through, but even that became absolutely exhausting by the time I was a teenager. I am convinced that my parents only had children as an obli-gation; otherwise they would be completely happy in their respective careers. My sister and I are the casualties in their search for happiness."

She led him over to a stall close to the end of the small path. The scent was sweet, and a man sat in front of a wide-mouth wok, sizzling oil sputtering in front of him. With a piping bag, he made little squig-gles with wet dough on the surface of the oil.

Jalebi.

Silas held up two fingers. The slender man, who had biceps that could probably crush a watermelon, nodded in response.

"So did your sister have the same problem in high school that you did?"

"Because of our age gap, my sister had to focus on taking care of me when she was in high school," Tara replied. "And when I no longer needed a babysitter, she was in college, working first at an internship in Dad's company, then in an entry-level job. I don't think she ever got the chance to be anything other than what my parents wanted her to be. That's why I rebelled so hard when I started high school. I tried to hide everything about my weird, eccentric childhood with my fanatical mother, who claims her beliefs are based in research, and my self-centered father."

"Tara, your secrets about your family, about you and Sunny Deol taking this religious trip, they're all out," he said. "What are you going to do now?"

"Yes, now my secrets are out," she repeated quietly. "And I have no idea what I'm supposed to do next."

"Well, first, you're free of pretending to be someone you're not. You're taking back ownership from your parents. That's a lot."

Tara hummed, watching as the man worked quickly. "Silas?"

"Yeah?"

He saw the exhaustion on her face. Whether she was ready to admit that she was able to make choices for her future, he wasn't sure. But the fact that she'd finally told him about her past was probably more than she'd wanted to do tonight.

"Let's just have dessert and get back," she said. "No more venting or advice."

"Sure," he said. "We can do that. And thanks. For helping me with my project."

"No problem. Hey, did you hear that 'Jalebi Baby' song by Tesher? It took me months to realize it was sexual."

He burst out laughing and handed her one of the orders of jalebi. The fried dough was covered in a sweet, sticky, bright-orange syrup, and it smelled divine. "I didn't even know there was a 'Jalebi Baby' song. But now I want to hear it."

"I brought my AirPods."

10

DAY 10: ROAD FROM PUNJAB TO JAMMU AND KASHMIR

Silas liked Tara.

Obviously, he thought she was beautiful; he'd noticed that the very first time he saw her at the airport—that and the fact that she was smart as hell.

But the one thing she'd made pretty clear in their time together was that she was starting over, and sometimes, when people started over, they needed to do things alone.

After a few more sleepless nights in Punjab, not wanting to miss the chance of Tara coming back to his room, offering to take him exploring after hours in the fun parts of the city, he resigned to spending time with her during the day.

And focusing on his pictures. Because now that he had a new direction, he needed to figure out if his game plan had shifted, too.

"Silas? I lost my shoes," Dax said, standing barefoot in the hotel hallway. "I can't leave Punjab without my shoes."

"Where were you the last time you had them?"

"Sleeping?"

"*Sleeping?* Did you check your bed?"

Dax shook his head. "Should I?"

"Probably, dude." Was Silas like that four years ago? He couldn't remember. If so, he'd have to send his parents an apology.

Dax walked back into his room. A second later, Silas heard, *"Found them!"*

"Come on!" he called out into the empty hallway. "The bus is going to leave without you if you don't hurry it up."

He hated that he was stuck rallying the late students. Tara had already climbed on board after breakfast, which meant that Silas had to race onto the bus if he wanted the chance to sit next to her. But for some reason, every kid in his group was determined to delay him that morning.

"We're literally going to be on the bus for the rest of our lives," Chetna said, exiting a door at the end of the hallway.

"We can't be out on the roads after dark," Amit said, exiting his room after Dax. "There are still bandits at night. Like the old-school Bollywood movies from the seventies. They'll stop the bus, and kidnap all of us for either ransom or human trafficking. Most likely human trafficking since we're all young. There's a lot of money in that."

Chetna froze, her eyes growing wide. "You're joking. He's joking, right?"

"Of course he's joking," Silas said, motioning to the elevators impatiently. He made a cut-it-out gesture at Amit, who gave him a *What did I do?* look before rolling his suitcase down the hall after everyone else.

By the time Silas loaded his suitcase into the bus bay and boarded the vehicle, most of the group was already inside. Chetna, traitor that she was, had taken the seat next to Tara. Silas cleared his throat to get her attention, then gave her a pleading expression.

Instead, Chetna rolled her eyes and shook her head. When he looked up, he saw the barest hint of a smile from Tara, but she kept her focus on the scenery out the window, her earbuds firmly in place.

With a sigh, he took the closest seat he could—two rows back, next to Faruk, who had their game console out and a travel pillow hooked around their neck. It didn't look like Mario was doing that hot in the race.

If his seatmate was going to game, Silas would do the same. Just as he booted up *Animal Crossing*, Chaya and Neil boarded the bus, looking more like movie stars than tour guides. Their large-frame aviators matched, and they wore billowing clothes that were both chic and classic. He looked at Neil's wide shoulders and square jaw for a moment longer than he probably should have.

A sharp elbow jabbed him in his rib. He turned to Faruk. "Yeah?"

"Can I ask you a question?" they whispered. "You like both Tara *and* Neil—"

"Whoa, whoa, whoa," Silas whispered back. "I don't *like* Neil. But you must admit the man looks like he's chiseled from brown marble. God told me that I should respectfully admire the way Neil was created."

The comment about Tara, though, he refused to acknowledge. Not yet.

Faruk nodded, their travel pillow sliding off their neck. "Bi?"

Silas nodded back.

Faruk's shoulders relaxed just a bit before they went back to their game. The bus hitched forward.

Silas barely heard Faruk's whisper a moment later. "Did you feel safe wearing your belt yesterday?"

His belt? For a second, he was confused; then he realized what Faruk was referring to. His slim corded pride belt that his parents bought him last Christmas.

"I grew up with two moms," Silas said. "They taught me how to be careful and be safe, but I had to learn what that meant for me. Do you feel safe?"

They shook their head. "Not always. I feel like people judge me here. They're always judging me. My parents made me take this trip after I told them. It was this or a camp in Florida, which felt so much more dangerous. Then I heard that your moms met on the trip."

This was what Tara was talking about, Silas realized with a jolt. The shift in the way queerness in India affected the diaspora. Silas didn't want to make assumptions about Faruk's parents, but having to go on a religious pilgrimage after coming out spoke volumes about their homelife. The fight was never over. It was just starting for some people.

"Joke's on your parents," Silas said lightly. "A lot of Hindu texts embrace queer identities. Most of the places we're going to will have histories supporting people like you and me, and our fellow queer friends."

The corner of Faruk's mouth curved upward. "That sounds awesome. Thanks."

"No problem. Hey, you know how I was doing that photojournalist project? Collecting pictures from our trip?"

"The one about conservation?"

"Yeah, except I'm changing my focus. It's about my moms, and about people like you and me. Think you can help me out? I have to do a ton of research."

"Yeah! That sounds cool."

~

The bus broke down almost three hours from their destination. For most of their drive, they'd been on a wide highway lined by one- or two-story buildings, but here, in the middle of nowhere, a plume of smoke billowed out from under the front hood before Chaya said something that sounded suspiciously like a swear. She pulled over onto the narrow shoulder right next to a large field.

There was a gasp, and then quiet spread over the bus.

"Everyone stay calm," Chaya said in her soft voice. "We'll just see what the problem is and be right back." She followed Neil off the bus. Silas could see the hood pop open from where he was sitting.

Since the vehicle was off, it got warm very quickly.

"I'm going to die," Sunny Deol choked from the back, fanning himself with the tablet he'd been using. "Every person for themselves! I'm getting off the bus."

Before anyone could stop him, he was out of his seat and rushing down the aisle and through the accordion doors.

"Yeah, I'm getting off, too," Dax said. It took less than thirty seconds for everyone else to follow.

Tara stood when her seatmate trailed behind the last of the passengers.

He nodded at her, then turned to Faruk, his camera in hand. "Shall we?"

"Sure," Faruk said.

When they stepped off the bus onto the side of the dusty road, Silas moved next to Tara to look at what was happening. Neil and Chaya were speaking in rapid Punjabi.

"What's going on?" Silas said, leaning down to whisper in Tara's ear.

She tilted her head, exposing the curve of her neck. "We've overheated. They just need to add some radiator fluid and let the bus cool a bit, and we can be back on our way."

"This is what I was talking about earlier," Amit said. "These remote highways are where bandits will find us. I think in certain states, you have to watch out because they'll get you in the middle of the day, too."

Chetna stomped a foot, pointing at Silas and Tara. "Make him stop that! He's freaking me out."

"And us!" Ina said, gesturing at her twin, Gina, who raised her hand.

Jhumpa and Ravi also raised their hands.

"You're fine with us," Chaya said, patting him on the shoulder. "We'll be okay here for twenty minutes or so."

"Oh my god," Gina said, looking at the field next to them. "Are those mustard flowers?" The beautiful green-stemmed plants had a pop of budding yellow at the top. They looked like chaotic wildflowers growing in rows. "I feel like they're always so much taller in the movies."

"This is surprising," Neil said, striding over to Gina and admiring the stretch of land, which was divided into perfect rectangles. What looked like a small gazebo stood in the middle of the field, in the distance. "Paddy harvesting is normally what we would see this time of year in this region. Maybe this farm wanted to have a small crop of mustard by September."

"Beth," Happy said, nudging her friend. "We have to have a Bollywood picture. You know, of us running through the fields?"

Silas had watched enough Bollywood movies to know what she was talking about. There was the iconic Shah Rukh Khan pose, with arms outstretched, standing in a mustard field, waiting for his heroine to run into his arms.

"Neil," Gina said, "do you think the owners of the land would mind if we took pictures in their field?"

"I'm sure he wouldn't mind, but I'd prefer you stay here for your safety," Neil said as Chaya called his name from the other side of the bus. Neil glanced at Silas, Tara, and Sunny. "Watch them, please."

"Killing all the fun, if you ask me," Sunny murmured.

"Neil is right," Tara said to Sunny. "Do you remember what happened when *we* ran through the fields?"

He grinned at her.

It was the first time Silas could see that they looked good together. They both had comparable heights and similar backgrounds. He, on the other hand, was different. He loved his Goan-Christian-Indo-Portuguese ancestry, and he knew his height and rich, dark skin made him look like a delicious snack, but he'd read and seen enough online to understand that some people were . . . specific about their taste. But the real question was if Tara cared. Some people would.

Their moment of peace was short lived, when Tara turned to Silas and said, "I'll be right back. I forgot my phone." She returned to the bus, leaving Silas and Sunny with the rest of the group.

"It would take two minutes to get a picture," Chetna said. "Two minutes in the field and we'll be back."

Before Silas could respond, Sunny looked over one shoulder and then the other and said, "Two minutes!"

It was like he released the floodgates. Everyone rushed over the bank and into the rows of mustard fields.

"Are you sure that's a good idea?" Silas asked.

"I remember when I took this tour," Sunny said, "it was so miserable. Any bit of joy was worth breaking the rules."

"Why do you say that?"

Sunny motioned to the scrambling group of students. "Just like me, most of these guys don't want to be here. This was not their first choice for a summer vacation. They haven't seen India through a positive lens, like so many people are privileged enough to do. They aren't going to family homes and eating with cousins. They aren't taking a day trip to the Taj Mahal, a canal ride in Kerala, or experiencing a Mumbai beach day. Their parents or their community thinks there is something wrong with them, or they have to do something to be a better kid. So if this gives them a good memory to associate with this trip, then they should have it."

The heat and humidity made Silas's shirt stick to his back as he watched the pure joy of everyone making connections to the India they'd seen on screen growing up.

"Yeah, I guess you're right. I have to capture this." From the road, he began taking close-ups and wide shots with the camera he'd brought with him. Then he called everyone's name and took a group picture. When he looked at the previous screen, he knew he had to send a copy to them all as their going-away present at the end of the trip.

"So you and Tara, huh?"

Silas wheeled around to look at Sunny. "What?"

"You and Tara. You're also making the best of this trip. Are you into each other?"

"Tara and I are friends," Silas said, then, unable to resist a dig, "which is more than I can say for you two, I guess."

To his surprise, Sunny winced. "Yeah, we aren't on the best of terms. We did this tour together and then swore to each other we'd never let on that both of us had spent the summer before high school checking out temples. Since none of the other kids in our group were from Jersey the year we'd gone, our secret was going to die with us."

"Until it . . . didn't."

Sunny's smile faded as the bus doors opened and Tara stepped off. "Until it didn't," he said.

Tara looked around, then out at the field. "What the hell? They were supposed to stay on the side of the road!"

"It's fine. Stop being so uptight," Sunny said.

"Silas!" she said.

"What? Sunny said the word, and they all went running. Is it really that big of a deal? I mean, look at them. They're having a blast."

"They won't be if one of them gets bitten," she said.

"Bitten?" Silas lowered his camera. "Bitten by what?"

Tara opened her mouth to answer when a shrill shriek came from the field. Everyone froze. The laughter died.

"Snake!" Dax shouted.

Before Silas could figure out what was happening, all ten kids ran through the fields toward them, screaming like something was nipping at their heels.

Sunny burst out laughing.

"Mustard fields often have snakes in them," Tara said over the sound. "We found one when my group went on the tour. Sunny, you should know better."

Sunny was still bent over, hands on his knees, trying to catch his breath.

When Neil and Chaya rounded the bus to find out what happened, some of the kids were still squealing.

"Did you see how big it was?"

"Did you guys get bitten?"

"It was probably a boa constrictor. We could've died!"

"There are no boa constrictors in Punjabi mustard fields, idiot."

"Well, you're not the one who saw it."

"You knew there were snakes out there?" Silas asked Tara.

"We both did," Tara said, pointing at Sunny. "They're pretty common in mustard fields."

Neil did his annoying whistle to get everyone to quiet down. "Enough, guys. The bus is just about ready. You can all go back inside."

Everyone rushed to return to their seats, as far away from the snake as possible. Finally, only Silas and Tara were left.

"Are you coming?" Tara asked, motioning to the bus.

Silas looked at the field and then back at her. It didn't seem fair that everyone else got their pictures, to have a moment of joy, and Tara didn't get hers. "Can you come here for a sec?"

"What? What is it?"

He took her wrist and pulled her until they were at the edge of the bank before it dipped into a drain between the road and the field. He flipped his phone camera on and held it up, angling it so the sunlight gave them the best glow. He framed the shot so their heads were centered, and the field stretched out behind them.

Tara tilted her chin up and posed, a smile at the ready. She'd probably looked exactly like that on her social-media feeds before she'd deleted them.

"Nope, I'm not taking a picture until you fix your face."

She glanced up at him, startled. "Fix my face? What the hell does that mean?"

He pulled her closer. "You're making a posed selfie face. Give me a Tara smile. The kind you make after eating street food in Punjab."

She was still looking at him when she flashed that genuine smile. He took the picture, capturing the moment just as he wanted to.

"There," he said. When she looked at the camera, he took another picture. "Thanks."

"You're welcome."

When they turned back to the bus, every single student's face was plastered against the windows, watching them.

"It's like they have nothing better to do," Tara murmured. "You know what? I'm glad they saw a snake and almost peed their pants."

Silas was still laughing as they got back on the bus.

11

Day 12: Jammu and Kashmir

Hotel Site before Amarnath Cave

Postcard dated July 21—one year ago:

Remember how we used to beg Mom to spend time at the temples in the mountains? India is a sauna in the summer, but the Himalayas are always wonderfully chilly. Now that I'm back, I took a trip to Jammu and Kashmir for a week just to get a break from the heat. The snowy peaks were as beautiful as I remembered. But at twelve thousand feet elevation, without you or our parents, I wasn't expecting the eerie silence. It's incredible how loud your thoughts can be when you're by yourself.

Miss you, munchkin.

Love,

Didi

Tara felt the tension building behind her eyeballs as her mother stared back at her on her phone screen. "I just don't understand why you won't talk to me."

"There is absolutely nothing to talk about," Tara said. She thought that her mother's guilt trips, her barrage of questioning, and all the invasive conversations would come to a stop now that she was almost halfway around the world. Instead, Tara realized they were getting worse. It was as if her mother was afraid she wouldn't come back. "I'm on a youth group temple tour to pilgrimage sites that I've been to before. The same youth group tour that you forced me to go on before high school right after you kicked out Didi, and the same one you helped me get as a job this time around. I have nothing to report back to you."

"Tara . . ."

"Okay, maybe some of the kids have never done laundry, and a few days ago, on our first laundry day, they learned invaluable life skills. This one kid, Amit, dyed his socks pink. Is that what you want to know?"

There was an edge of irritation in her mother's voice. "What about Sunny? Did you apologize for putting him in that predicament and make up?"

"What? No way. We have nothing to say to each other."

"Tara, be the bigger person."

Tara pinched the bridge of her nose. She was always wrong in her mother's eyes, always the person who had to make the first move. It was like her mother was punishing her because of her sister.

"This is why I really don't want to talk to you. You're always telling me how to live my life, which makes me want to not listen to you at all."

There was a stretch of silence, and Tara couldn't tell if it was her mother or if it was the spotty Wi-Fi. They were in the Himalayas now, and the small hotel lodge on the tour wasn't exactly in a bustling metropolis with 5G.

"How about we talk about this when you get home?" her mother asked gently. "Maybe your focus should be on the Amarnath Cave. It's one of the most sacred parts of your whole trip. Most Hindus never see it in their lifetime, and you're going to see it for the third time! The last time you went—"

"You and Dad dragged me on a four-day trek. Yeah, I remember." She'd refused to go on any more pilgrimages after that. She had been on enough, and she felt like her relationship with god was becoming more and more strained with every ritualistic act. Her mother, ever the academic, was too focused on her own work to see how much it hurt her to be grilled about spirituality when she was forced to go on these trips. How could Tara believe when religion was the cause of so many problems at home? It didn't bring her peace. It brought her sadness.

And she hated that. When she'd first started to understand what religion meant as a kid, it felt like magic. Connecting to the universe's messages was like exploring an endless library of philosophy and mythology. But then her mother would only let her check out certain books in that library, which built compounding resentment for her faith.

"You know, the Amarnath Cave is where Lord Shiva explained the meaning of life to his wife and consort Parvati, according to some Hindu mythology," Tara's mother continued. "You can at least try to think of this as a way for you to get some enlightenment about your future, your friends, and the decisions you've made recently."

Tara stood and walked to her window as her mother droned on about responsibility and dharma. Despite her mother's accusation, Tara was very much thinking about the Amarnath Cave and her future. Her bed was covered with sticky notes and a notebook filled with scenes for a story that involved the legend of the cave. Maybe writing her own story was a way for her to reconnect with the endless library she'd once thought was magical.

"Tara, are you listening?" her mother said, irritation in her tone.

"Yeah, Mom."

"Hahn Ji."

"Hahn Ji," she parroted. The light was just starting to shine over the snow-covered mountains in the distance, casting hues of pink, orange, and gold over the jutting peaks surrounding their hotel lodge. The views in Jammu and Kashmir near the Amarnath Cave were spectacular, the rich green foliage of the valleys contrasting with the white tips.

The last time she'd seen this view was the summer after sophomore year.

"Mom," she finally interrupted. "I have to get going. I'll talk to you when I'm back from the cave."

"Okay, please don't forget—"

"You're breaking up, sorry, bye!" She hung up.

Automatically, her finger hovered over the app that used to be her social-media go-to, like she used to check after every call.

"Nope, still gone," she mumbled. But it was getting easier to forget it was there. It had been a few days since the last time she'd gone to press the app.

Tara looked around at the simple, sparse room with a cold tiled floor, a single daybed, and an open bathroom without a separate shower stall. No, not a stall. This one was just a sloped tiled floor with a shower-head on the wall in one corner. It had been quite some time since she'd washed her hair in an open bathroom without getting the toilet, the sink, and pretty much everything wet, but Tara managed that morning. Thank god she brought her bath flip-flops.

Checking the time, she decided to head down for breakfast a few minutes early, when a hard knock echoed on her door.

"Who is it?" she asked, expecting Silas.

"It's Neil."

Uh-oh. Something must be up, she thought as she opened the door to her tour guide.

He looked haggard and annoyed, his hair still wet and slicked back after what looked like a hasty shower. "We need to have a quick meeting with you, Silas, and Sunny," he said in Hindi. "Do you have a minute?"

"Okay, now?"

Neil nodded and motioned for her to follow him.

Tara grabbed her keys and a sweatshirt before she followed Neil to a room three doors down. When she entered, it looked similar to hers, except it had a queen-size bed. Silas, Sunny, and Chaya were already standing there, shifting their weight from foot to foot.

"What happened?" Tara asked.

"Four out of ten of the kids have a stomachache," Sunny replied. "They're . . . incapacitated."

Oh no. Delhi belly. "Who?"

"Dax, Amit, Jhumpa, Ravi," Silas said. He motioned to Sunny. "*Someone* told them that drinking the water up here was totally fine."

"Hey, it's *glacier* water!" Sunny said. "I used to drink it all the time."

"That doesn't matter," Chaya said, irritation written plainly on her face. "But it was bound to happen to someone. I just didn't expect it to be at the Amarnath Cave. You have to be in the peak of health for this trip because of the altitude and strenuous hiking during the next two days."

"What do we do?" Tara asked. Just the thought of being sick on such a physical part of the tour made her queasy. "I know we're here for the week, but they aren't going to be able to do any of the hikes with altitude nausea if they're still throwing up. Even if we take a helicopter to base camp, it's going to be exhausting. The first half of the trek is the steepest, which means they have to be feeling better right now . . . what?"

All four heads in the room had turned to stare at her.

"What?" she repeated.

"I barely remember the hike from when we went together," Sunny said. "And I sure as heck wouldn't know what it was like being sick."

"This is my third trip to the cave," she said. "I got sick my second time, and it was the worst experience ever trying to make it up that mountain for five minutes of praying in front of a cavern with an ice stalagmite." Thinking of her mother, she added, "Not to mention, you shouldn't go to the Amarnath Cave if something is standing in your way. It's an . . . omen. My mother thinks that my going last time has affected my future."

"She's right." Neil sighed. "Not about your future, Tara, but about the trip. It's a bad omen. Getting sick or some sort of delay means you aren't ready to experience the pilgrimage, and you should not try to circumvent fate."

"Whoa," Silas said. "That's . . . intense."

Neil looked at Sunny and Silas. "Sunny, you must stay back. Silas, you should stay back, too. Tara and I will go with the remaining students."

Tara saw the shock and panic on Silas's face. "Wait, no, I have to go. I have—"

"Neil is right," Chaya said. "You should stay here with me and Sunny."

Tara thought of the pictures and remembered the ones he'd had in front of the Amarnath Cave. The ice lingam stood in the background of the picture with two teenagers, grinning from ear to ear.

"He should go because of Chetna and Beth," Tara blurted out.

Everyone stared at her again like she'd grown a second head.

"I'm just saying there will be a lot of inexperienced hikers who don't really want to be there. Silas is . . . good with them. And he makes Faruk feel safe. Meanwhile, the ones that are here will really be sleeping it off and hydrating."

"She has a point," Neil said to Chaya. "Beth's and Chetna's moms were concerned about this leg of the trip because it's so physical."

Chaya crossed her arms over her chest. "Okay. I guess it makes more sense for Silas to go as well. Sunny and I will manage the sick kids."

"I mean, I can go," Sunny said, pointing to his chest. "I bet I have more strength than Tara does, and I might be more help."

Before Tara could issue a cutting remark, Neil and Chaya burst out laughing.

"Tara is probably the only one I trust going on this trek without either myself or my wife," Neil said to Sunny.

Tara could feel her cheeks heat. She didn't think she'd ever been praised for knowing about religious pilgrimage facts. She turned toward the exit. "If that's the plan, I'm going to get breakfast. I'll meet the group at the bus out front?"

She heard Neil and Chaya thank her as she stepped into the hallway.

"Hey!" Silas's voice made her stop and wait for him to catch up in front of her room.

"Yeah?"

"Thanks," he said, combing his fingers through his hair. "I know I'm here for the kids, but I appreciate you supporting me in there. I really want to go on this trek."

Don't mention it was on the tip of her tongue. Instead, she said, "The cave is . . . an experience. It's really just a large opening in the side of a mountain with an ice-shaped lingam, but it's the people that really surprise you."

"How so?"

Tara shrugged. "Some people cry. Others are struck silent. It's like you're looking at one of the seven wonders and thinking, wow, this must be photoshopped. Not that I've seen any of the seven wonders other than the Taj Mahal. But it's the energy. And of course the Himalayas are . . . unreal. You'll like it."

Silas watched her with those clear brown eyes, that solemn mouth. "Can I tell you something?"

"What?"

"I really like your secrets, Tara Bajaj."

"My secrets?" She stared at him, startled. "What do you mean?"

"The skeletons in your closet that you didn't want anyone to see. I see them. And I like them. And I hope you realize soon that everyone else is starting to see them and like them, too."

There was an itch at the back of her throat, a tickle that she didn't quite know how to scratch. "People usually don't."

"First impressions are almost always wrong, anyway," he said with a laugh. "People will come around."

His comment was jarring. It was one of the best compliments she'd ever received, and it was delivered when she was being her true self. "I've been told I make a shitty first impression."

"You didn't with me. I saw you saving those seats at the airport, and I knew you were someone pretty awesome," he said with a laugh. He reached out and tugged on the end of her ponytail, sending tingles through her scalp. "Thanks for thinking of me in there, sunshine. I owe you one."

With that, he walked down the hall to a room on the left. Without another backward glance, he entered and shut the door behind him.

Tara stood there, twisting the end of her ponytail where he'd held it.

The sound of Chaya and Neil's door opening again, their voices carrying down the hall, made her jolt into action. She ran to her room quickly and slipped inside, her heart beating faster at the thought of Silas's words and the fact that he said them before touching her hair. She tucked the memory in the back of her mind, a special thought she'd have for later, and squared her shoulders. She needed to eat if she was going to hike all day.

12

Day 12: Jammu and Kashmir

Amarnath Cave

Silas knew the group had to sign waivers when they participated in the tour because of the strenuous path to the Amarnath Cave, but he didn't know how intense it would be until they were finally on their journey.

He was seated squeezed between Faruk and the thin metal wall of the helicopter as they took the flight to the base camp where they would continue the hike. His heart began to pound at the aerial views of the snow-peaked, jagged mountains. He'd only ever seen pictures of the Himalayas.

Only ever dreamed of seeing them in real life.

Their passes and registrations were reviewed at base camp. Silas watched as Neil slipped rupees to the rangers, who then gave them passage to the trail.

"What was that?" Silas murmured to Tara.

"The cave is only open for two and a half months out of the year. These guys sometimes only have work during this brief window. When festival season begins, sometimes they're here around the clock to manage population flow. They have to get money to feed their families when they can."

Silas nodded, waited for Tara to pass, and then stepped behind the students. They were pointed to the trail, and after a few muddy slopes, they joined the back of a line.

A ridiculously long line.

In fact, there were so many people that when they reached the first valley and saw the number of travelers, all six students let out an audible gasp or groan. There were people walking for *miles*.

It was beyond anything Silas could've prepared for. He tried his best to focus on the scenery and the breathtaking beauty around them. He burned through a memory card quickly, taking pictures of the green valleys, the blinding white snow, and the jagged cliff ledges, but that didn't stop him from feeling on edge. He didn't know why. Maybe it was the frenetic energy? Or maybe it was the soft sound of shloks and bhajans that so many pilgrims kept reciting, echoing in his ears.

Since he was taking up the rear of their group line, he kept looking past all the shorter heads to Tara, who was right in the middle, followed by more students, and then Neil at the front. They walked single file, with hundreds of people behind and in front of them. Unlike everyone else, Tara looked calm and collected.

"Are we almost there?" Beth said, huffing in front of him a half hour into their trek. They weren't on an incline, but the air was thin up here, and it was affecting all of them. As beautiful as the scenery was in the Himalayas, it was just as dangerous.

"You have to regulate your breathing," Neil said from the front. "Do you want the air pump, Beth?"

"I think it would be easier to use the air pump if we weren't walking in a line through a valley leading up behind another mountain to a mysterious cave with an ice sculpture shaped like a Shiva lingam," Gina said.

Beth ignored Gina and shook her head. "I don't need the pump," she said quietly, but her breathing was becoming concerning.

An hour later, they slowed to an almost standstill. Beth was taking big gasping breaths now, and Neil was trying to convince her to use the pump. The portable oxygen sensor indicated that she was doing okay, but she was starting to freak out. Silas watched as Tara ran a hand down her back in comfort. "When Neil says regulate your breathing, he means use all of your air passageways," she said quietly. "Try to remember that you are in control. There is nothing to panic about. I'll do it with you. Straighten your shoulders."

Beth immediately did as she was told.

Tara took her hands and placed one on her stomach and one on her chest. "Okay, you're going to relax your jaw, then take a big deep breath through your nostrils, but keep your mouth closed. Count if you have to. Then you let it out through your mouth, but purse your lips so you can control the airflow."

Beth did exactly as Tara instructed, then repeated it.

"Good. Keep doing that for fifteen minutes. I can set a timer if you want. As we're walking, count your breaths to match your steps. In through the nose, out the mouth. Okay?"

Silas could see from the back of Beth's head that she was nodding. The gasps were slowing until they were no longer audible.

Everyone was starting to trust Tara—starting to question all the rumors Sunny had shared and that they'd heard from their siblings or social media. And Tara just had to be herself to convince them she was different from what other people said about her.

When she looked over in his direction, he winked at her. She rolled her eyes and turned to face front again, but he caught the barest hint of a smile.

The line moved forward, and the landscape began to shift into snowy banks and wet mud. Thank god the tour had given them a packing list. Who knew they were going to see hundred-degree weather one minute and snow and ice another?

"Does everyone know the myth behind the Amarnath Cave?" Neil called out.

"Is this another history lesson?" Ina said.

"Yes. Do you know about the myth?"

"No," she said, putting her earbud back in.

"Depending on which region of India you're from," Faruk said. "It's different, right?"

"The general consensus is that the cave is where Shiva told his wife and consort the secrets of the universe, of divine life, but she fell asleep before she heard it all."

"I wouldn't want to know the secrets of the universe," Gina said. "Then there would be nothing exciting anymore."

"Is that why all of these people are here?" Chetna asked. She was also breathing heavily, and since her phone didn't have service, she couldn't do anything but listen to the conversation. "They all want the secrets of the universe or of divinity?"

"The myth says that if you visit the Amarnath Cave and you pray to the Shiva lingam, the ice stalagmite, then you will achieve moksha and be free from the cycle of birth, life, and death," Neil said. "You'll achieve divinity."

"Do you really believe that?" Ina asked.

Neil nodded. "Of course I do! And I want as many people as possible to experience these pilgrimages, to connect with the religion that unites so many of us."

"Or divides us," Faruk grumbled. Silas reached out and patted them on the shoulder.

"What do you think, Tara?" Gina asked. She turned from her position behind Neil. "Do you think that visiting the Shiva lingam is an experience that will give us divinity?"

Tara was quiet for a moment as they moved ahead, but Silas heard her let out an impatient huff of air.

"I think that people need to believe in something to feel like their life is worth living. They need to look forward to a happier moment. Whether it's getting into the college of your dreams or finding your soulmate." She let out a humorless laugh. "Or getting your dream job in your dream city and settling down in a house with a white picket fence. There is always something more. Even if it's a divine . . . end."

"That's very enlightened, Tara," Neil said. "But of course, I expect nothing less from the daughter of one of our most well-respected theology scholars."

"Your dad is a theology scholar?" Happy asked, spinning around and almost knocking Neil over with her pink backpack.

"My mom."

"I guess it makes sense that you're religious, then."

"I'm . . . not," Tara confessed. "I'm spiritual. Hinduism can be incredible. But certain interpretations and blind faith is a problem."

"I don't get it," Ina said. "So are you Hindu or not?"

"Yes, and no," Tara finally answered. "I believe in some of the philosophies and principles, but not the practice."

"But following Hinduism as a religion is finding the truth that applies to you through practice," Neil added. "So isn't it the same thing?"

The students all turned to look back at Tara.

"No," she said, her voice firm. "Based on who you are, your privilege, and your family, someone centuries ago wrote down a set of rituals to follow. Those rituals are how people practice their faith. Like if we were to go to do a pooja, there is a *way* to do the service. You accept the blessing with your right hand. You have to prep the status, use vermilion, and tie the red string around your left or right wrist depending on whether or not you're married. But being spiritual? Sometimes it's enough to just believe."

The group quieted, sitting with Tara's truth. Silas's moms both came from religious families, and although he knew so many relatives that thrived within religion, there were many who used religion as a guise for prejudice. Was that what had happened to Tara's sister, too?

The group trekked on, talking about what they liked so far on the trip, what they missed back home, and the food that they'd enjoyed the most so far on their adventure. Silas added commentary when he was asked for his opinion, but he was still focused on the conversation about religion and spirituality. He tried to think about how his moms had felt on this very walk over thirty years ago. Did they have the same conversations? Did they lose sight of religion because of who they were and whom they loved? And was it the truth of queer representation in Hindu mythology that kept them grounded in their faith all this time?

As they hiked in the mud and cold, he watched people who had so much less than they had, all seeking spiritual guidance. Silas wrestled with guilt for how little he knew about his personal belief systems and the ones that he was raised believing as truth.

Finally, they headed over the last cresting peak into the valley where the cave was set in the side of a mountain. They were so close to their destination.

"We have barely five minutes on that platform," Neil said over his shoulder. "Be prepared."

"We hiked all this way for five minutes?" Happy asked. "That seems unfair."

"I don't think I want more than five minutes," Faruk said. "It's cold up here." They looked back at Silas. "Do you think that's enough time for your picture?"

"It's going to have to be," Silas said. "There is a famous Sri Lankan travel photographer who once waited two months to get this picture of a rare bird. And when it appeared, this photographer had only thirty seconds. When people ask him if he thinks he got the perfect shot, he says, it's perfect because it had to be. It was a once-in-a-lifetime moment."

When their line slowed to a stop, the students groaned. Silas tapped on Faruk's shoulder and leaned down to speak in their ear. "Hey, can you all move up so I can talk to Tara about the picture?"

Faruk sighed and shook their head. "Why don't you just ask her now? It's not like we all don't know about your photo project."

"Because I don't want Neil to think that I'm prioritizing my work over you guys when we get into the cave."

Ina turned and hissed, "But technically you are. You have to put us first."

Silas leaned forward and hissed back, "I'm asking you to move in front of Tara so I can talk to her, not turn around and never get the chance of moksha."

Chetna cleared her throat. All three of them looked up.

She pointed at Tara, who stood with her arms crossed over her chest, staring at Silas.

"What?" she said, her eyebrows pinched, the corners of her mouth turned down.

"Oh, uh." He grinned. "I know the last time I asked you about my picture project, my . . . er, topic wasn't great. I'm changing the essay, but I'm still going to frame the essay around the same type of pictures. The past meets present. I was wondering if you would want to be in my cave picture." He took out his phone and held it for her to see the image. "You'll balance the photo."

She glanced at it and shook her head. "Silas, this is supposed to be about you and your moms and your legacy. I'll watch the group while you take the shot."

He wanted to argue, but he could already see the resolve on her face.

"Shut. Down," Happy said in a singsong voice. Beth, Ina, and Gina shushed her.

The line moved forward, inching closer to their destination. There were armed guards now at various checkpoints in line. An iron railing jutted out from the rocky ground, attempting to keep the line single file. A tall torch burned brightly in the distance.

"Hey, Tara?" Faruk called out.

"Yes?"

"My mother says that if you do something nice for someone, you balance your karma scales. Do you think that if you help us on this trip, that you'll balance your karma scales from what happened during your senior year?"

Silence fell over their group. The only noise that could be heard was the chanting, muffled from a distance.

"I think whatever I do," she called out, "I'm already too late. I'll always be in debt, trying to balance the scales for the rest of my life."

The silence between them was deafening now. Silas wanted to reach out and hold her hand, but this was still a solo trip for her. Tara had to figure this out for herself.

"You know, you can probably give karma a nudge," Neil said. "People often assume that karma is its own entity, but we have the opportunity to control good things happening to us."

"What could she possibly do to control good karma?" Chetna asked suspiciously. She reached for her phone again, fiddling with it before putting it away.

"Be herself," Silas said.

Tara turned to look back at him, surprise in her expression.

"I feel like I'm missing something," Faruk mumbled.

Just then, the drums and music from the prayer service echoed through the valley. Their line moved forward at a quicker pace now, and the deep ravine between towering mountains came into view. The ground was gray and black and rocky, with dirty snow at the base stretching to pristine white at the cliffs. Silas could see the mass of people gathered at the mouth of the cave—a large opening in the side of the mountain—ready to see the ice stalagmite.

Silas had never seen anything like it in his life. When his moms had visited, the trek hadn't been as popular as it was now because of how difficult it was to get up into the mountains, but with the helicopters and guides who now drove so much tourism to the cave, this was otherworldly.

In contrast, the Golden Temple, with its pristine white walls and interiors, its sense of calm and silence, was very different from this pilgrimage. Now, the scenery around them was breathtakingly rugged; the feeling of man felt out of place. He could almost believe the stories of a god hiding secrets here.

"What are you going to do?" Faruk asked as they moved closer and closer to the temple.

"I'll set up my tripod, take the photo of just myself, and go with it."

"I can watch your tripod for you."

"Thanks."

They climbed a rocky path that was steeper than Silas had anticipated when he'd first seen it from a distance, then ascended a small platform where they waited for their moment in front of the iron fence that blocked anyone from approaching the stalagmite. Despite the many ceremonies going on at the same time, Silas could see the exact corner where he would have to stand for his picture.

Still, the crowd of people would mean that he'd have to do some photoshopping.

As they approached the cave opening, Silas took a moment to pause and stare up at the stalagmite in the cave once it came into view.

"Oh my god," he whispered.

It was *huge*. It reached at least a few stories, and it was definitely in the shape of a Shiva lingam. What was even more fascinating was how preserved it was year over year over year. But as Tara had said, it was the people around him who fed this frenetic energy. It wasn't desperation, no—naming it as such would do a disservice to the feeling. It was more reverence and awe, more gratitude and love.

For a moment, he wondered if he'd ever show much clarity, love, and devotion for something greater than himself.

"We're next," Neil called out.

Silas's heart began to pound to the drums. It was just one picture, one in a series. And were all his options for a future outside wedding photography lost if he didn't win this contest? No, absolutely not.

But he really, really wanted this. Because if he was able to nail this competition, it would mean that he was being celebrated for his South Asian identity in a way that was more than the connection he had through his mothers. Like the Amarnath Cave, like the Shiva lingam, his work would be a part of a greater story.

He took a moment to retrieve the tripod from his backpack and began setting it up. Then he attached the camera to the head of the tripod and synced the remote just as they reached the iron fence in front of the mouth of the cave.

People were speaking in so many different languages around him that it made his hands shake, but he focused on the exact position he needed the camera to be in before crossing the large rock platform in front of the mouth of the cave, ignoring the few irritated shouts he was sure were pointed in his direction. Then he waited for his moment.

Neil and the kids were in the process of folding their hands and standing reverently in front of the fenced-in stalagmite. Silas took a few shots focusing on their expressions, their posture, then them as a group, because having them in his photo collection was important, too. Like a superhero, Faruk squeezed through some of the lingering patrons and stood behind Silas's camera moments later for Silas to get the one pose he'd been hoping for.

"Go ahead," they said. "I think we have to leave soon."

Silas didn't waste any time. He quickly got into position according to his moms' old photographs and smiled. Faruk took the picture.

Silas held up a thumb and flipped it up and down. Faruk scanned the camera screen and then made an okay motion with the palm of their hand.

Someone yelled in his direction. In English, Neil said, "We have to leave now," to the group.

"Just one more shot!" Silas said desperately, pressing his remote, even though he wasn't even in position yet. He just needed this one shot. Who knew if he'd ever be able to go back to the Amarnath Cave for this opportunity again?

Before Neil could respond, Tara stepped up and pointed at his camera.

"Come on, let's do this quickly; otherwise, they're going to drag us away."

Silas didn't hesitate to lean in just like in his moms' photo; then he smiled and pressed his remote clicker a few times. "Done!"

And then he was racing to grab his things and make room for the next group of people. At the last moment, he looked over his shoulder at the Shiva lingam and let out a deep breath.

I've never been good at praying, so I won't start now. But maybe I can just put in a request. I just want this whole experience to mean something. Is that too vague? I'm not sure.

Oh, one more thing. Can you give Tara whatever she's been looking for? I think she deserves it. Because I have a feeling that she's blaming karma because she doesn't like what happened to her, when really it might have been protecting her from a shitty future.

Anyway, thanks.

Silas closed his eyes for a moment, then followed his group down into the valley and back toward the helicopter launch area.

A few hours later, he stopped Tara and pulled her aside when they were waiting for their ride back to the hotel.

"Thank you," he said. "I know I've said it a hundred times coming back from the cave, but really. I don't know if any of the shots are good, but you've improved my chances by being in one of them."

Tara shrugged. "You looked panicked. And since this was your one chance at getting a picture at the Amarnath Cave, I reacted."

He was so tempted to tuck the curl behind her ear, the one that fluttered in the wind over the smooth curve of her cheek. "Thank you. For everything."

"You're welcome," she said. "And thank you."

"For what?"

"For not treating me like everyone else has for the last four months. I don't think I'm the reason why the group is no longer avoiding me like a plague. I think it's because of you."

"You're welcome," he said, then gave in to his urge and smoothed her curl back. "Will you help me with the rest of the pictures, too?"

She let out a deep sigh. "I have one condition."

Out of the corner of his eye, he saw the entire group watching them. Good lord, he couldn't even have a normal conversation without an audience.

He returned his focus to Tara. "Name it."

"You don't share them on social media. You use them for your photojournalist thing, and that's it. I like being hidden away more than I care to admit."

"Done," he said.

Her face was a study in skepticism. "Really? Done? Just like that?"

"Just like that," Silas said. "This is important to me. You're doing me a huge favor."

The sound of copter blades whirred in the distance. Tara looked up, shielding her eyes from the sun's glare on the snow, then turned back to Silas.

"I can't wait to get back," she said.

Personally, the trip was going way too fast for his liking. But he nodded, then followed her toward the safety zone where they had to wait to board their ride.

He felt an elbow in his ribs and turned to Happy, who had sidled up next to him. "You have a little drool right here," she said, tapping the corner of her mouth.

"You know what? I hope you prayed in the Amarnath Cave for god to give you a better sense of humor." But he absently brushed at his mouth anyway.

13

DAY 15: JAMMU AND KASHMIR

NEAR BALTAL BASE CAMP

Postcard dated May 5—last year:

There is this strange gap in our mindset when it comes to romance. Love stories can exist in books and on screen, but when it comes to South Asians falling in love in real life, it feels almost shameful. Thankfully that is changing. Mom and Dad, I know you read Tara's postcards. Please tell me you're not feeding her the same toxicity about romance that you fed me? Because, Tara, whatever they've told you isn't true in the real world. Love is thrilling, and scary, but never something to be ashamed of. It's always worth the fall.

Miss you, munchkin.

Love,

Didi

It took Tara longer than she cared to admit to realize that she liked Silas.

He was sweet and open with her, and his brief touches felt like a low-grade electric buzz against her skin, just shocking enough to raise a trail of goose bumps.

This was different from what she was used to. Jai had been by far her longest and most serious relationship, but it felt exhausting toward the end. Even after she'd shown all of who she was to him, she still spent so much time trying to be the person she thought he wanted her to be when they first met.

There was no subterfuge with Silas. From the moment they met, he saw all of her. She felt comfortable around him. And that was both scary and exciting at the same time. Maybe it was more than friendliness from him. Maybe he liked her, too.

A few nights after the Amarnath Cave, after a day of touring the smaller local temples, Tara had just changed into her pajamas and scrubbed her face clean when there was a knock on her door. She dropped her phone next to her laptop, which was opened to a draft of the story she'd been working on, and crossed the room to answer it. Silas stood on the other side, freshly showered, holding up two McDonald's bags.

"What are you—"

"Shh!" he said, sliding past her into the room. "I think Neil and Chaya are still up. It took me forever to sneak out and grab these."

He held up the bags. Damn, she could already smell the masala fries. Tara quickly peeked in the hallway, then closed the door.

"What's the occasion?" she asked, motioning to the desk chair.

Silas sat and held out a bag for her to take. "I was craving these fries. It's not street food, but I couldn't go another day in India without trying these again. I brought you some to thank you for the cave picture."

"You already thanked me." She sat cross-legged at the edge of her bed, facing him. "You had no problem getting these?"

"None," Silas said with a grin. "I did a lot of hand gestures and the few Hindi words I know. They did a lot of hand gestures and a few English words they knew, and it worked great!"

When she opened the bag, she saw the same order she'd gotten in Delhi the last time they ate fast food together. That was . . . sweet of him.

Silas shoved a handful of fries into his mouth and chewed. "Man, the food at these hotels is just as good as Neil promised. But McDonald's has been doing us dirty in the US. This is the real showstopper."

"I dream about this stuff back in the States," Tara replied, popping another fry into her mouth. It felt surreal to be eating with a guy she'd met only a few weeks ago at the start of a youth group temple trip, but if she was still on the path of being honest with herself, there was nowhere else she'd rather be.

They unwrapped their food and began munching on aloo tikki burgers and paneer sandwiches.

"What's with the laptop?" Silas asked, nodding at the bed.

"It's nothing," she said reflexively.

Silas hummed. "Okay."

Tara looked at the computer and then back at him. "Okay?"

"Yeah."

She expected him to push, to ask her for more details. But maybe that was because she expected everyone to push and ask for details about what she was doing and whom she was with. But in retrospect, Silas had never pushed her.

"It's a story," she finally admitted. "When I was a kid, and my sister and I would have to do these pilgrimages with our mom. We didn't have computers or Wi-Fi, and we'd finish reading the books we brought with us by the halfway point. My sister would say, 'Munchkin, tell me a story.' And I'd create something out of nothing. And my sister would add on to it and throw curve balls like 'Oh, a chudayal came one night!' and I'd have to go with it."

Silas scrunched his nose. "A chudayal?"

Tara smiled at the memory of when she would ask her sister and her mother the same question. "A chudayal is colloquially known as a witch. But some folklore says that it's a cursed woman who comes back after suffering an atrocious death at the hands of a man, and that she's out for revenge against the man. They only come out at night."

Silas leaned forward, snatching a fry from her hand. "Please tell me your story is about a chudayal."

"It's about four rakshasis, actually." They were so vivid in her mind that she itched even now to write them into existence. Her high school creative-writing teacher used to say that a story has promise if it keeps calling to her, and Tara felt that call.

Silas leaned back in his chair, a tikki burger in one hand. "Rakshasis are demons, right? That's cool."

Tara was very aware of his knees peeking out from his board shorts. They were just knees—except they were a naked part of him. A flash of memory from when he had on shorts and nothing else had her cheeks warming.

He said something, and she blinked in confusion. "What was that?"

"I said, it sounds like you had *some* fun on these pilgrimages, right?"

She laughed and heard the bitterness in the sound. "We had to make our fun."

"But something changed."

"Silas—"

"No, no, you don't have to tell me." He held up his hands like he always did when he asked questions and she shut him down. "I just want to know you. But if you don't want to talk about it, then—"

"I want to talk about it," she whispered, surprising herself. She wrapped the half-eaten burger back up and set it down on the flattened paper bag. "I want to talk about it," she repeated more firmly. "But it's hard. Because I sound like a spoiled brat, the same spoiled brat I tried to make people believe that I was for so long."

"We have all night," Silas said, stretching out his legs. "Or until you get sleepy and kick me out."

She smiled. "I guess it starts with Savitri Didi. My sister was super patient like that, too. She's about eleven years older than me."

"Wow, that's quite an age gap."

"Yeah, I was a bit of a surprise," Tara said with a laugh. "I never felt unwelcome, just . . . unexpected. Anyway, you already know about my parents. My mom specializes in North Indian sects, communities, and religious studies. My father is an executive at a huge entertainment conglomerate. I was shaped by my parents' interests first. I was the kid of the religious parents who would go to community Diwali parties to talk about Hinduism, or the kid of the Disney adult."

Silas winced. He held up a hand as if waiting to be called on. "I think I got the rest after that. You went on this youth group trip with Sunny, who had a thing for you, and then you both swore you would never tell anyone ever about this trip—"

Her jaw dropped. "Wait, how did you know about that part?"

"Sunny filled me in," he said with a shrug. "When you went to go get your phone after the bus broke down."

"That was, like, a week ago!" she said indignantly. He'd known that about her for so long, and didn't bother telling her?

But then again, what opportunity had he had? She wasn't exactly open about her secrets. Not as much as Silas.

"Just so you know, anything that comes out of Sunny Deol's mouth is a lie. Even if, oddly enough, the one thing he told you was the truth."

Silas sobered. "I heard that he dated your best friend . . ."

Tara brushed her hands against the napkin in her lap. "I think Umma was just someone I felt like I was supposed to be friends with to fit in."

"That's . . . I mean, I get it."

Tara studied his blank expression and scoffed. "Don't hold back now."

"Okay, fine. That's very . . . efficient of you."

"Still holding back, but just know that I'm pretty sure Umma felt the same way. I needed someone who already had friends at Rutgers High, and Umma was that person. I took her to my community Holi party freshman year, and she met Sunny there. They hit it off, and they were on and off together since that moment. Sunny and I pretended like we'd never met before that party. His parents have a complicated passion for organized religion, too."

Now that she was telling him everything, it all came out quickly, like a clogged water pipe that was finally clearing.

"What happened?"

"I met Jai. He was a dancer at a different school, but his family went to the same community events. I was with Jai for about three years, and he found out all my secrets and was okay with them. But I wasn't okay that he knew. We ended up breaking up, a few times actually, until he found someone who was perfect for him."

"Do you—" Silas cleared his throat, staring at the wrapper that he'd begun tearing piece by piece in his lap. "Do you, uh, still love him?"

"Not romantically," she said, smiling. Oh yeah, Silas had to at least think she was cute if he was asking.

"Oh. Cool. What happened?"

The sound of late-night rickshaw motors hummed outside the window. She tossed the wrapper remnants back into the paper bag and folded the edge down. "Long story short, Jai's new girlfriend was one of the best classical dancers in the *world*—"

Silas let out a low whistle. "World?"

"Yup. World. But she choked at a competition, and people found out that her mother slept with one of the judges. My team, Umma specifically, decided to try to use that information against Jai's dance team to force them out of the competition so we'd win regionals."

The look of disgust on his face was exactly what she'd hoped to see.

Silas crumpled up his bag as well and set it on the desk behind him, next to her makeup bag. He linked his fingers together and leaned forward, elbows on his knees. "Tara, did you tell Jai they were doing this?"

"Yeah," she said. "Yeah, I did. I may have been a bitch, but I wasn't a cheat. And there was no way in hell I was okay with someone using another person's secrets against them like that."

"Yeah, I can see how that would bother you."

The knots in her stomach eased. Of course he could. Because now he knew just as much, if not more, about her than Jai did when they were dating.

Tara told Silas the rest.

The fact that Sunny had been feeding Umma lies. That Tara had used Sunny's text messages he'd sent her in confidence after their temple tour, to tell off Umma. Afterward, she was seen as the cheater, the asshole, the backstabber. For four months, she was ridiculed, shunned, and cast out of all the friend groups she'd once been a part of.

"God, that sucks so bad," he said quietly. "I'm so sorry, Tara. No one should ever have to go through that."

Tara shrugged. "It is what it is. I've had time to accept it." Not that the thought didn't burn her every time she looked at Sunny Deol across the dining hall or in any of their temple excursions.

"The way you stuck to your principles is still freaking amazing." He stood and began to pace the room. "What does your sister say about all this?"

"My sister?"

Silas nodded. "Yeah, you mentioned that you used to travel together when your mom brought you to India as a kid. You sounded close."

Tara felt a familiar ache in her chest at the thought of Didi. That was the last secret, the one that even Jai didn't know about. She wasn't ashamed of her sister, but she was ashamed of the way her parents treated Savitri.

Tara stood because she needed to do something with her hands. After grabbing her journal on the bedside table, she untucked the stack of postcards from the back and held them out for Silas to see.

Silas stood, took the cards from her, and began flipping through them. "Some of these are in India."

The postmarks were obvious, even though the images on the post-cards were generic. "A few months ago, they were arriving from Europe, so I guess she must be back in the homeland."

Silas ran a long finger over the edge of one of the cards. "Why does your sister send you postcards?"

Tara could feel the scratchiness at the back of her throat even before the words came out. "When I was in elementary school, Didi developed an addiction. She was in college by then, hooked on opioids and other painkillers. My parents put her in rehab centers, hiding her away like a dirty secret."

Silas put down the postcards, and there, standing on the tiled hotel floor next to her bed, he held open his arms. Tara didn't hesitate to step into them. She sighed at the warm feeling of his hands pressed against her back.

"She started working at Dad's company after graduating from college," Tara finally said against the soft fabric of his T-shirt. "But she wasn't getting better. Something happened, and Mom kicked her out. When Didi threatened to take me with her because she thought my parents were going to suffocate me, too, Mom panicked and filed a restraining order against my sister."

"Oh my god."

The steady beat of Silas's heart thudded under her ear, comforting her.

"She sends you postcards," Silas said softly, "so that your parents can read what she's writing. Is that why they don't try to stop you two from communicating?"

"Yeah. She was gone, and then six months later, I went on the group tour."

"Oh man." He squeezed Tara's shoulders. She closed her eyes. No matter how old the scars were, sometimes they still hurt with enough pressure.

After a moment, she pulled away. "You know what's funny? Sunny figured it out. His mom and my mom have somewhat of a relationship, and I think his mom ended up telling him at some point. But all through high school, and even after we had a big blowout, he never told anyone."

"Maybe he's a douche with standards?"

Tara smiled. "Who knows?"

Silas reached for the postcards again and flipped through the most recent ones. He looked at each image closely. "You know, I bet that restraining order has expired by now."

"Wait, what?"

Silas held out the card Tara had gotten the week before she left. It had a picture of India Gate on the front. "Your mom had to sign it since you were a minor at the time, right? Now that you're eighteen, I doubt it's still valid. You can, in theory, reach out to your sister."

It hadn't even crossed her mind, partly because she'd been so busy with her life imploding, but now . . .

She shook her head. "I don't even know the first thing about getting in touch with her."

"Does anyone in your family talk to her? Other than you and these postcards."

"My dad, but I doubt he'd give up the contact information so easily."

Silas handed back the stack. "I don't see why not. You're an adult. All you have to do is ask him when your mom isn't there."

So many thoughts, so many questions. "Savitri Didi . . . she could be here in India."

"There's only one way to find out." He strode toward the door as hope began to take root in her heart. Her mind clouded with possibilities.

"Hey," she called out before he left. "Thanks."

Silas winked at her, and she felt the heat rise up her neck and into her cheeks.

He pressed an ear to the door, waited a moment, then slowly unlocked it. After opening it a fraction, he peeked out into the hallway.

"See you later, sunshine," he whispered. With those parting words, he was gone.

Tara put her journal back on the table and locked the door. She thought about it for a moment before she sat in the desk chair Silas had vacated and picked up her phone.

"There is only one way to find out," she said to herself before making the call.

"Hello? Tara, is everything okay?" The voice came fast and crisp.

"Hi, Dad," Tara said, taking a deep breath. "Yeah, it's fine. I know you're probably already at work, but I have a question. And—please don't tell Mom."

14

Day 18: Jammu and Kashmir

Vaishno Devi Temple

Sometimes, pictures couldn't capture stunning beauty. Sometimes, Silas had to just experience it in real life. Nestled at the foot of a large mountain, lush with summer green, was the entrance to one of the holiest places in North India. The location was marked with an open archway in carved stone. At the top were conical shapes in white marble, accented with spires.

As Chaya parked the bus in the tour lot, Silas asked Tara about the pilgrimage.

"How much hiking are we doing today?"

"Almost seven miles uphill one way," she said. "It's in your tour-guide packet."

He balked. "You're bullshitting me."

"No, I read it this morning."

"Not about the tour packet, about the hiking. We're walking over fourteen miles today?"

She grinned at what had to be a horrified look on his face. "Silas, the whole purpose of this trip is more than the psychological and spiritual enlightenment for the students. It's the physical work you put into getting closer to god, too. If we were coming to this temple thirty years ago, they would've made us crawl on our hands and knees through a small cavern tunnel to get inside. Now, they've opened it all up and we get to just stroll in."

"I feel like we aren't paid enough for this," he muttered. He looked up at the wide serpentine path on the side of the mountain that was supposed to lead to a white temple at the top. It was early in the morning, but there were already so many people there. Even though they were in the Himalayas, today was hot and humid. "Then again, there are worse jobs than seeing a temple built on the site where a goddess fought a demon."

"That's not what you said a few nights ago," Tara mused.

"What happened a few nights ago?"

The voice grated on Silas's nerves even before he turned. Sunny stood with his hands on the straps of his backpack, his fanny pack cocked to one side, and his hair standing on its ends. "What happened a few nights ago?" he repeated.

"At dinner," Silas responded smoothly. "The kids were talking about the worst summer jobs. I feel like we lucked out, you know what I mean?"

Sunny looked back and forth between them. "I don't remember anyone talking about jobs."

Silas clapped him on the shoulder. "Well, how could you listen to all four tables at the same time?"

Sunny stiffened. "Whatever. Tara? Maybe you and I can walk together. We can catch up. You know. Like good old times."

"No."

"I think it would be a good idea if we did," he repeated.

"We've managed just fine for almost half of this trip, Sunny," she said smoothly. "Let's not ruin it now."

Before Sunny or Silas could respond, Chaya stepped up next to them. "While the three of you are busy gossiping," she said, "your students are trying to climb onto someone's mule."

Silas looked over, his jaw dropping. Amit and Dax were haggling with a man holding the reins of a mule. Silas bolted, stepping between the man and his students before Dax could reach for his wallet.

"Oh, hey there, sorry about that. Americans. You know how it is."

The man shook his head, as if understanding every word.

Silas ushered Amit and Dax away. "You two are seriously going to get me in trouble," he murmured.

"Dude, do you know how cheap a mule ride is up to the top?" Dax said. "Walking is so unnecessary."

"Walking builds character and shows your physical commitment to getting closer to god," Silas said, thinking of Tara's words.

"I think you're making that up," Amit replied.

Silas had no idea if it was true, but there was no way he would admit that.

"Okay, everyone," Neil called out from his spot next to the bus. He brushed at his perfectly groomed 'stache. He wore pressed jeans and a fitted kurta top. "We're going to start our hike to the top. Does anyone have to use the washroom now? The next one is in two kilometers."

No one raised their hands.

"Great. As we begin the trek, the path becomes narrow, and there is walking traffic in two directions. We'll stop at the next tea staller in a few kilometers. Please always stay on the correct side of the walking path. Chaya will lead, and I will take the rear. Junior guides will follow every two or three students. Everyone understand?"

Every head nodded.

"Our goal is to be back down here by dinner. Onward!"

"His cheerfulness is so annoying," Beth muttered.

"Come on, kid," Silas replied. "Take some pictures for your social, breathe in the fresh mountain air, and focus on that spirituality."

"Are *you* always this cheerful?" Jhumpa asked him as she passed. "Or is it a new thing?"

"Always been a happy kid. You all should try it sometime."

Tara raised an eyebrow at him as she passed. He winked back, then wiped his smile off his face as two more students went by, grumbling something about how his being so happy was disturbing.

Silas fell in line after his group and started the trek up the mountain.

He took a deep breath, settling in for the long hike. Tara's ponytail bobbed ahead of him. She'd put in her familiar AirPods, unbothered by the rush of visitors going the opposite way. She'd probably done this pilgrimage a dozen times.

"Hey there, Silas."

He turned around and gave Sunny a tense smile. "What's up?"

The dude inched closer, leaning forward to talk. "I don't want to be the third wheel or anything, but if you and Tara are hanging, I could use the company. I'm exhausting playing *Mario Bros.* in my room every night by myself."

Silas felt bad for lying to the guy, but if he made Tara uncomfortable, there was no way that Silas would contribute to that feeling. "Uh, yeah, sure. But we don't hang out. I'm working on my photo project at night."

"Then maybe I'll ask Tara if she's up to hang."

"Considering the animosity between you two, and the way you told everyone her business, I doubt she'd say yes."

"She told my business first," Sunny hissed. He stepped up and squeezed next to him on their side of the walking path. "I think you've only gotten one side of the story, my dude."

"I've gotten all I need, *my dude.*"

Even if Tara hadn't told him about their history first, there was nothing genuine about the way Sunny spoke about Tara. He was a walking, talking red flag.

"So then you *are* close," Sunny said. "How do you guys know each other?"

He was almost as tall as Silas, and when he leaned over, he was practically breathing in Silas's ear.

"We met at the airport," Silas finally said.

"Ah, cool, cool."

"Dude, aren't you supposed to be behind two students?"

Sunny leaned closer as if sharing a secret. "No, thanks. Then I'd have to talk to hero number one, if you know what I mean."

Silas looked over his shoulder at Neil, who wore his aviator sunglasses and had a grin on his face. He looked like he was having the best time, even though he and Chaya had been doing this same exact tour for a few years.

"Yeah, he does look like a hero," Silas said.

"When Tara and I took this trip, it was a bunch of older people who were both senior and junior tour guides," Sunny said. "But our moms were determined for us to go. They made us pray together every night. Thank god Neil and Chaya give us our own time."

Silas let out a sigh. "What is it that you want? I feel like you're on a fishing expedition."

"He sure sounds like it," Chetna said, turning and glaring at Sunny even as she kept up her pace.

Sunny scowled at her. "I'm not on any fishing expedition." He made a shooing motion at Chetna until she turned around. "I'm here more as an old . . . acquaintance of Tara's. You're spending a lot of time together on this trip, ya know? I'm just looking out for her."

Silas wanted to call bullshit, but there were way too many people listening in. Even with Tara so far up ahead, there was still a chance she'd catch wind that they were talking about her. Instead, he gave Sunny an easy smile.

"We're on a tour of all the religious pilgrimage sites in North India. This is not Rutgers High or wherever you went to school. I'm sure she can take care of herself."

A loud shout from behind made everyone in their tour slow and move to the side. A group of four men carrying a woman on a palanquin needed to get through. The woman looked at least eighty years old. She was dressed in a white sari and carried a mala wrapped around her hand. The beads of the prayer necklace rattled with each step.

A grieving widow. She had sad eyes. This was probably a trek for her husband's last rites.

The four men carrying her wore shirts with the temple's name on the back and worn open-toe sandals. Another worker carted a collapsed wheelchair close behind. They moved like this was an everyday stroll for them. Silas remembered reading that there were only three ways to get to the top of the mountain, where the Vaishno Devi temple was situated. By mule or horse, by foot, or by palanquin. Now he'd seen all three.

"That is the life, huh?" Sunny said as they started walking again.

This dude was going to get punched by someone before the trip was over, Silas thought as he continued up the hill behind Chetna.

"As I was saying," Sunny continued. "As someone who knows Tara, I feel like I wouldn't be upholding the bro code if I didn't warn you. She's an ice princess. Just because she talks to you doesn't mean she's interested."

"Did you learn that the hard way?"

Sunny let out a humorless laugh. "Yeah, you could say that. But like I told you already, we've known each other a long time."

Up front, Chaya held her hand up, asking everyone to pause. In the distance, the line had stalled behind two mules who wanted to stop traffic to say hello to each other.

Silas took the moment as an opportunity to lean in close to his ear so Beth and Chetna or any of the other students couldn't hear. "I know exactly how long you've known Tara and how badly you messed with her relationships," he said quietly. His voice went hard. "And if you think for a moment that I would ever trust you and your warnings over something she says, you've lost your mind. I don't know what you're trying to do here, but I'm not falling for it. You're probably better off walking with Neil."

"Wow, she's got you hooked already, huh?" Sunny replied in the same quiet tone. He backed away. "That's how she was with me, too, when we did this tour before high school. Dude, what do you think is going to happen when we're back in the States? Do you think she's going to be the same person she is with you now? No way. She'll start over in her liberal-arts college, she'll reset her personality, and the people who don't know her there will think she's the hottest shit because she's mean and smart. Where do you think that's going to leave you?"

Silas had no idea. Tara was on a journey, and she seemed to want to be on that journey alone. But regardless of how true—and unsettling—Sunny's comments might be, Silas would never confide in someone like this guy.

"Maybe going to the back and having a chat with Neil will be good for your soul. Everyone needs a little redemption, you know?"

Sunny's gaze sharpened, his lips thinning. "I'm just trying to help."

"Noted," Silas replied. He watched as Sunny wove through his group until he reached Neil and held up his hand with a "hey" as if he'd intended to join their tour guide all along.

What a tool, Silas thought. When he faced forward again, he met Tara's gaze. She stood with her arms crossed, a questioning expression on her face. Silas shook his head, then mouthed, *I'll tell you later.*

"You two are gross," Faruk said, peeking out from behind Tara's back. "Seriously, gross."

Silas shook his head. There was always a critic.

15

Day 22: Himachal Pradesh

Thirty-Eight Days until Flight AA293 from DEL to JFK

Shimla

Postcard dated September 12—four years ago:

The next time Mom takes you to India, listen to the sounds around you. The animals, the trees, the engines. It's all so different from what you would hear in the States. And if you're in the mountains? It's even better. It's a song that brings the deepest part of your soul to life.

Miss you, munchkin.

Love,

Didi

WhatsApp message dated 7/28 to 91-6097851000:

Hi, Didi. It's your favorite little sister. It's been a long time. Dad gave me your number. I hope you don't mind. I'm eighteen now, so I thought I'd reach out because Mom and Dad can't stop me. If that's okay? Since you're writing postcards, I figured you wouldn't mind.

Your last one was from India, and I was hoping you might still be here. I'm working for the youth group temple tour. You know, the one that you had to take as well? Except I'm a junior guide. Maybe you would be interested in meeting up? Miss you, Didi.

Tara was too young to remember the last time she visited Shimla. It hadn't been a stop on her temple tour four years ago, and the hill station was too touristy in the summer for her mother's liking. The last time they visited as a family was because Tara's father had distant relatives that wanted to meet.

As the bus traveled toward the vacation city, it hugged the curves of the mountains that were practically vibrant neon green on one side with sheer cliffs and a ninety-degree drop on the other. Clouds hovered over peaks in the distance.

Everything was so lush. The colors almost seemed like they'd come out of a fairy tale. And the city center itself? Tara had to actively work to keep her mouth from falling open. The architecture had been influenced by the Europeans, no doubt, with all the steeples and sloping rooflines with marble archways at the entrances. It was so different from the beautiful ancient temples and structures they'd visited in Punjab and Jammu and Kashmir. No, this place had colonizers stamped all over it.

"Shimla used to be the summer capital of India during British rule," Neil said from the front of the bus, confirming Tara's thoughts. He stood, grabbing his seat rest for balance as he addressed the group. "Then it was part of the state of Punjab before it became a part of

Himachal Pradesh. This is the perfect place for relaxation because of its scenery, fresh air, and slow pace. The retreat house we'll be joining is going to be self-maintained. That means chores!"

Every single student groaned.

Chaya expertly drove into a narrow lane with labeled parking. "But first," she called out. "We're going to have lunch at one of the outdoor cafés. Welcome to Shimla!"

The students cheered at the mention of lunch.

"I feel like so many of these nerds are missing the point of this whole trip," Silas muttered next to her.

Tara had to laugh. He wasn't wrong. But then again, since most of them had made it clear they didn't want to be here in the first place, it didn't matter whether they were missing the point.

The humming of the engine stopped as Chaya finished her parking job, and a burst of tourists flooded past their bus toward a narrow pathway with shops on one side and scenery on the other. A church stood in the distance on top of a hill, and beyond that were rich green mountains that rolled into valleys.

"Grab your backpacks, everyone," Chaya said. She flipped her ponytail over one shoulder and motioned for Silas and Tara to get off the bus first, since they were seated in the front.

While the group huddled together on the side of the road, waiting for everyone to disembark, Tara leaned into her hip and stretched, releasing a steady stream of cracks.

"Whoa," Gina said, eyes widening at the sound of Tara's body adjusting. "Your body cracks like my grandmother's."

"Thanks," she said, smiling. "It's the years of classical and Bollywood dance, I guess."

"Are you going to join a team again in college?" Happy asked.

Tara looked at the curious expressions in front of her. A few of them were probably going to try out for teams, based on the trending dances they'd done in temple parking lots over the last month. "Dance was fun," she said slowly. It had given her a direction and sense of purpose when she felt like she didn't have any. Until it wasn't anymore. "It no longer makes me happy."

"But you were *so good*," Happy said. "I remember watching your team compete at regionals. It was amazing."

"Just because you're good at something doesn't mean you have to stick with it, though," Tara said.

"Oh my god, that's so true," Ina said. "I mean, I'm great at math. Doesn't mean I'm going to be an engineer."

Gina elbowed her. "That's literally what you tell everyone you want to be."

"Oh, shut up."

"Can I ask you a question?" Jhumpa asked, tugging on the strap of her crossbody. "If it was just fun for you, then why did you compete? That's a lot of work for just 'fun.'"

Most of the kids had gotten off the bus by now and were staring at her expectantly. She locked eyes with Silas over their heads. He smiled at her and then mouthed the words *tell them*.

Tara cleared her throat. "In my family, it was either eat or get eaten," she said. "If I didn't push back on my parents with a reason why I wasn't at temple or volunteering at my dad's work programs, then I'd be stuck doing what they wanted me to do. Dance was my excuse."

And the ability to step into someone else's life by acting it out on the dance floor? That had been the most freeing experience for her.

Happy, Jhumpa, Ina, and Gina looked at each other and then back at her.

"If you don't want to be a dancer," Ina started, "then what *do* you want to do? Are you going to major in premed or something?"

The stereotypical Desi career path wasn't for her. That was probably the one redeeming quality her parents had. They were fine with whatever she wanted to do.

"I don't know yet," Tara said finally.

They cringed. "Yikes, that must be scary," Happy said.

"Yeah, but also kind of freeing. I can check out my options, you know?"

Neil let out one of his annoying pay-attention-to-me whistles and then pointed at a restaurant sign farther down the street, next to another that featured a large Nike logo. "We'll eat first. Plenty of time to walk the Mall later to see the views."

"There's a mall?" Beth asked, cheering up.

"Yeah, it even has outlets," Sunny said.

There was a whoop of cheers.

"Sunny," Chaya said, sighing his name with such irritation.

"Fine, it's not outlets," Sunny said. "It's just a wide street for people to walk down to see Shimla views."

Tara was a fan of retail therapy and wouldn't mind a mall herself, especially since the ones in India were so gorgeous. But as they traveled en masse to the small restaurant with its long tables and plastic chairs and with the scent of heaven wafting out of an open kitchen in the back, this didn't seem like such a bad place, either.

She caught Sunny's eye from the end of the table as they moved to sit down, and he smiled at her, mouthing the word *hi*. She ignored him and opened the plastic menu in front of her. A sandal nudged her bare leg, and she looked up. Silas wiggled his eyebrows like a clown. She practically snorted.

"Hey, Tara," Amit said from next to Silas. "Have you seen some of the pictures that Silas has been taking? They're pretty amazing."

"I haven't."

Silas had showed up again at her door the night before with snacks and his laptop, and she'd been able to review every shot he'd taken since the start of the trip, but like hell she would admit that to these gossipmongers.

Amit began rambling about the project, with Faruk and Dax chiming in. As plates of food were delivered to the table, the conversation shifted, and Neil and Chaya briefed what their time in Shimla would be like.

Lunch ended quickly, much like it always did, but because there was so much food and the yoga retreat had a communal kitchen on their floor, they were able to pack the leftovers in plastic food containers and carry them out in bags.

The group poured out of the tiny restaurant less than an hour after they had arrived and began walking toward the Mall, where they were supposed to meet the bus.

The open street had valleys on either side and was lined with shops and restaurants up to a wide cobblestone square with a church. "Wow, this place is amazing," Beth said, taking a deep breath. There was a half wall with lookout points for people to stop and take pictures.

"That's the retreat center," Neil called out, pointing to a large complex in the distance, nestled on a neighboring mountain slope.

"Sunny, are there any samosas in the bag you have?" Ravi asked.

Tara turned to watch as Sunny moved over to rest one of the plastic bags he'd brought from the restaurant on the half wall so he could open it.

"Yeah," she heard him say. "There are a couple in here. Do you want one now? Oh, hey, little buddy."

At first, she had no idea whom Sunny was talking to. And then a small, furry monkey popped up from behind the wall. It was so tiny it could probably fit in the plastic bag.

"Oh no," she heard Chaya and Neil say in unison.

The monkey inched closer to the bag and began sniffing it. It used its little fingers to poke and prod, jumping at the sound of the plastic.

"You're so cute," Sunny said. "Hey, guys? Take a picture of me, will you? Silas, do you have your camera on you? I want to post this. No one is going to believe how close I am to one of these things. We barely got to see monkeys the last time I was in India."

Before anyone could move, a second monkey popped up from behind the half wall. It made a chittering sound and inched closer to inspect the bag.

"I know monkeys are in the wild around here, but it's amazing how close they are right now," Silas said, stepping up next to her.

Tara wasn't a huge fan of Sunny, but her stomach twisted. "Yeah, Sunny has absolutely no idea how much danger he's in."

"Danger?" Silas snorted. "Look how tiny and cute they are."

"Sunny? You need to back away," Neil said.

A third monkey popped up at that moment. The three began closing in on the bag.

Sunny snatched it up and stepped away from the wall. "Okay, y'all. This has been fun." He let out a nervous laugh. "But I'm going to take my samosas and go."

The monkeys hopped off the wall and began advancing toward him in slow, measured movements.

"Oh shit," Silas said.

"Um, guys?" Sunny called out over his shoulder. "What's happening?"

"They want the food," Chaya called back.

"What do I do?"

Before Chaya could respond, Sunny let out a piercing scream as the monkeys jumped forward. He turned and bolted across the Mall. The three small monkeys, all screeching and baring their teeth, ran after him.

The crowded Mall watched, laughing as Sunny ran in a figure eight. Chaya and Neil kept calling, "Drop the food!"

Tara couldn't help herself—she hadn't seen something that funny in a long time. Now that it was obvious Sunny wasn't in serious danger, her entire body shook as she braced her hands on her knees and roared with laughter. And for the first time in forever, she felt the lightness of pure, unadulterated joy in her chest.

When Sunny finally dropped the bag of food, she quieted and wiped her eyes. Some of the kids and Silas were staring at her with strange looks on their faces.

"What?" she asked.

"Nothing," Silas said quietly. "You sound beautiful when you laugh."

Amit, Dax, Faruk, Beth, Chetna, Ina, Gina, Jhumpa, Ravi, and Happy all let out groans and boos.

16

Day 29: Uttarakhand

Thirty-One Days until Flight AA293 from DEL to JFK

Chota Char Dham: Yamunotri

Silas wasn't much for yoga, but the retreat in Shimla was like a valve inside him opening up. When they started their first day just focusing on breathing, he felt both frustrated and at ease. Frustrated because so many people had told him to try yoga and at ease because he went through the exercises with his group, and they were all struggling together.

And then things started to click.

The best word he could use to describe it was *grounded*. He was centered and could focus his thoughts. For once, he wasn't thinking about whether he was Desi enough on this trip through India. So what if most of his friends weren't brown? That he didn't speak the language and he didn't watch the movies? How important was all that, anyway? In theory, he'd always known none of that mattered, but feeling it was different.

As if validating his experience, everyone else in the group also looked more grounded and centered. Even Tara, although Silas knew she probably had her breakthrough moment after the monkey bait experience with Sunny. She'd smiled readily, even joked with the kids. That night, she'd even asked him if he wanted to take a walk—and she'd looped her arm around his waist before he dropped an arm around her shoulders.

He hoped that this was a permanent change. He wanted her to be like this from now on, not just during the trip like Sunny suggested.

On the first tour in Shimla, Tara surprised him again. She stood next to his side and let him take a picture at the retreat house gazebo overlooking the valley and the green mountains in the distance. Tara didn't stiffen when he pulled her closer. He felt her fingers brush against the soft cotton of his T-shirt at his back, and when he finished taking the picture, she didn't pull away. Her touch lingered for just a moment longer.

After leaving Shimla, they traveled back into the snow-peaked Himalayas, the weather playing tricks on them, and the heat returned full force. By the time they arrived in Yamunotri, the first of the four holy sites known as Chota Char Dham, the bus was warm and filled with terrified passengers after the treacherous drive along narrow single-lane roads hugging the cliffs. If they looked out the window, all they would see is how close the bus was to a cliff edge without a railing.

"Come on, everyone," Chaya said. As they got off the bus at their hotel destination, she looked as exhausted as Silas felt. "We'll get you all checked in and ready for dinner tonight."

The students waited in front of the one-story structure carved into the side of the valley, while Neil, Silas, and Sunny pulled all the bags for everyone out of the undercarriage of the bus. The entrance to the hotel had an A-frame design, but the body was more of a simple rectangle. A blast of cold air came through the opening doors of the lobby. Eerily, there were no people around.

"Is it just me, or does this place remind anyone of those Indian horror movies where people come to die?" Amit asked.

"Great," Happy said. "First, we almost died on that cliff road, and now I'm going to have nightmares about haunted hotels in India."

Silas grabbed his bag and scanned the gravel road leading up to the hotel entrance. They were off the beaten path, but close enough to the main street that they could walk if they wanted to. The downfall was that there were no streetlamps in the vicinity. The sun was already starting to set, and tiny lights flickered in the valley down below.

"What are you going to do on your night off?" Chaya asked him, taking her bag from him.

"What?"

"Your night off," she repeated. "Don't you remember? You get two nights off. Today and the last day. Neil and I are responsible for dinner duty tonight. You, Tara, and Sunny all have the opportunity to eat at one of the restaurants. There aren't very many options, and you'll have to stay close, but it's your choice. Or you can eat with us."

Silas's brain went into overdrive. No way—if he had a night off away from his group that didn't involve sneaking, he was going to take it. And he was going to take Tara with him.

"Excuse me for a moment," he said to Chaya.

Tara had just put in her AirPods when he stepped up next to her and tapped her on her shoulder.

"We have tonight off," he whispered when she removed her AirPods. He tried to ignore the way her jasmine scent made his stomach flutter. "Neil and Chaya are on dinner duty. I don't think we're going to find a McDonald's in town, but what do you think about risking our stomachs again for some street food?"

Her eyes lit up. "Count me in."

"Great."

"Great."

"It's a date," Silas said.

Her cheeks tinted in color. "Yeah, okay."

"Great."

There was a noise, and Silas looked up to see Faruk standing with their arms crossed. "You're telling me we're stuck with zero entertainment at dinner today?" They shook their head and began pushing their suitcase after the rest of the group.

"Glad we're good for something," Tara murmured.

Silas nodded, but he couldn't get himself to care. He was going on a date. With Tara. In the middle of the Himalayan mountains.

~

After discovering that they had an abysmal lack of cell service, Silas knew they had to wing it when it came to directions. He waited until he was sure everyone was in their rooms before he walked down the hall to where Tara was staying and knocked. When she opened the door, his stomach fluttered.

"Hi," he said.

"Hi."

He took in her outfit. She wore wide-leg linen pants and a collared shirt tied at the waist, sparkly juttis, and jhumkas winking in her ears. "You look gorgeous."

"Look at you in pants—and a T-shirt that doesn't have a vintage logo on it."

He ran a hand down his striped button-down. "Please don't tell my mom this came in handy. She's the one who forced me to bring it."

"I didn't think I'd get a chance to wear these." She flicked one of her earrings. "Thanks for the opportunity."

"Maybe we'll see some in the shops downtown so you can get some more. Ready to go?"

"Give me a second." She grabbed a small purse he'd seen her use during dinners. "Ready. Hopefully we won't run into Sunny."

"I hope not, either." Her eyes were lined with a smoky dark kajal that made them look bigger than normal. When she pursed her lips, his attention fractured as he focused on her raspberry-red lipstick.

"Silas?"

"Hu—what?" They were standing in the empty hallway now, her room door locked behind her.

"I asked what's with the backpack?"

"I have my camera, just in case we have the opportunity for pictures."

"Oh. Is there another picture to re-create here in town?"

He paused at the exit of the hotel and turned to face her. "No. Tonight we make our own memories."

"Got it," she said. Was it his imagination, or was she blushing?

She reached into her purse and flashed her notebook at him. "Also guilty. For the same reasons."

"I'm glad you understand," he said. He held out a hand, and to his giddy surprise, she twined her fingers with his as easily as if they'd done it a dozen times.

They made their way down to the main road and walked in the general direction of the center of town.

When they turned the corner, they found an alley bustling with street stalls and the sound and scent of sizzling Uttarakhand street food.

"Are you ready for round two?" Tara asked, squeezing his hand.

"Round one was one of my favorite nights on this trip so far. Let's see if we can top that."

"Let's start over here. The last time my mom brought me to Yamunotri, I had the best chili momos. I've been craving some."

Silas had no idea what that was, but he followed Tara to the first stall on the left and listened as she ordered in Hindi. When she reached for her wallet to pull out rupees, Silas stopped her.

"Person who asks for the date, pays for the date."

Tara's eyebrows raised nearly to her hairline. "That rule is . . . genius. Totally takes out the guesswork."

"Yup." He handed over a few rupees. "Let me guess. When you were Before-Tara, the guy always paid?"

"No, actually," Tara said. "With Jai, we always split it. He hated that, though. His family didn't come from money, and whenever I told him I wanted to split the bill, he thought I was feeling sorry for him."

"But you weren't."

Tara shook her head. "I didn't want to owe him more than I already did. He felt . . . safe, and that was invaluable to me."

"That's a hell of a price, Tara Bajaj."

"It was. And sorry. It's weird talking about someone else when . . . well."

"I think you can talk to me about anything."

The vendor handed over two cups made of dried leaves and two bamboo forks. In the cup was a heaping mound of green momo dumplings.

"Cheers," Silas said, tapping his bamboo fork against hers.

Huddled next to the open food stall, underneath a tarp overhang, on a stone-and-dirt alleyway crowded with people, Silas ate the fried dumpling, which was smothered in a spicy green sauce.

"This is *incredible*," he sighed before biting into his second momo. It practically melted in his mouth.

"Just like I remembered it," Tara said. She was smiling now, and Silas was momentarily distracted by how beautiful she looked in the dimming light. "By the way, Yamunotri is the one temple that I really think you'll enjoy."

"Why is that?"

"Because it's a photographer's dream," she said. "It's squeezed between these two massive mountains, and the trees practically grow sideways on the mountain faces. It's so green it's neon, and you can hear all this wildlife. It's incredible."

Her face practically glowed at the memory in the moonlight.

"Hey—Tara?"

"Yeah?"

"I wasn't going to tell you, but I really want to."

"Tell me what?" she asked, looking up at him.

He handed her the empty disposable carton, his bamboo fork hooked on the end, then wiped his sweaty hands on his pants. The words came out, tumbling over each other. "We're on a temple tour in the Himalayas. I have plans. Like, a lot of plans. To travel, to take photos, to expand my family business. To go to college. And you! You have plans, too. You're writing your book, and healing after *a lot* has happened in your life."

"Okay," she said slowly. "Is that what you wanted to tell me?"

"I like you," he blurted out. "I like you a lot, and of course, I want to be with you, but we're literally junior spiritual guides for a bunch of overly involved rising high schoolers, so we can't even *be* together other than like this. And I know you need your time to—"

"I like you, too," she interrupted.

"You—what?"

"Silas, I really like you." She tossed their cartons in the nearby trash receptacle, then wiped her palms on her thighs. "And it's kind of amazing that you said it first. I've never had that before, and it makes me feel like I can be myself now." She lifted her eyes to his. "That's important to me. Even if I'm still trying to figure out who I am, I know that feeling like myself is important. And you're . . . so great about seeing the real me. So yes, of course I like you."

It was like his brain crashed, and he had to do a mental reboot. "Say what now?"

She laughed, her face glowing in the dim light. "I said I like you, too. But you're right. We're in this very weird place. And just, I don't know, saying it out loud feels new and weird and honest and scary all at once. What do you think about just . . . spending time together? We can figure out the rest later."

He took a deep breath. "Yes. Yeah, of course. I can do that. Sure."

He could spend time with her. *And fall in love with her in the process.*

Silas took Tara's hands in his and squeezed until she looked up at him again. "One more thing. I just want to say—you did nothing wrong when you told your ex about the rumors. You did nothing wrong when you told your dance director, and fine, it was a bit much to post old texts online, but we all make mistakes. I'm sorry that the internet exploded around you, but you are so much better for it now."

Tara's hands trembled. "It's a wonder you could like someone that messy."

He snorted. "How could I not? You're smart as hell, with your multiple languages and insane fact recollection and dance trophies and all the books you've read and all the ones you want to read. You hid this part of yourself that went to India and amusement parks for years without anyone knowing, but now you're owning it. I like you because of all the secrets that make you *you*."

At first, she didn't respond. Then, after looking left and right as if making sure that no one was paying attention to them, she stood on her toes and pressed a soft, sweet kiss against his lips. It lasted seconds, but every aching moment of it was burned into his brain.

Wow.

She pulled back, but Silas followed her mouth to kiss her once, twice more, trying to memorize the softness, the shock of pleasure through his system, before letting go.

"You're special, Silas D'Souza-Gupta," she whispered when she pulled away.

"I am?" he replied, flustered. He cleared his throat. "I mean, I know. No, that's terrible to say. You know what? Why don't we eat some more? You know. Food."

She nodded. When Silas moved aside to let her lead the way, they almost ran into a group of women who were openly staring at them.

"Shameless," one of them muttered before they pushed past Silas and Tara.

Kissing in public in a small town next to a religious site probably wasn't the most respectful thing to do, but Silas couldn't stop himself from grinning.

"My mother would've had a cow if she saw that," Tara murmured.

"A holy cow?"

She burst out laughing. "I'd say that's racist if it wasn't so perfect."

17

Day 32: Uttarakhand

Twenty-Eight Days until Flight AA293 from DEL to JFK

Chota Char Dham Site Two: Gangotri

Postcard dated August 8—two years ago:

It makes me sad how much I'm missing with you. Your first crush, first date, first boyfriend. First high school dance, prom, graduation. I'm so sorry I'm not there, but just know that you don't need me. You don't need anybody. You're incredibly strong and resilient all on your own.

Miss you, munchkin.

Didi

Silas liked her. There was something so straightforward and innocent yet unbelievably hot about the way he put his feelings out there for her. Like an adult. Someone who was unapologetic about the way they felt.

She couldn't say Jai wasn't the same way, but Jai was different. Jai had been with Before-Tara. It was unfair of her to be Before-Tara with such a great person, but who knew if they would've met if she hadn't been that version of herself.

With Silas, she was After-Tara. No, that wasn't right. She was just Tara.

And that kiss was . . . amazing.

"Tara?"

She blinked, shaking her head. "Yeah?" She looked at Happy, who had tapped her on the arm, then took out her AirPods. "What's up?"

Happy pointed at the small white marble temple situated at the base of the Gangotri glacier. "Is this really where the Ganga River begins?"

It was the middle of the day, but the air was crisp and the sun burned brightly, reflecting off the ice and snowcaps. The sound of rushing water echoed with chanting and music.

"That's what they say."

Happy squinted. "Why are so many people dressed like they're going swimming with their flip-flops on? It's actually cold up here."

Tara glanced around, her eyes tracking Silas's movement as he took pictures of the surrounding area. "Uh, it's because they're going swimming. The Ganga has healing properties. People with cancer, blood disorders, and skin disorders come here to be healed through natural remedies."

"Does it ever work?" Happy asked, skepticism painted across her face.

"Some say it does. Why, do you want to take a dip?"

Happy scrunched up her nose. "Did you . . . did you just make a joke?"

"Absolutely not, that was a serious question."

"Okay, then no. Definitely not," Happy said.

Tara hesitated, then said, "You should buy one of those little water vessels they're selling at the market stands and scoop up some water for your mom. We use Ganga water in prayer rituals at home, and I'm sure she'd like it."

Happy's eyes widened. "Oh my god, that's a great idea. Thanks!"

"You're welcome," Tara said as Happy ran off toward the stalls. It wasn't until she was farther away that Tara let out a giggle. She was actually connecting with the students.

Before she could put her AirPods back in, Chaya called her name. She turned to see the tour guide approaching her, a simple bag slung over one shoulder and her hair swept back in a French braid.

"What's up?"

"I was wondering if you could do me a favor?" Chaya asked. "Chetna went back to the bus. She's really upset and doesn't want to talk to anyone. I'm a little worried about her. Would you mind going and checking on her? I think she'll respond best to you."

Tara balked. "Oh, I'm not good with comforting—"

"Please?" Chaya said.

That sounded more like a firm order than a request. "Uh, yeah. Okay, fine."

Tara began the slow trek back to the bus. Not only did Tara suck at first impressions, she also was terrible at comforting people in times of need; that's why no one came to her for advice. She could probably count on one hand the times even Umma had asked her to listen to her vent.

Silas caught her eye. He gave her a questioning look.

She shrugged, then pointed to the bus. He nodded and mouthed the words *good luck*.

The bus was parked in a small lot on a plateau carved into the side of the mountain. It was surrounded by jagged white cliff peaks and the sound of running water in the distance.

Tara pushed at the accordion door and climbed on board. It was warm inside since the air circulation was off. Chetna sat in the second to last row in the back next to the window, her headphones on and her phone clutched in one hand. She glanced at Tara, then looked away just as quickly. She let out a sniffle.

Tears. Tara's gut twisted.

She walked to the back of the bus and sat in the aisle seat across from Chetna's row, not knowing what else to do.

They sat for a few minutes, until Chetna's small, wavery voice interrupted the silence. "Chaya and Neil sent you after me?"

Tara nodded.

"Are you supposed to drag me back out there to pretend we're connecting with god?"

That was an interesting way of putting things. That's probably exactly how some of the students felt. Like they were pretending to connect with god, to a religion their parents believed in but that they had no context for. For the first time, Tara had to wonder if she was luckier than most. Having her mom meant having a better understanding of spirituality and its complexity, and she could separate her truth from what everyone expected her to believe.

"If you don't want to go out there," Tara finally said, "I'll just sit with you here."

Chetna didn't say anything, so Tara reached in her pocket for her AirPods. Before she could put them in, there was a loud sniffle.

"My boyfriend broke up with me," Chetna confessed. "He broke up with me, and he's dating one of my friends now. They're both starting at the same high school as me in the fall."

Ouch. That sucked so much.

Tara thought about what she would do in that situation, and then what Silas would do. "Do you need a hug?"

Chetna shook her head and kept looking out the window. "That's weird."

"Yeah, I think so, too," Tara muttered. "Uh, how long were you together?"

She sniffled again. "Since the winter formal. Since January fifth at two thirty. He's why my parents wanted me to go on this trip. They thought that maybe if I became more, I don't know, religious, I'd stop dating. I think they just don't understand. They just don't want me to have fun or anything until my grades go up."

The lie was on the tip of her tongue, but Tara swallowed it back. "My parents are still trying to change me, to this day. I think it's because they didn't realize raising kids in a place different from India meant they'd have to change, too."

They sat in silence, Chetna sniffling.

"I really liked him," she whispered. "We got . . . caught, and then my mom met someone at temple who suggested I come on this trip. He cost me my summer."

Tara had to bite her tongue from saying something about how that was way too short of a relationship to cry over a boy. "Uh, have you talked to your friend?" *And told her what a jerk she is for stabbing you in the back?*

Chetna shook her head. "She sent me a text message that says, 'I'm sorry. We fell in love. I think we're better together than you guys were, anyway.' I told her everything about our relationship! And she used it against me." Another sob.

Tara closed her eyes and dropped her head back against the seat. She felt like she was having flashbacks of her own messy life crumbling from a few months before.

"Can I ask you something?" she said. "Are you more upset about your friend, or about your boyfriend?"

Chetna wiped her nose with the sleeve of her sweatshirt. "Does it matter?"

"No, I guess it doesn't. They're both trash people."

Chetna's sniffling stopped. She turned to face Tara. "What did you say?"

"I said they're both trash. The guy who broke your trust and hurt your feelings, and the friend who knew that you were in a relationship and deliberately hurt you by putting her desires over your friendship. I can't tell you why they did what they did, but holding on to the grudge means that you're still thinking about them, and do they really deserve your time?"

For a moment, Tara was sure that Chetna would snap at her or tell her to get off the bus for insulting her friend and ex-boyfriend. She wiped her eyes with her sleeve, smearing her mascara. "How do you do it?"

"Do what?"

"Not care. I wish I didn't care so much right now, either."

Tara couldn't lie to her. She saw so much of herself in that sad face that it wouldn't be fair to say anything but the truth. She pulled her hair off the back of her neck. The warm bus was starting to cause it to stick to her nape.

"I do care," she said slowly. "I care . . . so much sometimes. When I started high school, I had just finished this same youth group trip. My sister had left home, and I didn't know when I'd see her again. I pretended to be someone different because I was worried about what people would say. And you know what? All those memes online were right. None of them mattered."

Chetna watched her with sad, teary eyes. Then she held out her phone. "Will you hold this for me? I don't want to text her back, and I don't want to text him and tell him how mean it was for him to do that to me. At least not yet. Maybe when I get back. Until then, I'm going to focus on me. I'm going to end my summer the way I want it to end."

Tara looked down at Chetna's smudged screen. All the social-media apps she used to post on incessantly were prominently on display across the top row.

Okay, maybe she wasn't done with the old Tara quite yet. A part of her would have loved to exact the type of revenge that used to make her laugh. Instead, she said, "Why don't you shoot a video first? You're literally at one of the most scenic places in the world. Do a dance up here with these incredible views and post it. Smile through the whole thing. It might even make you feel better. And it's the memory you'll take with you from this place. Not crying in a bus."

Chetna's eyes lit up. "You don't think that's blasphemous or something? Dancing in front of the temple?"

"Indian dance has always been a form of prayer. It's a way to worship and a way to express yourself. I think if there was any place on earth to dance, it would be at a Hindu temple in the mountains."

Chetna nodded. "Yeah. I could do that. Do you think you can teach me something to do? Me and Beth, Happy, Jhumpa, Ina, and Gina?"

"Sure." It had been a long time, but she could try.

"You know so much stuff about religion and history," Chetna said. "You could be a lead tour guide, you know."

Tara made a face. "Absolutely not. Neil and Chaya are saints for wanting to do this every summer, but I spent too much of my childhood at temples already."

"Then what are you going to do? In college, I mean."

She thought about her stories. About the mythology she was weaving into a rich fantasy that kept pulling her to her laptop each night. "I'm going to write." She'd never vocalized those words before, but it was the correct answer. "I'm going to write an epic adventure. Gods, goddesses, all of it."

"Wow. I can't wait to read it."

Tara smiled at her. "If I finish it, then I'll send it to you. But until then, we're stuck. Let's get the rest of the group so we can do our dance." Chetna stood, but Tara waved at her to sit down. "You can't do the dance looking like that." She pulled out a small makeup pouch from her backpack, which she'd set on the seat next to her, and removed a makeup wipe and a compact mirror. "You'll need to reapply. Maybe fill in your brows. Then comb your hair."

Chetna gave her a trembling smile. "Okay, I can do that."

"Take your time." She left her emergency repair kit for Chetna to use, then got up to leave. She was halfway down the aisle toward the bus exit when Chetna called her name. "Yeah?"

"I don't believe the stuff Sunny said about you," she said with a soft smile. "That you were jealous and that you tried to break him up with his girlfriend. I never did. And I know it's probably the reason why you're out on this trip. But I'm glad you're here."

"Thanks," Tara said slowly, noticing Silas approaching the bus, the other students chatting behind him. "I'm glad I'm here, too."

She opened the accordion doors to the bus exit and accepted Silas's hand as he helped her to the ground.

He adjusted his backward hat, his hair a little overgrown and curling out over his temples. "Everything okay?"

"Yeah, I think so," Tara said. "She's just getting herself together."

"Cool," Silas said.

Tara looked up at him, squinting against the light. When he squeezed her hand, she smiled. "Do you want to go back and get a few more shots? In case the one we took when we arrived wasn't the right one?"

"Yeah, that sounds great." He cocked his head when a buzzing sound came from her backpack. "Is that your phone?"

"Holy shit, I did not expect us to have cell reception up here." Tara retrieved her cell and read her screen. It was a notification from WhatsApp. Her jaw dropped when she saw the name. "It's my sister," she said. "She's in India."

18

Day 35: Uttarakhand

Twenty-Five Days until Flight AA293 from DEL to JFK

Chota Char Dham Site Two: Gangotri

Time was running out. There was less than a month left until they flew back home, so by some unspoken decision, Silas and Tara were trying to spend as many hours together as they could without getting caught. But from the moment they started, it was as if the universe was hell bent on keeping them apart.

There was the time when half the students wanted to do spa day things with Tara.

Then there was the evening where Faruk, Amit, Dax, and Ravi invited Silas over for video games.

But tonight. Tonight he was going to watch a movie with Tara.

He tucked his computer under one arm, and after listening at his door for a few minutes, he opened it a crack. He winced when the hinges squeaked just a bit. The lodge they were staying at for the next two temples that made up the Chota Char Dham temple circuit was more on the rustic side, with dingy white tile flooring and a poorly lit corridor. But the views? He'd seen mountains and valleys and untouched terrain, but India was more special than he could've ever imagined because of how *real* it all felt.

He tiptoed as quickly as he could to Tara's room and entered through the unlocked door.

Tara looked up from the journal she was writing in at the small corner desk. An open laptop sat next to her, with a playlist humming in the background. A scatter of makeup tubes and containers he'd seen on previous visits covered one edge of the desk. In another corner was a basket of washed and pressed clothes from the group's laundry day.

"Were you able to secure the goods?" he whispered as he closed her door slowly.

She reached under the desk and pulled out a brown paper bag. "I just want you to know that Chaya and the rest of the girls are to thank for this. If the students hadn't all rebelled before lunch and said we needed to go to a threading parlor to get our eyebrows done, I wouldn't have had an opportunity to wander and get some extra food."

He stood next to her chair, looking down at her beautiful glowing face, her brows and upper lip still slightly red. He ran a thumb over the corner of her mouth, then leaned down to kiss between her eyebrows. "They look like a work of art."

"India's hair-removal services are first class, just like the food," she said as she handed him the bag. "Today, I have both. It's a good day."

"And you have a response from your sister," he said, pulling out two bottles of orange Fanta and two foil-wrapped potato tikki burgers. He was happy that he'd saved room after dinner at the hotel. "What are you going to do about that?"

Tara took one of the burgers. "I honestly don't know. She's in a pretty accessible part of Delhi and can meet me anywhere, apparently.

And since we have free rein of the city on our last day of the tour, I think I'm going to see her."

"Are you going to tell your parents?"

"I'm not sure," Tara said. Her voice wavered. "God, I can't believe I'm going to see her again after four years. If I say something to Mom, she's going to ruin it for me, I just know it."

"I think you probably should tell her," Silas said, sitting on the edge of her bed and taking a bite of the delicious fried potato patty.

Her eyes widened. *"Why?"*

"It's so when she does find out, she won't be upset that the news didn't come from you. Your dad is going to tell her if you don't do it first. I don't know if your parents are like mine, but there are no secrets when it comes to family." Well, there was one tiny truth he hadn't confessed to his moms yet. Silas still hadn't told them that he didn't want to be a family photographer, but he was getting around to it. Soon.

"There are secrets between my parents," Tara said softly, pulling a piece of her bun and tossing it in her mouth. "I honestly don't know if Mom even knows that Dad still talks to my sister. And I don't know if Dad realizes how much happier he is when he doesn't have to go to temple. I don't think either of them know anything about me other than what they hear from other people."

Silas hated to see the sadness on her face. He was lucky to have two loving role models in his life who trusted him and loved him the way he was. But it was clear that Tara thought something broke between them when her mother hurt her sister.

"Can I ask you something?" he finally said.

She chewed and swallowed, then dabbed at the corner of her mouth with a napkin. "Yeah, of course."

"We've been on this trip for a month now."

"Yeah, it's going a lot faster than I thought it would."

Too fast, Silas thought. "What are your thoughts about your situation and karma?"

"That it's a philosophy much more complicated than a meme or T-shirt logo."

He laughed. "Yes, that we know. But the basic concept is that what you put out into the universe, you will get in return, right?"

"Sort of, yes. Why?"

"What if it's not just about good deeds? What if it's about confrontation, and truth, and laughter, and tears? What if karma is about all of it?"

Tara looked pensive for a moment, then put her sandwich down, wiped her hands on her pants, and turned to her computer. After typing something in a search bar, she pulled up a university web page that had a picture of a woman who looked a lot like an older Tara in the top left corner. "There are three types of karma," she said. "Sanchita, which is an accumulation of past deeds that are now coming into fruition. Prarabdha, which is past karma that affects the life you live today. And then there is agami, which is karma that people can create right here, right now in the current moment."

Silas hummed, thinking of everything everyone had told him about her and everything she'd said about herself. There was still that little itch, the irritation in the back of his brain that Sunny had started at Vaishno Devi. That itch was becoming harder and harder to ignore. Would Tara move on when they got home? Would she run away from what they had? He knew from the moment he met her that she was on a journey. Was he part of that journey now?

"Silas?"

"Yeah," he said, shaking his head. "I think all of that means that karma isn't really about doing something bad and getting hurt."

She turned in her chair. "What?"

"I think what karma really means is that whatever you put into the world, you have the potential to create happiness." Like giving a relationship a chance even if it started on a youth group temple tour.

Like his moms started their relationship.

Tara's eyes narrowed. "Are you telling me this because you want me to tell my mom about my sister?"

He laughed, then leaned down and pressed a soft kiss against her glossy lips. "You have time to make the right choice for yourself. But maybe instead of pushing people away, keeping things inside, and making assumptions about how people are going to react to you, you could just do something for yourself?"

"The last time I did that," she mumbled, "the entire school thought I was a home-wrecking bitch, and I made enemies with the entire Bollywood dance team."

"They didn't deserve you."

Her hands cupped his cheeks, running over his soft scruff, as she kissed him. She tasted like spicy chutney, the sweet butter from the toasted bun, and something soft and uniquely Tara. Silas wanted to pick her up, to take her to the bed, to kiss her as long as she'd let him.

She pulled back, her hands fisting his shirt, as if hearing his unspoken thought. "Silas?"

"Yeah?"

"Are you going to remember me when we go back to our lives?"

"W-what?"

Before he could process what she was saying, or even how to address it, there was a sharp knock at her door. Silas sprang back, hitting the side of the bed and almost falling to the floor.

Tara's eyes went wide. "Who is it?" she called out, her voice reedy.

"It's Chaya. Do you have a minute?"

"Uh, yeah, one sec." She motioned to her bed, and Silas didn't hesitate to dive underneath it. He heard the crinkle of paper, and the clink of a Fanta bottle before Tara's flip-flops slapped against the tile toward her door. It screeched open. "Hi," he heard her say. "Is everything okay?"

"We have a situation," Chaya said quietly. "There may be a mixed-gender party, and we need to separate the students. Neil is going to talk to Faruk, Amit, Dax, and Ravi, but we have to interrupt them first. Is that . . . is that tikki I smell?"

Tara let out a nervous laugh. "I grabbed some when we went out for our eyebrows. Don't worry, no one left the hotel after hours. I just had to treat myself, ya know?"

Silas heard Chaya hum. "I didn't see you holding them when we came back to the hotel."

He caught his breath, listening to her footsteps enter the room.

"Anyway, as I was saying, we have a problem, and I would like your help in breaking them up."

Tara's flip-flops got louder as she moved closer. "I mean, I can just do it myself. Why don't you go back to your room, and then you and Neil can do your thing once they're in the right rooms again?"

"Oh no, I'll stay with you. And I might get Sunny and Silas to come and help, too, depending on which boys are in the room. I'm not sure how nefarious the situation is."

Silas had to bite back a snort. Based on what he knew about the kids, they were probably either trying to prank the girls or challenge them in some sort of multiplayer game.

"You know what? I'll get Silas and Sunny," Tara said awkwardly.

Chaya hummed again. "No need. Silas? Since you're here now, why don't you join us?"

"Busted," he murmured. He got to his feet, pointing at the empty floor in front of him. "Oh, look at that, Tara. I found it. The back to your earring. Uh, glad I could come by and help. I know how blind you are when it comes to those things. You know, from what you've told me. I'm just going to head back to my room now, and—"

Chaya held up a hand to stop him, then motioned to the computer on the bed. "If you were really here looking for an earring back, you wouldn't have brought your laptop with you."

Silas shrugged, smiling sheepishly. "Um—I was going to go through pictures to see if I have any with her earring in it, so I'd know what it looks like?"

Chaya raised one arched brow and shook her head. Then she pointed at both Tara and Silas. "Listen, since you're both over eighteen and adults, as well as junior guides on this trip, you have some leniency. But please don't tell any of the students that you're spending time together; otherwise, we'll have a harder time disciplining them if they break the rules."

Silas nodded. Tara did the same.

"Good. Now come on."

Silas gave Tara a look, and she wiped her brow. His thoughts exactly. Close call.

A close call for everything.

The walk to the students' rooms gave him more time to think about the whopping question she'd laid at his feet. Obviously, his answer was yes, of course he wanted to see her after their trip was over. But was she asking only because she didn't think they'd have a future together? Did *she* want to see him when they returned to the States?

Silas thought about Sunny's warning again. *Do you think she's going to be the same person she is with you now? No way. She'll start over in her liberal-arts college, she'll reset her personality, and the people who don't know her there will think she's the hottest shit because she's mean and smart.*

They'd just stepped out into the hallway when another door opened at the end of the hall. Sunny stepped outside, phone in hand, holding it up to the ceiling.

"Damn cell recep—hey, what's going on?"

"I was helping Tara find an earring," Silas blurted out. Tara elbowed him hard in the ribs. "Uff—I mean, we're on a mission."

Sunny's gaze narrowed. "What kind of a mission?"

"We're breaking up a mixed-gender party," Chaya said softly. "Please lower your voice."

Sunny still looked skeptical. He scratched his abs across his fitted shirt, and Silas felt the need to emphasize his own. He had abs. He worked out, too. Did Tara notice Sunny's abs? No, of course not. Sunny was not competition. He was the enemy.

"Who am I busting?" Sunny asked.

"You'll stand behind me so I can do the busting," Chaya said.

Silas followed Tara, who followed Chaya down to the end of the hall. Sunny stepped in line next to them until they reached the last door on the left, where they could hear giggling coming from inside, as well as a loud laugh that sounded very much like Ravi.

Chaya didn't waste any time. She knocked hard three times.

There were whispers of *"Shit"* and *"Oh no"* inside, along with *"My mom is going to kill me."*

Silas looked down at Tara and smirked. At least it wasn't them, he thought.

Finally, Beth opened the door. Her eyes widened when she saw all four of them waiting for her. She looked straight at Silas and said, "I can explain."

"Busted!" he said in a singsong voice.

"Beth?" Chaya said. "Who else is here with you?"

She sighed, and the hinges creaked loud enough to probably wake the whole hallway. Inside, Jhumpa, Happy, Ina, Gina, and Chetna sat on the beds and on the floor, looking up at a laptop screen positioned on the dresser.

Ina shrugged. "Sorry! We may have gotten too noisy. But it's just us. Gina, Chetna, and I can go back next door if—"

"I'd check under the bed," Tara said calmly.

Silas turned to look at her, along with Chaya and Sunny.

"What?" she said. "They're like mini Silases. If that's where he'd hide, I bet you that's where the other guys are."

Sunny crossed his arms over his chest and glared at Tara and Silas. "And how would you know that Silas would hide under the bed?"

Silas laughed awkwardly. "What? It's just so . . . obvious. I mean, isn't that where you would hide?"

"Well, no. My first choice would be—"

"You all can come out now," Chaya said, her voice sharp.

There were grumbles, and the bed shifted as Faruk emerged first. Then Dax and Amit. Last, Ravi came out. His short mop of hair had a dust bunny in it. "We were just playing video games," he said, hands held high. "I swear."

"Then where are your controllers?" Sunny asked.

"Yeah, check their Netflix history," Silas added.

The echoes of noes ricocheted off the walls as Beth and Dax dove for the laptop and shut it before shuffling it away.

"Okay, back to your rooms," Chaya said.

The ones who weren't supposed to be there walked out, single file, heads hung as Chaya promised to come to each of them for a talk.

Faruk stopped in front of Silas and motioned for him to lean down. When he did, Faruk said, "That was a boomer move. We know where you sleep at night."

"I've been at this longer than you have," Silas replied.

They shook their head before leaving. Dax held up a hand as if he didn't want to even hear what Silas had to say.

Then Amit dragged a finger across his neck before walking away. Ravi did the same.

"I feel like that was excessive," Tara said when they were all gone.

Chaya stepped into the girls' room and turned to close the door. "Thank you," she said to the junior guides. "Now you can go. We'll handle it from here."

Sunny took one look at Silas, then at Tara. He shook his head and returned to his room.

"I wonder what that was about," Tara mused. She began walking in the direction of her room as well. "I should probably get to bed."

A part of him felt a pang of regret at not being able to spend more time with her, especially when they had so little, but he needed some time, too. Despite the hilarity of the kids watching Netflix after dark, her question stuck in his head.

Tara was incredible, but while she was figuring out what was important to her, his goal was the photography competition.

Wasn't it?

"I'll see you tomorrow," he said, and turned to walk away.

19

Twenty Days until Flight AA293 from DEL to JFK

Rishikesh Spiritual Center

WhatsApp message dated 8/15 to Tara Bajaj:

> I hope you don't mind me texting you instead of sending another postcard. I'm assuming Mom doesn't know we're meeting up. Anyway, here is a picture of my view. I'm currently at the beach but looking forward to meeting you back in Delhi. Do you remember when the tour bus broke down on the way to that spiritual family center Dad was desperate to see? It was the first time we'd gone to the beach with our parents. I think they hated it, but you had a BLAST. I wish I could remember it more clearly myself.
>
> See you soon, munchkin.

The monsoons had arrived.

Torrential rain came in spurts, then raced across the mountains in a single sheet. They were standing in the dry heat one minute as they watched the rain clouds rush in—warm water soaking like a shower straight to the skin. The rain cooled the hot earth until steam circled Tara's feet like a dream cloud.

Staying in Rishikesh at the start of the monsoons was better than she remembered. The communal yoga spiritual retreat house was a few hours from Kedarnath, the next stop on the Chota Char Dham temple circuit, which required hiking twenty-one kilometers in the Garhwal Himalayan range. The A-frame retreat center had wooden ceilings, mosquito netting around the beds, and large patio doors that opened into a shared green space. At night, peacocks and other birds sang and rustled sweetly in the trees, barely audible against the rain showers. The cool night breeze would filter in through the windows, along with the scent of jasmine. Since the first evening at the center, Silas came to her room, and they lay together, curled against each other's side, listening to the night's music.

The days were just as special. Tara met the students in a large hall with walls that opened to the sounds of rustling trees and wildlife, where a PhD student taught them how to meditate.

Tara knew the basic principles because she'd been on the tour before, but she absolutely hated the practice. This time, when she tried to focus on being in the moment, it was easy implementing the habits that her mother had drilled into her.

She was starting to understand what peace felt like.

This was something she didn't get with her phone constantly in hand. To clear through the noise and embrace silence. She didn't know if she'd ever have this type of moment again when she was back home. Maybe if she started hiking or something. She'd hiked the Himalayas. Why couldn't she hike in the Poconos when she went to college in Pennsylvania?

Writing, hiking, and meditating could be a part of the new Tara. And Silas.

"Okay, everyone, let's meet for lunch in one hour," Neil said from the front of the studio hall. He was wearing athletic shorts and a tank top that showed off his unusually large muscles. Next to him, Chaya wore a matching athleisure set. They looked like they had just arrived for brunch at the hottest new spot in Mumbai, instead of sweating it out in the heat.

Tara stood from the mat and quickly rolled it up to put in the corner with the rest as she thought about the shower she desperately needed. Maybe she could get herself together to look as great as her tour guides before dinner.

"Hey," Silas said. She felt the graze of his fingers along the waistband of her leggings. "Guess who has another night off tonight?"

"Um, you do?"

"And surprise, surprise: so do you," he said. His grin sparked a riot of butterflies in her chest. "Apparently Neil and Chaya are being generous and want to give us an extra one because the trip has been so chill so far."

"Tara?" Her name came out like a whine. She turned to see Jhumpa, Beth, Happy, Ina, Gina, and Chetna standing in the corner. "We need you for a second."

Their request silenced the butterflies just as quickly as they'd started. "What's going on?"

"Can you come here, please? It's *private*."

Tara had no idea what that meant, but she shrugged. "They need me," she said to Silas.

He squeezed her hand. "Then I guess you better go. I'm going to take Faruk out to town for some shots. Let me know if you need anything."

Tara squeezed his hand back, their silent gesture, and walked over to the group on bare feet. "What's up?"

They huddled closer to her, as if she was one of their trusted confidants.

"We have a problem," Beth said. "Chaya and Neil gave us *chores*."

She couldn't hide her smile. "That's nothing new. What kind of chores?"

"We're supposed to make lunch for everyone," Chetna complained. "Our entire group. In one hour. Like a cooking show. Do any of us look like we know how to make Indian food?" She motioned to the group.

Every student shook their head.

"Didn't you have cooking duty when we were in Shimla?"

"We were just told what to do in Shimla," Happy said. "The kitchen staff handed us things and that was it. But now we have zero guidance."

"Does it have to be Indian food?"

They all shrugged.

Tara thought about the tour she had gone on four years ago. They had constant adult supervision in the kitchens whenever they were on cooking duty. "None of you know how to cook at all? Not even, like . . . daal?"

"Do *you* know how to make daal?" Happy asked.

Tara snorted. "Please. Even my parents don't know how to cook daal. We had someone drop off Indian food twice a week when I was growing up."

"What are we supposed to do?" Gina asked, her hands on her hips. "The guys and Faruk are supposed to make lunch tomorrow, and we have to be better than them. I refuse to deal with them bragging."

Tara thought about asking Silas, but he'd mentioned that he was heading into town to get some shots. She then thought about the few friends she had back home. Jai's girlfriend, Radha, was a great cook, but it was probably too late in the States.

"As much as I hate him, there is one person I know who can help us," Tara admitted. "Sunny is actually a really good cook."

Every single jaw dropped.

"How do you know?" Jhumpa blurted out.

"Our moms are friends, so my mom tells me everything his mom shares. Also, he used to date my ex-best—uh, my dance team co-captain. I think he cooked for her last Valentine's Day."

"We need whatever we can get," Beth said. "Fast."

"We'll go get him," Gina said, gesturing to her sister. "You guys go to the kitchen and get started."

Tara followed Jhumpa, Chetna, Happy, and Beth to the communal kitchen, which had stainless-steel counters, a double-wide fridge, and large ovens. Open shelving revealed dozens of spices, dried herbs, and seasonings, and on the counter were large stainless-steel bowls filled with fresh fruit and vegetables. Two older women wearing white saris stood at one end of the island, cutting off the stems of baby eggplants, slicing them in half, and pouring tablespoons of spice mix in the seams.

"Are we interrupting?" Tara asked them in Hindi.

"Nahin, beta," one of them said. Then in English, "Just let us know if you need help. We're volunteers, but we can get someone at the center if you need."

"Thank you," Tara answered.

"I hear you guys are looking for a savior!" Sunny said, his voice booming. He was shirtless under a half-sleeve sweatshirt and wore Bermuda shorts with pineapples on them. "What can I do to be of service?"

"They need to make lunch," Tara told him. "And you're the only one who knows how to cook out of . . . most of us."

Sunny laughed. And then his smile slipped. "Wait, seriously? None of you know how to cook?"

"Our mom makes everything," Gina said. "She'd rather we not enter her domain."

Everyone else nodded as if to confirm their mothers were the same.

"Okay," Sunny said. He cleared his throat. "First things first. I'm doing it for all of you, not for you," he said, pointing at Tara.

"Fine by me," she replied. Over the past few weeks, she'd developed an indifference toward Sunny. Whatever he'd said to the group about her hadn't worked. Most of them approached her freely now, asking her questions or opinions about one thing or another.

He rubbed his hands together. "Good. Now. What is everyone in the mood for?"

"Chole!"

"Chaat."

"Masala paneer."

"Vindaloo?"

"I could really go for some fried chicken."

The older women at the end of the counter gasped.

Beth, who had made the chicken comment, cowered. "It's a joke. I mean, of course it's a joke."

Sunny thought about it, then said, "How about fried cauliflower? Gobi manchurian . . . tacos?"

The cheer was deafening. Sunny began by ordering everyone to wash their hands, put up their hair, and stand at different stations. People were given knives and tools to chop, mix, stir, or deep-fry. Tara managed the fry machine because every time it sputtered, Jhumpa and Happy let out an ear-piercing shriek.

Sunny worked on the sauce, mixing it with a competency she recalled from when they took the trip together. He stood next to her, smiling at the conversation around him. He was a jerk, but he was a jerk who liked the kids.

"Thanks," she said, leaning over a bit so he could hear over the kitchen noise. "For doing this with them."

He didn't say anything at first, instead focusing on whipping the sauce in the bowl in front of him. "It's my job."

She nodded.

"Hey, what's the name of the school you're going to?"

He nodded when she told him. "Oddly enough, my mom asked me to apply there, too. I got in with some scholarship."

"Cool. But you're going to Berkeley with Umma, right?"

He didn't say anything.

A few seconds later, he poured the sauce into a large, heated wok, where it sputtered and spit before calming to a gentle simmer. Then he snapped his fingers.

"I forgot. My mom wanted a picture of us. You know, family friends and all. It's the least you can do for—"

"Yeah, yeah," she said. "It's fine." Regardless of how upset she and Sunny were with each other, Tara knew their parents would never disrupt their friendship on behalf of their children. It always angered Tara when they prioritized community over family, but she doubted her mother would ever change.

Sunny held up a phone and angled it, and Tara leaned in to smile.

Then she remembered Silas's comment about a real smile. At the last minute, she stuck out her tongue.

Sunny chuckled and took the picture. "Thanks."

"You're welcome," she replied. They went back to working silently on lunch side by side.

~

Tara didn't expect lunch to be as good as it was, but everything came together. More importantly, the group had fun making the meal. She was smiling when she re-entered her room. She had two hours to herself before dinner that night, and all she wanted to do was write about characters who constantly nipped at each other with wicked banter like the students in her group tour.

Spending time with Silas and the kids was better for her healing process than she'd ever imagined. She was happy, truly happy.

Just as she was ready to strip out of her clothes and walk into the adjoining bath, a smile still on her face, her phone rang. Her pulse jumped when she saw her mother's face on her screen. Tara quickly answered. "Mom? Is everything okay? It's early there."

"Hi, honey," her mom said in a tired voice. "Everything is fine. I'm working on summer-semester papers and time got away from me. I'm calling because I wanted to talk to you about something. But first, how are you? Is everything okay there?"

Tara knew that tone. In her mother's eyes, she'd done something wrong. This was exactly how her mother always started her lectures. Tara sat at the edge of the bed and pinched the bridge of her nose. "I'm fine. It's hot and rains a lot now."

"That's good," she said absently.

"Mom? What is it?"

"Tara, I thought we had trust. I thought we had open communication."

Her stomach twisted in knots. She covered it with her hand, eyes closed. "Dad told you about Didi."

"Why didn't you come to me?" her mother asked.

"Would you have given me Didi's number?"

"I didn't even know your father was still talking to her after the last time she asked for money almost four years ago! I'm surrounded by a houseful of liars, and I don't know what I did to deserve this deceit."

The sharp accusation was hurtful and cutting.

"Maybe it's karma, Mom."

"Tara!" her mother shrieked. "Your sister is sick. She has a disease, and she is going to ruin your life if you let her into it. You will constantly want to help her, but she cannot be helped."

"Why?" Tara burst out. She got to her feet and paced across her hotel room. "Why can't she be helped? Why did you abandon her like that when she needed you?" Her eyes filled with tears as her chest tightened. "You *failed* her."

"As her family, we stuck by her side for a long time! I didn't *abandon* her. I did the best I could as her mother! I prayed—"

"Your prayers are meaningless," Tara snapped. "You are always focusing on what's best for yourself. Or for god. Or in the name of god. But you're never doing the best for your children." Tears began streaming in earnest down her cheeks, burning her skin. "You *and* Dad."

"I knew I should've stopped those postcards a long time ago. They were against the restraining order, but—"

"But what? You realized that I would've left, too, right? Why do you think I wanted to go to Berkeley with all my other friends, Mom? It's clear across the country from you."

There was a long pause. Then her mother said firmly, "Tara, you need to stop crying. This is an adult conversation. You need to respond maturely. Take a deep breath and we'll talk about how to address this together. Just because you aren't happy, you can't blame your parents for the rest of your life."

"You're right. Which is why we're not going to address anything together." She looked down at the phone, her hand shaking. "I have over two weeks left on this trip, and I'm going to meet Didi if I want to. I will have a relationship with her if I choose to do so without you getting involved. And, Mom? If you try to get in my way or hurt her in any way because of this, you'll lose both daughters."

She hung up the phone and threw it across the room. It hit the wall with an echoing thud and fell onto her bed.

In a race against the sobs bubbling in her chest, she tore off her clothes and stepped into the adjoining bath. The water was ice cold when she turned the knob and stepped under the rainfall spout. That's when she began to cry.

20

Day 45: Uttarakhand

Fifteen Days until Flight AA293 from DEL to JFK

Haridwar

Haridwar was hot and muggy, but Silas didn't mind. Especially when one night after the rains, he and Tara sneaked out to go down to the marketplace, where they walked into tiny shops and ate at a sit-down restaurant for the first time together.

He took pictures. Tons of them. For his photojournalism competition, of course, and for himself. With Tara's help, he began researching and reading articles on the long bus rides from location to location. His notes were piling up, and Tara edited each one for him, showing him yet another side of herself. She was so generous, and she cared. Even when he was rambling about feeling connected to a Desi identity, she didn't laugh at him or tell him his concerns were meaningless. If it was important to him, it was important to her.

It was two weeks until the end of their trip, and Silas was starting to see his story about timeless love that was celebrated by god and condemned by man.

Maybe that was because more and more of his pictures—and his time—included Tara Bajaj. He fell in love with her during moonlight strolls, long conversations about spirituality, and shared meals on late nights.

He dreaded what would happen when the trip came to an end.

The sound of thunder rumbled in the background as their bus pulled up the circular drive in front of their next hotel. Silas could hear the kids' sigh of relief as they all got off the bus and waited to unload their bags. Most of the luggage was caked with stains and dust now, but that seemed to be the least of everyone's problems.

Because of the looming monsoons, the air was thick, sweltering, and sticky, and there wasn't a day where every person on the trip did not have a bug bite that required some sort of anti-itch cream. Happy got it the worst with red welts all over her arms and legs. Silas watched as she inched over to Tara and leaned against her side.

"You sure you're okay?" Tara asked quietly.

"Yeah," Happy replied. "I just don't want to go to the temple tomorrow." Her lower lip wobbled as she scratched her triceps. "I'm tired of all of this."

Tara's eyes widened at Happy's search for comfort. She looped one hesitant arm around her shoulder. "I've been so many times," she told the girl. "If you want to stay back, I'll ask Chaya if you and I can miss tomorrow."

Hope shimmered in Happy's eyes. "Please?" she said, her voice cracking.

Silas could see the recognition on Tara's face. He'd learned a little bit more about her childhood, her long history of traveling with her parents as they went in search of knowledge, joy, or religion. If Happy was miserable going to temple, Tara understood those feelings.

"I'm going to do my best to get you out of it."

Yeah, there was no question about it. He was in love with Tara, and he had no idea if he should tell her first. Or tell her at all.

Neil whistled. Everyone groaned in response.

"When is he going to stop doing that?"

"Never. He's been at it for this whole trip."

"I hope no one buys him an actual whistle."

"You all know what is expected of you by now," Neil said, trusty tablet in hand. "We're going to go in, hand over our passports, check in, take back our passports, go to our rooms, get settled, and meet for dinner. Tomorrow is Haridwar. It will be hot, so we are going to be starting earlier than what is in your itinerary to avoid weather delays and crowds. Inside we go!"

There was another round of groans. Then, like all the other times, the students moved en masse toward the reception desk to get checked in.

"Chaya? I have to do laundry again."

"Neil, do you think they'll have chicken for dinner? I didn't think I'd miss American food as much because I ate so much at home."

"Hey, Sunny, are we playing Mario tonight?"

Silas grinned as he followed behind, helping Happy carry her bag. He loved listening to all of them pick at each other, laugh, talk about memories, or recollect moments with their families. He never had this growing up. He'd mostly gone on quiet holidays with his moms or other family friends.

The noise on this trip felt like that of family.

"Can we switch rooms?" Dax asked Neil, pointing to Ravi. "Amit and I have unfinished business."

"No, we don't," Amit said. "I beat you fair and square. I'm not doing a rematch."

"You're all supposed to be using your free time to reflect on your spirituality," Neil said with a deep sigh. "No switching."

They trudged up the stairs and into a long hallway. Neil and Chaya had been able to secure a private section of the hotel, which was both good and bad. Good because the kids were separate from the rest of the guests, but bad, Silas thought, because they were probably going to be running around the halls until Chaya and Neil told the junior guides to deal with the rowdiness. Silas glanced over his shoulder at Tara, who smiled before walking into her room two doors down.

"See you all at dinner," Neil called out just as Silas closed his door. "We have a long day tomorrow, so rest as much as you can."

A long day, Silas mused. He dropped his luggage in the closet, then unpacked the print photos from his moms' trip. Since he had some time before dinner, he could work on his project. The Haridwar leg of the trip would be the most difficult to capture because something had changed in the photos.

After lining up the pictures in order, then going location by location on his laptop, he landed on the last photo in the series where Mom was on one side of the group and Mama was on the other. Mama was laughing with her arms slung around a few other students, but Mom was much more subdued. Instead, she had her polite face on, something Silas would recognize anywhere. Had they fought? What had happened between them?

He was about to call them, now that it was late enough in the morning their time, when he heard a soft knock on his door.

Silas got up to answer. In front of him stood Dax, Ravi, Amit, and Faruk. They pushed past him into his room.

"Uh, come on in, I guess."

"Have you seen it?" Dax asked, his face ashen.

Silas looked back and forth at all of them. Something was wrong. "Have I seen what?"

"The picture."

He thought of his mothers' photo first. "What picture? What are you guys talking about?"

Amit held out his phone. It took Silas a minute to realize whom he was looking at. He took the phone and brought it closer to his face. The image was on a familiar social-media platform with a caption under it.

Sunny held the camera up at an angle. He was smiling ear to ear, and Tara was sticking out her tongue, her eyes sparkling. They looked like they were in a kitchen. There was another picture in the carousel, and when Silas swiped, he saw a younger Tara and Sunny in a similar pose, wearing backpacks and standing on a mountain. Silas read the caption.

> I know I've been offline for most of the summer, but that's because I've been traveling with this familiar face. Met ten years ago when our parents became friends. Traveled India together over the summer four years ago. We're at it again seeing some of our favorite places. Can't wait to see what college brings with T at my side. (No more Berkeley for me. Go . . . mules? That's a terrible mascot.)

"I can't believe they're going to college together," Ravi said quietly.

"Do you think she knew about Sunny going to her school?" Faruk asked.

"She had to know," Dax said. "They're family friends. Family friends know everything about each other, right?"

"That means she's been playing Silas the whole time," Amit replied. "That's dirty."

"No," Silas said. He handed back the phone, shaking his head vehemently. There had been too many quiet nights, too many secrets shared with him. Tara would've told him if Sunny was going to be in her future.

But what if it was true? What if she was just waiting for the opportunity to break it to him? He felt his heart clench, squeezing painfully at the thought of losing her. To someone who obviously didn't understand her truth and her secrets.

No, he thought. There was no way he'd just let that happen without saying something. Without asking for her to tell him why she'd knowingly be with Sunny after *being* together in every way.

The sound of doors opening in the hallway had him stepping outside. Tara stood there, shock on her face. Chetna, Beth, Jhumpa, Happy, Ina, and Gina surrounded her.

"She didn't know," Chetna blurted out.

"We were all in the kitchen when he took that picture," Happy added.

"He's just using her," Jhumpa said, her voice thin and shaky.

Dax pushed in front of him, hands fisted at his side. "None of it is a lie, though, right? I mean, they went on this same trip together, and now they're going to college together."

Another hotel door opened, and Sunny stepped out. He leaned against the doorjamb, a smug expression on his face. "Oh hey. What are y'all doing out here?"

"Douche nozzle!" Happy shouted. She sniffled.

Chaos broke. All the students began hurling insults at each other, fighting about who knew what and what was truth versus what was a lie. Then Silas looked at Tara's face, and he knew instinctively that his biggest fear was happening.

She was going to run.

Silas held up his hands in the shape of a T. The hallway noise dropped to barely audible whispers.

"Go back to your rooms," he said. When the students behind him began to argue, he cut them off. "I don't want to have to call Neil and Chaya."

They waited, all ten of them staring at each other, then at Silas and Tara, as if debating how far they should push and rebel. Then Tara nodded her head. There were sighs, and even a few watery sniffles, as if the students had been betrayed, before they hung their heads and walked back to their rooms. Then there was only Sunny, Silas, and Tara in the hallway.

Silas didn't hesitate. He crossed the distance between himself and Tara and ushered her back into her room. There was little satisfaction in seeing the irritated look on Sunny's face when he closed the door.

"I d-didn't know," Tara said when Silas turned to face her. Her fingers dove into her hair at her temples. "I don't understand why he would want to go to a small college in Pennsylvania. I mean, I picked it because I didn't think anyone at my school would want that. Why would he want to be there, too? That was my fresh start!"

"Maybe he still has feelings for you."

Silas watched first confusion and then shock cross her face. "You don't think I'd actually be interested in someone like him—"

"No," Silas said. Now that he saw her reaction to the picture, he knew. He *knew*. "No. We've spent hours together. Weeks. I know you now. I understand you, Tara. I also trust you. But what are you feeling?" He rubbed his hands up and down her arms.

"What am I feeling? I—I'm pissed! I'm pissed he's using me to get back at Umma for dumping him. I mean, that's the only logical reason for doing something like that. I'm off social media. I have no friends." When she giggled, there was no humor in the sound.

"Are you going to post something to prove him wrong?" Silas said. He had so many pictures of Tara . . . of both of them together. He could fill both their social-media accounts with all their photos and make room for even more memories with her.

Tara crossed her arms over her chest, as if to ward off a chill. Her face was still pale, and Silas was sure it was because she was remembering the first time her business was splashed online. "Why would I? I don't have any accounts anymore. I have nothing to prove."

"What if I asked you to do it for me?"

Her eyes widened. "For *you*? Why would you want me to post something on social media for you?"

"Because it matters," he said. His heart was pounding hard and fast in his chest. "Because I want you to tell everyone that Sunny is wrong. I want you to fight his bullshit. This is not your high school anymore. He knows that, and he's taking advantage of you. That's not fair to you, and honestly, that's not fair to me."

"Silas, the last time I fought back, I was ostracized."

"You did the right thing!" He had to work hard at lowering his voice, at controlling his tone. "They started the bullying, and when you wouldn't have it, you fought back. I'm sorry that it didn't work and that you were outnumbered, but you're not in high school anymore."

"If you believe me, then why is it so important to you that I say anything?" Tara cried. She crossed the room to her window, facing out to the hot afternoon sky. "Why can't we just ignore Sunny?"

"I want you to tell everyone that you're with me!" he shouted. "I'm sick of watching you trying to circumnavigate anything that hurts you. I'm afraid that you're going to put me in that category, too. That you'll run away from *me*."

Tara spun on her heels to look at him. "That's not true! I'm here with you, aren't I?"

"Because you have to be," he said evenly. "What's going to happen when we get home?"

There was a buzzing silence in the room, the barest hint of shuffling out in the hall. Silas took a minute to count backward from ten and ran his hands through his hair. It was too long now. The ends curled over the nape of his neck, and he had to wear a backward hat to keep it off his face.

"What do you want me to say? That I'm going to be the same person when we get back as I am now?"

She'd painted her nails late one night with the group, and the bright-purple polish was shocking on her fingers.

There was a long silence. "I think you just want us to have a summer thing," he finally said. "I'm a temporary party journey."

"Silas," she whispered. She had tears in her eyes now. "You believe Sunny, don't you? Like all those other people I used to know, you think I'm a shitty person, that I would use you like that."

His gut twisted. "No, Tara. I think you're incredible. But you're still so damn scared. And you're still trying to figure out who you are."

"What is that even supposed to mean?" she said, stepping toward him. "I reported my entire dance team, the only friends I had, because I stood up for what I believed in. I know myself enough to stand up for what I think is right."

"You stood up for Jai," he said, shoving his hands in his pockets.

"Wait a minute, you don't get to tell me about my choices," she said, her voice rising. "You don't get to tell me what I want."

"Then what do you want?" he said.

Tara inched forward again, but there was still so much space separating them. "I want us to just go back to the way things were before this dumb picture. It doesn't affect either of us."

"Then why are you scared to tell Sunny he's wrong on a public platform?"

"Because it doesn't matter!" Her shriek was louder than he'd ever heard her raise her voice.

The hurt twisted inside him, frustrating the hell out of him. He could see how to unknot it, but he didn't have the power to do so himself. He moved to the door. "I'm going to go."

"Wait," she said. She grabbed his arm, holding it tightly. Her eyes were wide, shining with tears. "Where are you going?"

"To my room," Silas said. "Then maybe to town. I need to think. I just need . . . I need space. You understand that."

He stepped around her and yanked open the door. He heard scurrying down the tiled hall floors, but when he looked out, no one was there.

Without a backward glance, he left Tara to her tears while he nursed a broken heart.

21

Day 47: Uttarakhand

Thirteen Days until Flight AA293 from DEL to JFK

Haridwar

WhatsApp message dated 8/22 to Savitri Bajaj:

> TARA: Didi, Mom found out. If she tries to make things difficult
> for you in any way, although I don't know how she'd do that,
> please let me know. I'll deal with her. Are you still okay to meet
> when we reach Delhi?
>
> (Read 11:45 p.m.)

WhatsApp message dated 8/22 from Chaya-Tour Lead:

CHAYA: Feel free to sleep in. We're not going to Haridwar today. Can't leave the hotel. Warnings of landslides from the monsoon rains mean we are here for the day for our safety.

TARA: Okay.

CHAYA: Are you okay?

TARA: Fine. Thanks.

Tara turned on the bedside light at the rumbling sound of thunder. The storm had started late at night, and now, in the earliest hours of morning, it was violent and vicious. The windows rattled like they were thin sheets of plastic instead of reinforced glass. The lights flickered overhead.

Her laptop sat open on the bed next to her, and the cursor blinked on a blank page. Her story of gods and demons had been coming together so quickly, but now she'd finally stalled. She had no idea what her characters were supposed to do next.

After twenty minutes of staring at her phone uneasily with no one to call or text, and without Silas by her side, she got up and put on a sweatshirt over her pajama top. Tara dug a pair of flip-flops out of the front compartment of her suitcase and pocketed her hotel-room key card and ID before opening her door and stepping out into the eerily quiet hallway.

Thunder rumbled again. She looked back at Silas's door. Her chest ached from all the tears she'd shed.

"Tea," she whispered to herself. "Didi used to make me tea."

There had to be a small kitchenette in the lobby like most Radisson hotels in the States. Because of the storm, she opted for the stairs instead of the elevator and was pleasantly surprised to see a few people behind the front desk.

"Ma'am, is there anything we can help you with?" one of the women asked when she saw Tara.

Tara responded in Hindi. "I'm just looking for some chai. Is there any?"

The woman nodded and pointed her to the kitchenette. "There is only dip-dip, but if you want it boiled, I can ask the kitchen."

"That's okay," Tara said. "I'll have the dip-dip." In the kitchenette, she found a white ceramic mug and a Lipton tea bag. She hooked the string around the handle of the mug. There was a hot-water dispenser, and she poured the filtered hot water over the tea bag.

After adding pasteurized milk, she nuked the mug of tea in the microwave until it barely bubbled before dropping in two sugar cubes. There were Parle-G digestive biscuits on a small platter, and after taking one of the individually wrapped packages, Tara sat in front of the unlit fireplace in the lobby lounge. The lights flickered again, but she took solace in the sound of easy conversation at the reception desk behind her.

She'd just dunked her biscuit into her tea and popped it in her mouth when a figure moved to stand next to her. Tara looked up and almost choked.

Sunny's hair stood on end. He'd also opted for a sweatshirt over his athletic shorts at this early hour. There were dark circles around his eyes behind black-framed glasses. "I knew I heard someone leave. It's three in the morning."

Tara grabbed the rest of her cookie pack and her hotel key card and stood.

"No, wait," he said, holding out a hand. "Just . . . wait."

"No," she replied, stepping around him.

When she was halfway across the lobby, he called out, "I just did what you did to me. It wasn't personal."

Tara stopped, her grip tightening on the mug until her hand warmed. "It's *always* been personal."

He motioned to the armchair she'd just vacated. "Two minutes? You don't have to stay, but I want you to. Please. Two minutes."

She looked down at the chair, then back at his face. She was so tired. The idea of starting over, starting new, was intoxicating, but it hadn't worked. It never did. She always felt ensnared by her past. She might as well face it.

"Two minutes," she said quietly, and sat back down.

He took the seat across from her and braced his elbows on his knees. The fridge in the kitchenette hummed softly over the thunder rolling outside. After a stretch of silence, Tara was about to get up again when Sunny spoke.

"Do you still believe in god?"

"What?"

He looked up at her, eyes solemn. "I don't think I do anymore. I don't think I have for a long time." He scrubbed his hands over his face. "I don't know why I told you that. Please don't tell your parents. They'll tell mine, and then . . . Just don't."

She shook her head. After another sip from her tea to try to settle her stomach, Tara said, "Why do you want to know?"

"It's . . . important."

She sighed, and then thought about his question for a moment longer before responding. "Sometimes I believe in the god I'm told to believe in, but mostly, it's about their stories, and what they represent in their various forms. The teachings."

"How?" he asked. "How can you possibly believe when religion is a business? In India, in the diaspora. Hell, the Western world is ruled by the business of god. Churches are tax havens, right? Believing in god costs people money, and their homes and their lives. Our moms? Their existence is all about the business of god."

Tara curled up in the armchair and pulled on the string of her tea bag. The tea bag dipped in and out of the water. Dip-dip tea.

"Tara . . ."

"There's believing in god and believing in believing, I guess," she finally said.

It was Sunny's turn to look at her with confusion on his face.

"Some people claim that god is supposed to do something for you, right?" Sunny nodded.

"Other people understand that regardless of what god is, the act of believing in something outside of yourself will make you a better person."

He scoffed. "Which do you think our moms believe in?"

Tara wanted to say something inspirational, like their moms believed in them. But she couldn't get herself to hide the truth.

"Our moms believe in a version of a god that makes them feel better about the decisions they make," Tara said quietly. "And there is nothing that we can do to change that."

He got to his feet in a rush. "It pisses me off so much," he said. He paced back and forth in front of the fireplace. "These pilgrimage sites in India? They actively enforce casteist practices. Did you know that?"

Tara nodded. "And discriminate against people with disabilities. And charge higher prices for people from the diaspora. The list goes on and on. But India isn't the only place that does it. This is a problem that exists for everyone who wants religion. Of course, that's probably not what pilgrimage tours want to advertise." She thought of Chaya and Neil and how they would react if Tara told them the same thing she was telling Sunny.

Sunny swept his arms wide. "If we say something about it, we're told, 'Oh, you don't understand.' We're just supposed to shut up, and go to temple, and follow the rituals of our family's version of Hinduism. Then we move out, and we do the exact same thing to our kids that we were taught growing up. We never question it. How are we not part of the problem?"

"We don't have to be, Sunny. Who said we do?"

"But, Tara, the minute we start arguing, we're told that it's not our business to ask questions. We aren't Indian *enough* to understand. We're not from here. And that's how they keep the diaspora kids in check. That's how they get us to keep pushing casteism. By telling us we aren't Indian enough to understand, or we're too privileged to ask questions. So we should follow along for the sake of tradition."

She thought about the same conversation she'd had with Silas about his photo series and began to realize how truly thin the line was between where she came from and where she belonged.

"I don't know what you want me to say."

"I want you to tell me the truth. Would you willingly go on a religious pilgrimage after this tour?"

"No," she said. This was the last temple tour she'd ever take. Not because she was rejecting her faith. In retrospect, she loved these monuments, these symbols of Hinduism. But she was no longer required to worship there.

She put her tea down on the side table with a thud.

This was going to be her last pilgrimage tour.

She was done after this.

As beautiful and peaceful and majestic as some of the temples were . . . she was free from obligation. Her heart fluttered, and she pressed a hand to her chest. *Holy shit.*

"Yeah," Sunny said. He collapsed in his chair and ran his hands through his messy hair. "Umma was going to break up with me at the end of senior year."

Tara was taken aback. "Wait a minute. After your last break, I thought things were good. That you two were supposed to go to California together."

"I thought so, too," Sunny said. "I have my mom to blame for that. She would always compare you two whenever Umma was over. Umma was so jealous. Then Umma and I would fight, and she would throw you in my face."

"What the hell?" she said, loud enough to attract attention. When she looked around the lobby, though, she saw that there was now only one person behind the reception desk. The storm had quieted. "Why would Umma be jealous of me? Your mom is just as fanatical as my mom, except mine hides it better."

"Umma saw you as competition, Tara. She always did."

He had just confirmed his motive for texting Umma lies about her. "I knew you were trying to make her believe that I was trash."

"I was so desperate." His hands shook as he waved them in a wide circle. "Those texts were just to convince her that I would *never*, because she wasn't listening to the truth. But she still cut things off. I'm sorry for giving her that ammunition against you."

Tara thought about his apology, about the way he looked now, and about everything that had passed. She glanced down at her phone in her lap. "I'm sorry I shared your texts from all those years ago," she said. "I regret that. I wanted to hurt her for the way she hurt me."

He smiled ruefully. "But in the end, it was you and me who got burned. Mostly you. And it all started when we didn't want anyone to know that we went to India before high school."

Tara had to laugh at that. "Why did we hate it so much?" she asked, smiling for the first time. "We were so embarrassed by it, even though we were both going to a school in New Jersey with so many Desis. The kids on this trip are having such a good time."

"Maybe they like it better because of Chaya and Neil? Our senior guides were older than our parents, remember?"

Tara thought about it for a moment, then said, "It's Silas. Silas makes it all seem . . . special."

Sunny reached out with his sneakered foot and nudged her leg. "It's you, too."

"*Me?*"

He nodded. "I had such a thing for you back then. You were so smart and knew everything about the trip. All of us felt so awkward. So *American*. And we hated being there because our parents didn't understand us in some way or another. But there you were. You were the only one who wasn't a fish out of water. That's why it always surprised me that you wanted to keep it a secret. But hey, if we didn't talk about it, that meant that no one would know about me and my family, either."

It was rare for her to think of how Before-Tara wanted nothing to do with the people who made her look and feel and act a certain way.

And After-Tara? After-Tara was a lot happier.

She stood, picking up her now-empty mug, its quickly cooling tea bag still inside. "Why did you post that picture, Sunny?"

Sunny rubbed the back of his neck. His cheeks had a tinge of red in them. "I love her, you know? Umma. She's a bit much sometimes, but I love her. I saw that she was hanging out with this new guy, and I figured if I could make her jealous one last time, she'd be hurting as much as I was, and so would you."

"The problem is, you didn't hurt me. I'm no longer on social media, remember? I couldn't care less. Instead, you hurt a great guy who is innocent in our mess."

He didn't reply.

She passed his chair and went to the kitchenette to put her mug in the sink. Then, before she walked to the elevator bank, she called out Sunny's name.

He looked up, eyes wide. He was alone in the lobby now. Out of place. Out of touch.

"I believe in god," she said slowly. "But I believe in believing more."

She walked back upstairs to her floor. Just as she reached her door, Chaya stepped out of her room, wearing running shoes. She looked up with surprise and whispered, "Tara? Is everything—"

"Couldn't sleep. Went to have some tea," she said in Hindi. "Where are you off to?"

Chaya looked down at her clothes and said softly, "The rain has let up. I'm going to go to the gardens for a walk and some meditation. Would you . . . like to join me?"

Tara nodded. "Give me a second to change?"

"Yes, I'll wait here."

Tara walked back into her room and flipped on the overhead light. Her computer screen saver was up. It was a picture of her and Silas standing in front of Kedarnath, framed by its white jagged peaks in the background. The small temple in the corner left was surrounded by a shoulder-high wooden fence. His arms were wrapped around her waist, her hand in the air.

Tara smiled at the image. She knew what she had to do. Maybe meditating would help her figure out how to do it.

22

Day 50: New Delhi

Ten Days until Flight AA293 from DEL to JFK

"Music doesn't sound the same anymore," Silas said. "Like there's no more love in it."

Mama grunted, and he could feel her judgment through his computer screen. "Silas. You're being dramatic again."

"You know, you're both supposed to be supportive," he replied. "Not call me dramatic."

Mom also chuckled, only irritating him more.

"Come on, guys!"

"Honey," Mom said. "You're sitting in your hotel, sulking."

He stared at the two beautiful faces looking back at him. He couldn't believe he'd be seeing them again in ten days. He missed them. The homesickness had come unexpectedly on the trip, and he was ready to be with family again, even though he'd miss the friends he'd made.

"You know, yesterday when we left Haridwar and came back to Delhi, I sat with some of the kids, and she didn't even look at me when she got on the bus. She just sat in her usual spot."

Mama raised a brow. "Is that usual spot next to where your usual spot used to be before you chose to sit next to the kids?"

He crossed his arms over his chest and slouched. "You know what? Neither of you are being supportive right now."

They laughed at him again.

"Well, maybe focus on what you can control," Mama said. "When you get back, you'll be packing up and moving out a few weeks later. Isn't that exciting?"

"How can either of you think of college when I'm heartbroken?" he burst out.

Heartbroken. Yes, that is exactly it.

He rubbed the heel of his palm against his chest to try to dull the ache. He had only ten days left, and he might not see Tara again after that.

If he was being honest with himself, that was what was keeping him up at night.

His mothers looked at each other, then at him. "You know," Mama said, "we weren't together from the moment we took the trip, Silas. We were kids who had feelings that we couldn't figure out because we were from these religious families."

"I know," Silas said. "But neither of you gave up on each other! You stayed in touch; you decided to go to the same college because of your feelings! I feel like Tara is ready to give up before we even get started. Which means that she isn't really into me, and this was just a summer distraction."

No. Even as the words came out of his mouth, he knew that wasn't true. They'd been together day in and day out for the last two months. They had been able to read each other's signals within weeks.

And they'd *been* together. That meant something.

"Maybe she just needs to process before you guys talk again. Have you told Tara that you want to hash it out?" Mom asked.

"Not yet," Silas said quietly. "I'll tell her tomorrow." He looked around his hotel room. It was the nicest one they'd stayed in since they arrived in India. Despite that, Silas would trade it for another night at one of the retreat centers.

"Is it raining a lot there?" Mama asked.

"All the time now," Silas replied. He looked out the window at the gray, wet evening light. "In Haridwar, because of the mudslides nearby, the Ganga looked brownish, and Neil said it wasn't safe to take a dip for the holy cleanse. It's the same color as the brown floodwater in Delhi."

Mom turned to Mama, grinning. "Oh my gosh, do you remember when we did the bath in Haridwar? One of the kids on our tour tripped and went under, and everyone almost lost their mind."

Mama started laughing. "That was the big moment for all of us! Everyone was so scared. Silas, we're sorry you couldn't experience that. It's supposed to be the highlight. Submerging yourself in the holy river together as a bonding experience."

"Yeah, I think I'm good," Silas said. He could only imagine what Dax, Amit, Faruk, Ravi, and the rest would do in that situation.

He was about to sign off when Mom held up a finger. "Oh my gosh, I almost forgot," she said. "You got a big packet in the mail. It looks important." She left the screen and returned with a fat manila envelope. "It's from *Global Conservators Magazine*. Did you sign up for a subscription?"

Silas shook his head. His palms began to sweat. He'd been meaning to tell his moms about the competition, but he didn't want to hurt their feelings. They'd always talked about their photography business as a family thing. Almost as if it was expected that he would join the fray during wedding season. Maybe it was his fault that he never told them he wanted to try other things.

He had to tell them now.

"I, uh, I'm participating in their photojournalism competition. That's probably the print version of all their rules and guidelines."

Mom gasped. "Silas! That's great! What's the competition for?"

He shifted in his seat. The truth might hurt their feelings, and that was the last thing he ever wanted to do.

"It's for a chance to be featured in the magazine. And there is an internship for photographers who want to pursue nature photojournalism. If I don't win, I still get exposure . . ."

His moms were quiet for a moment. They looked at each other, their graying hair at their temples above their earlobes. Their sweatshirts and T-shirts faded with age indicative of an off day.

"Did you think we wouldn't be supportive?" Mom said. "That sounds like a good opportunity. Why didn't you tell us?"

"Because we always talk about wedding photography as the family business," Silas said. "That we're in the industry of capturing moments that make people smile. I want to do something . . . different. And we're in this together, right? This affects you. If I don't join you . . ."

He squeezed his palms tightly in his lap, his knuckles white as his fingers laced together.

"We want you to be happy," Mama said softly. Her words came through his computer speakers clearly, the connection so stable and crisp that he couldn't misunderstand. "And if you think that's what's best for your art, then wonderful. We never expected for you to follow in our footsteps. We just wanted you to have options."

"Beta," Mom started. "Just dedicate your heart and soul to it. Be the best photographer and photojournalist you want to be. That's all we ever wanted from you. And for you to be able to pay rent so you can move out."

He snorted with laughter.

They'd told him that before, that they wanted Silas to be happy. But he wanted them to be proud, too.

"I don't know if I'll win or even make finals," he said.

"Then you try somewhere else," Mama replied. Her ever-practical advice was always so comforting. "Silas, you're young! We never want you to feel the same way we were made to feel. Like you have to figure it all out now. You don't need all the answers. Life is a journey, and sometimes it takes years to figure out all the hidden pockets of yourself."

He thought about Tara, and how he'd told her that she was on a journey, and she didn't know what she wanted yet. Was it unfair for him to demand that she have the answers when clearly neither did he?

"I mean, you do have to figure out the writing part now if you are entering a photojournalism competition," Mom added. "Your spelling has always been atrocious."

He laughed again, even though he knew there had to be some level of disappointment they weren't sharing about how he wasn't ready to jump into the fold. Or maybe that was his fear talking. His scapegoat.

"The shots I'm going to submit to the competition," he said, clearing his throat, "they're a commentary on South Asian queer identities. I re-created some of your key images from your trip . . ."

"You re-created some of them for the competition?" Mom asked, her eyes wide, her mouth agape. "Can you show us? I want to see!"

Silas grinned. "When I get home. I'm going to clean up some of the images first."

"This is why you wanted to go," Mom said softly. "So you'd have the chance to take the pictures for this competition, not just for us."

He scratched the back of his neck, debating whether to tell the truth or to keep it for himself. "It was for me, too," he finally said. "I thought my Desi identity was because of where I was born, and because of you two. But now it feels weird talking about identity in absolutes. That's what Tara called it, anyway. Identity doesn't have to be an absolute, right?"

Mom clasped her hands together. "You're so smart, Silas. You'll always figure it out. Sometimes you just need some time."

Silas nodded, ignoring what sounded like a faint knock. It was probably the room next to his. He motioned to the package. "What do you think? Do I have a chance?"

His moms nodded in unison.

"I think you're going to be incredible, no matter what you do," Mama said.

He took a deep breath, his heart filled with love. "There is some stiff competition out there," he said. "What if none of this pans out?"

"There is always another way," Mom said patiently. "And if you burn like a dumpster fire, we can expand into destination weddings or something to give you an opportunity to travel."

He grinned. "I love you both."

"We love you, too," they said.

There was a more persistent knock now. He jumped, his pulse racing just a bit faster at the memories of the past few weeks of after-dark hotel visits. Someone was definitely at his door.

"I have to go. Someone is here."

His moms blew him kisses, and the screen closed.

It was 10:00 p.m. It could be Chaya and Neil with information about their tour of the Hanuman Mandir tomorrow. A part of him hoped that it was. He didn't know if he could take any more rejection.

He crossed the room. When he opened the door, he smelled the jasmine and coconut first.

Then he saw Tara's wide eyes, her braided hair draped over one shoulder.

"Hi," she whispered.

"Hi," he whispered back.

Her eyes began to water. "If you're free . . . want to come with me to eat some chole bhature?"

He couldn't say no. Not when he wanted so badly to spend as much time with her as possible before returning home. "Okay."

"Can you bring your camera? And your umbrella. It's raining. Again."

That was a new request, he thought. But he walked back into his room and put on his water shoes before grabbing his room card, phone, and the small waterproof day pack with his equipment inside. He had enough juice left for the rest of the night and the right lens already packed.

Silas followed Tara out of the hotel and onto the street.

"I can't believe we made it seven weeks without taking public transportation," she said.

"Wait, why do we need to take—"

She held up a hand, and the rumbling roar of a small motor grew louder until a rickshaw pulled up in front of the hotel. The three-wheeled motor vehicle had a yellow top and a green bottom half, and it was a third of the size of a compact sedan. The man in the single seat behind the wheel didn't even look at them.

"Oh my god, we're taking a rickshaw!" he said. He'd seen many of them over the past two months, but because of the bus, or their location, he hadn't had the opportunity to sit in one.

Tara motioned for Silas to get in first in the ridiculously small bench seat behind the driver. He ducked his head, held on to the roofline of the open three-wheeled vehicle, tucked his bag on his lap, and squeezed to one side so Tara could get in the other.

She said something in Hindi to the driver, who nodded his head in the side-to-side motion that Silas had learned to interpret as a yes . . . or a maybe, depending on the context. They jolted forward, which definitely meant it was a yes.

Then the rickshaw was moving fast, wind blowing in his face, water splashing at their feet from the rains pooling on the roads. The smells and sights of late-night Delhi consumed him: an earthiness from monsoons, diesel exhaust, and the scents of spice from passing restaurants.

Less than two minutes later, they pulled up to a street corner. The ever-familiar power lines hung overhead, and groups of people milled out front in a jumble of black umbrellas.

"Food carts aren't allowed to operate this late in Delhi," Tara said, opening her own umbrella. "But my sister mentioned this place when I asked her for some restaurant recommendations."

"Where are we exactly?" Silas asked as she paid for the rickshaw and they got out from the back.

"Follow me," Tara said in response.

They walked to the end of the block and turned the corner. Inside was an alley with a few overhead lights; a web of cable, phone, and electric wires; and a trickle of people walking slowly over cobblestone roads.

"Welcome to Chandni Chowk."

Tara led him through what looked like a maze of alleys lined with a mix of high-end shops, family-owned boutiques, and wholesale retailers.

"Chandni Chowk was established by the Mughal emperor Shah Jahan," she said, her voice modulated as if she were reciting a history lesson she'd once had to memorize.

"Shah Jahan, as in the guy who made the Taj Mahal?"

"One and the same. Chandni Chowk literally translates as Moonlight Square. Originally, it had a pool of water in the center of the market that reflected the moonlight and glowed so brightly that it illuminated all the surroundings. There is a fountain in that spot now."

"It's still a market?"

"One of the more famous ones. On weekends in the middle of the afternoon, it's impossible to get through." She motioned to the six-foot-wide path. "If you can imagine, this is filled with a rush of people, handcarts, delivery vans, and rickshaws. In heavy rain, it's even more intense."

"That sounds dangerous," Silas said, trying to imagine what the chaos would look like. He'd love to come back and see it.

"It's like Rockefeller Plaza on Christmas Eve."

They stopped in front of the only brightly lit restaurant on the block. It was narrow and squeezed between two larger buildings. The signs were dusty and old. Half the lights were out on the marquee. But inside, the downstairs level had a bright, modern marble order counter. Through the windows, he could see a wide-open seating space with white tables and chairs upstairs.

Tara led him inside after they shook off their umbrellas and covered them with the provided plastic wrap so they didn't drip all over the slippery tile floors. After they ordered two chole bhature platters, they were given a table card and then walked up the spiral metal stairs to the second floor. A couple was sitting in the corner, finishing their meal. Tara chose a table closest to the window and sat down.

"I should feel awful considering all the second dinners we've eaten on this trip," Silas said, trying to suppress some of the nerves bubbling in his gut.

Tara didn't respond. They sat in awkward silence for a few minutes, until finally a woman put a tray on their table, overflowing with puffed, yeasty bread and helpings of chole that smelled so fragrant Silas's mouth began to water. Fine slices of ginger garnished the top.

"Oh my god," he said reverently.

"I will never get enough of this," Tara said. After they used the hand sanitizer she retrieved from her purse, she tore off a corner of the bread, then used it as a scoop to pick up some of the chickpeas. Silas did the same.

The flavor bomb in his mouth was enough to make him want to stand up and dance.

"I'm going to miss this," he said after swallowing.

"Silas?" Tara said.

Here it comes, he thought. The brush-off and the apology. She'd try to be kind and make it hurt less, but Silas knew it was going to sting. He wiped his hands on the napkin.

"Yeah?"

"I'm not going to post anything on social media," she said quietly.

His stomach was churning now. Maybe they should've had this conversation before they started eating. He should get up and go. He looked at his camera bag next to him, ready to grab it, and then realized she'd asked him to bring it. There had to be a reason.

He sat back in his chair. "Tara—"

"I'm not going to post on social media," she continued, "because being online wasn't healthy for me. Some people can do it. Some people *love* it, and yeah, it would be great to eventually connect with everyone in this group to see what they're all up to. But I don't think I'm ready yet."

He nodded. For the first time, he began to understand her reaction to the picture. "I'm so sorry, I didn't realize when I asked you that—"

"No, no, it's fine," she said. "Really. It's just not for me."

Was *he* still for her, though? He waited, hands in his lap, appetite gone.

The last thing he expected was for Tara to start to cry. His panic meter went up to a ten in the space of a heartbeat.

"You know what? I didn't realize I was a crier," she said. She picked up a napkin and dabbed at the big soulful tears rolling down her cheeks. "God, I hope there are no chilis on this; otherwise, my eyes are going to burn."

"Oh, Tara. I'm so sorry. I—look, do you want me to go? I'll go. Just don't do that." He grabbed his wad of napkins and held them out for her. "I can go—"

She gurgled a laugh. "I didn't expect you to be scared of a few tears."

"I'm scared of *your* tears." He smiled nervously. "I love you, and I don't want you to be hurting like that."

The recognition on her face made him falter for a moment.

"I love you," he said again. "And I care about you. I know what I am, and I'm better when I'm with you."

Tara sniffed. Then, to his surprise, she said, "When we go on our next trip, can we just do foodie stuff? I'd like to avoid religious pilgrimage sites, please."

He was out of his chair before she could finish her sentence. She tilted her head back to look up at him, her lashes damp with tears just as his lips met hers.

She kissed him back, spicy and sweet, their mouths pressed so hard against each other that he never wanted to stop. The scent of her imprinted in his brain; he would always associate it with her. Her hands cupped his wrists. He reveled in that moment with her.

"That's a hell of a way to keep a guy waiting," he said against her mouth, then kissed her again, bursting with love for her.

"It took me a while to come around to it," she said, her voice wavering. "When we get back, it's going to be a weird adjustment, but I want to be with you, Silas."

"If we can hike the Himalayas, we can do anything." He kissed her again, holding her close, sinking into the feel of her lips under his.

When he finally pulled back, their noses brushed. Tara whispered, "I love you, too. We're only eighteen. We're going to college. We definitely don't have all the answers, and god sure as hell won't be able to tell us. But I know, right now, that I will always love you, Silas D'Souza-Gupta."

In the late-night hush of Chandni Chowk in the streets of New Delhi, against the quiet sound of warm rain, Silas knew his epic love story with this incredible person had just begun.

23

Day 56: New Delhi

Four Days until Flight AA293 from DEL to JFK

WhatsApp message dated 9/1 to Tara Bajaj:

Here is the address. Can't wait to see you, munchkin.

The day Tara went out to meet her sister, she could barely focus. It was her last day off as a junior guide, and the first one she hadn't spent with Silas. She needed to see Didi by herself.

Savitri Bajaj had been like a mother figure to Tara when their mom was too busy for most of their lives. When Savitri Didi left, Tara grieved. Every time she received a postcard, it triggered a rush of sadness and longing all over again.

Which probably explained why she was filled with nerves and fear. Was Savitri the same? Was she still using? Was she happy and healthy and safe?

Would she ever come home?

Her brief, infrequent text messages felt . . . friendly. Not as full of love and hope and heart as Tara was aching for. But maybe Didi was scared, too?

Tara took a car service to a location on the far side of the city and stepped out in front of a large shopping complex made of glass and steel. An overhead sign bracketed the entrance into the bustling shopping and restaurant complex: Select Citywalk.

After plugging the café name into her phone, Tara tried her best to keep her nausea under control as she walked from the drop-off point to where she was meeting her sister.

A thick crowd stood in front of the café. It was hard to see specific faces in the rain and dimming light.

And then, as if she'd willed it into being, the crowd parted. She slowed to a stop as Savitri Bajaj came into view.

Didi looked so much older than Tara remembered. She wore capris that fell to midcalf and rain boots that looked oddly fun with the rest of her outfit. Her black hair, which used to curl and fly everywhere, was pinned on top of her head. A crossbody bag the color of sunflowers rested against her hip, and her umbrella was a clear dome over her head. Phone in hand, Savitri turned slowly until her eyes locked with Tara's.

The last time they'd seen each other, Didi had been painfully gaunt, with dark bags under her eyes, screaming at their mother. There were tears back then, just as there were now.

Tara's heart clenched. She let out a sob and started jogging, then running. Her sister did the same, her umbrella falling just as quickly, and like always, Didi opened her arms wide, and Tara fell against her sister.

As those arms closed around her, Tara had memories of being held just like this, tightly against Didi's slender, soft body, forever protected.

They sobbed together, holding each other close, until Tara could feel the rain soak through her clothes.

When the sobs slowed, Didi pulled away, her mascara leaving black streaks against her cheeks. She cupped Tara's face. "I'm so sorry," she said. "I'm so sorry I wasn't there for you for so many years."

"It's not your fault," Tara sobbed. "It's not your fault. It's their fault. Please don't leave me again, Didi. Please don't go."

Her sister shook her head hard. "Never. Never again."

They hugged again, holding each other tight. All their fears, their memories, and their hopes circled around them like the casual onlookers in the middle of the heavy rain.

By the time they were able to compose themselves and the sobs began to slow, their hair was soaking wet and their clothes were limp and in terrible shape. They looked up at the café sign, and then at all the people staring at them, before they laughed.

"Want to come see my place?" Didi said hesitantly. "Or we can go to your hotel and sit in the lobby . . ."

Tara shook her head. The years had fallen away. This was her older sister. The one person who always saw her. "I want to see where you live."

"It's temporary since I'll probably be traveling again soon, but it's really nice. Come on."

They called a car, and while they waited, Didi gripped her hand hard and said, "I want to know everything. Start at the beginning. Tell me what I missed as if we are experiencing the moments all over again."

They talked nonstop during the fifteen-minute ride, hands clutched together as if scared one or the other would leave again. They paused only for the few minutes that Tara's mouth dropped at the apartment building her sister was staying in. It was a modern structure with an art deco aesthetic and a doorman. Since New Delhi was like any other city, she knew the rent had to be expensive.

Didi didn't seem to notice her confusion or awkwardness and motioned Tara inside the glass-and-chrome lobby and then upstairs to the spacious one-bedroom with floor-to-ceiling windows that revealed a gorgeous night view of the city. A single low-backed couch, a small coffee table, and a TV stand with a flat screen sat in the living room.

"Let's get some clothes and change. I'll make chai," she said in Hindi. Her accent was sharper. It didn't have the hint of American anymore.

Tara changed and sat in a T-shirt and leggings that smelled like her sister. She felt a pang of regret that she'd lost so much time with her, but they were together now. "Didi?"

"Mm-hm?" Her sister stood in front of a small cooktop, adding spices to a pot of water.

"I don't want to ruin our time together, but I have spent the last few years trying to figure it out. What happened between you and Mom? Why did she kick you out?"

Her sister's shoulders tensed.

"You don't have to tell me if you don't want to, but I only heard their story. That you'd relapsed and you wouldn't go back to rehab—"

Her laugh was hard and humorless. "That place was *not* rehab," she said, looking at Tara over her shoulder. "It was a religious center that took Mom and Dad's money and tried to pray the addiction away. Mom and Dad wouldn't listen to me, and I relapsed a third time because of it. I had barely finished college and was working as a copyeditor in Dad's office. My boss reported me for coming to work high. Then they reported it to Dad. I got fired, and they tried to admit me to that center again. They even tried to get a court order to take the decision out of my hands."

"Why didn't I know any of this?"

"Tara," Didi said. She set out two mugs at the open island that separated the kitchen from the living room. "You were what, thirteen? I hated that I could barely function during our time together. I didn't want you to worry about me."

"But then they kicked you out."

"But then they kicked me out," Didi said calmly. "And it sucked, and I missed you more than anything, but after a really hard year, I got help, I got clean, and I found focus in a job that I really like."

Her sister poured the chai through a strainer, then wiped up the drops on the white counter with a towel. Then she carried both mugs to the coffee table. Her drying hair frizzed and drooped to the side.

"I can't believe you opted to be a junior guide on the temple tour. I've been here for six months, and I refuse to go anywhere near those pilgrimage sites."

"It was the only job I could get that would pay me enough to set me up for college," Tara said. "Otherwise, I would've been stuck working at home and risking seeing everyone from high school."

"It was that bad, huh? I'm sorry I wasn't there."

Tara took a sip of the hot chai, and fresh tears formed in her throat. It tasted just like Didi always used to make it. She put the cup down before her trembling hand spilled it all over the floor.

"Didi?"

"Yeah, munchkin?"

"Are you happy?"

Sadness crossed Savitri's face, but she smiled. "I am now."

"Since you're clean, will you come back home?"

The smile faded. Her sister shook her head slowly. "I'm sorry, Tara. I can't. It's not . . . healthy for me. The risk of relapse is high. I've been in the States, but New Jersey is . . . off limits. I hope you understand."

Tara squeezed her sister's hands. "Will you come and visit me in Pennsylvania if you have time then?"

Her sister grinned. "What, now that you're eighteen and Mom can't stop me? You'll be sick of seeing me so much."

Tara couldn't wait. She knew it was expensive to fly back and forth, but—

"Oh my god," she said, sitting up straight. "I don't even know what you do for work! Is this Dad-money or you-money?"

Didi grinned. "Dad gives me, like, a few bucks here and there for my birthday or Diwali. I think it's his way of trying to take care of me, even though he doesn't want Mom to know." She motioned to the apartment. "This is me-money."

Her eyes widened. She looked around at the expensively furnished place. She was so proud of her sister, so proud of everything that she'd done to get this far, but there were still so many gaps in their history. "What do you *do*?"

"I'm a producer for a media company."

Tara's mouth fell open. "What?"

"I know, wild, right? I basically organize people and sets and photographers for our feature articles. They rent these apartments while we're working on shoots and stories. We just launched a streaming channel, so that's why I've been in India this long."

Tara's mind raced. "How did you even get a job like that?"

"Working at Dad's company as long as I did, between interning and then copyediting media contracts, I was able to make a few friends of my own. And then I was willing to travel and stay in remote locations as a trainee."

"Thanks to Mom," they said in unison, and laughed.

"I always wondered why she insisted on camping or staying in communal homes," Didi mused. "We could afford better places. Obviously."

"It's her way of wrestling with guilt," Tara said.

Didi brushed a curl off Tara's face. "And thankfully, because of that experience, I was able to find a career."

"What company do you produce for?"

"Global Conservators Magazine."

Tara's jaw dropped. "Oh my god," she said. "Silas is going to flip."

"Who's Silas?"

Tara tucked her feet under her, leaning against her sister's side. Didi wrapped an arm around her shoulder.

"Silas," Tara started, "is the reason why I believe again."

Epilogue

New York City

Four Years after Silas and Tara's Youth Group Temple Tour

"It's a big week for you," Mom said, straightening Silas's tie before running a hand down his jacket. "Graduations, Tara signing with an agent at such a young age, your first showing—"

"Darling, don't forget his job opportunity," Mama said.

They stood in a large gallery with white walls and pale pine floors in Greenwich Village. The staff had just finished setting up the drinks and a small table of snacks. His mothers had gone all out to support him—they'd even taken a trip to Costco in the suburbs to stock up for the event. They'd also sent everyone they knew from their client portfolio the invitation.

"You guys are going to make me throw up," Silas said.

"Swallow, honey," Mama said. "There is a cleaning fee here."

Silas looked around at the simple framed photos on the walls. It was the collection he'd submitted as part of his entry into the *Global*

Conservators Magazine contest all those years ago. He hadn't won, but he'd made the finals, and that was better than he could've asked for.

He turned to make sure everything was in place before they opened the doors, and saw Tara standing in the corner, wearing a simple black dress and heels. A line formed between her eyebrows as she concentrated on her phone.

"Is she okay?" Mom asked softly.

"She will be," Silas replied. "Her sister can't come for her graduation because her parents are going to be there. I know her dad wants to see Savitri Didi again, but things are still tense with her mom."

"It'll take time," Mom said. "She's strong."

"Stronger than anyone I know."

The bells above the front door chimed. *Showtime,* he thought.

When the first person walked through the door, his jaw dropped. *"Amit?"*

"Wow, have you gotten shorter?"

The kid's crackling voice had been replaced with a deeper timbre. He'd shot up in height, towering at six feet now. Before Silas could cross the room to give him a hug, a group of people entered from behind him.

Silas's heart pounded.

Faruk.

Dax.

Ravi.

Beth.

Ina.

Gina.

Happy.

Chetna.

And Jhumpa.

"Oh my god!" Tara burst out, coming to Silas's side. She looked just as shocked as he felt. "Look at all of you!"

"Surprise!" Gina shouted.

They rushed at each other, hugging and shrieking with joy. Tara had tears in her eyes, as usual, and Silas had to wipe away one of his own.

"What are you all doing here?" Silas asked. He'd seen them on social media, growing into their own, and they'd exchanged happy-birthday messages and DMs of support throughout high school. Tara had even met up with Chetna at one point, and their picture had inspired a flood of comments from the group.

"We wanted to come and see your show before we all went off for college and did, like, senior-week stuff," Faruk said. "We almost all didn't make it."

Everyone looked at Dax. "What? I'm going to be a junior guide on the temple tour this year. I had to work around Chaya and Neil's schedule."

Silas wasn't surprised at all that Dax would choose to go back. Out of all of them, he was the one who was the most skeptical, and appeared to have changed the most.

"You're all so much taller than I remember," Tara said softly. "It's so good to see you. Want to come out to dinner with us after the show?"

They nodded, cheering together.

"But a place with chicken," Ravi added.

They all groaned. Ravi had been the biggest complainer when it came to the vegetarian meals on the trip.

Silas's heart felt full. He couldn't believe his family was together in one place. "Come on," he said, motioning to all of them. "Before more people show up. I want to show you something."

They moved en masse to the back of the gallery, where one of the largest pictures hung in the center of the wall. The picture included ten kids, Silas and Tara standing in the middle. It had been taken on their last day of the tour, at India Gate, during a miracle moment in the middle of the monsoons where the sky was clear and the morning rush hadn't yet begun. They'd leaned in together, supporting each other.

"This is my favorite one," he said quietly, dropping an arm around Tara's shoulders.

When he looked down at her shining eyes, he saw only love. They'd been together now for four years, and although it wasn't all easy, especially when they were going to school in two different states, they were now living together.

"Thanks," he said to her, then looked around at the group. "Thanks to all of you. For being there with me."

They stood quietly, remembering that day at India Gate together.

"I looked so good," Faruk said.

Everyone laughed.

ACKNOWLEDGMENTS

In the 1960s, Sushil Punj, my mother's father, left India and took trains through the Middle East into Europe in search of a better life. He eventually settled in Queens, New York, and brought his wife, Mohani Punj, and their three children over once he'd secured a job in the fashion district, where he worked until his retirement. He passed away in 2008 from complications caused by ALS. My grandmother lived almost a decade and a half longer and passed in 2022 while I was writing this book.

Their legacy connects to my father, who came to the US in 1983 after marrying my mother. My father's family is still located in India, with a few relatives venturing beyond the borders in recent years.

My siblings and I were all born and raised in the US.

I know I've said this about every book I've written, but this was the most difficult project yet because I had to explore my relationship to ancestry. There are themes about identity, about sharing your true self, and about being Desi in the diaspora in this book. Are we Indian enough? Are we too Indian? And are we selfish for even asking the question in the first place?

As a South Asian writer from the North, I know that I have to balance addressing my privilege with writing a story about bicultural experiences. Religion is often an area that highlights privileges, as well as discrimination. I wrestled with both of these as I sat down to write this book, but I knew this was a story that I wanted to tell as a part of my personal spiritual journey.

First and foremost, thank you to my parents, for giving me the tools throughout my life to be able to face these hard questions about who I am and what I want to believe.

I also have to thank my sensitivity readers. There were a lot. For those who helped me navigate queer representation in the diaspora, to those who helped with my "unlikeable" character. I appreciate all of you for your patience and support. Special shout-out to my uncle Vice Admiral Dinesh Prabhakar IN (Ret.), who was one of the best editors I've ever had. The research about landscape, the pilgrimage sites, and the local atmosphere came to life in my head because he was able to walk me through all of it.

For Joy Tutela. Thank you for being my agent all these years. Your support, mentorship, and partnership are part of the reason why I have this career in the first place. To Lauren McKellar for your incredible guidance and coaching.

To my editor at Skyscape, Carmen Johnson, for being so patient, kind, and supportive, as well as Larissa, Emma, Laura, and Phyllis for the incredible notes. Thank you to the entire Skyscape team for shepherding me through this new process of a reimagined publishing industry.

To Namrata Patel for being my writing-sprints partner in crime. From the 6:00 a.m. wake-up calls to the weekend at a random New Jersey Marriott where we were able to finish our stories together. Your friendship has been a gift.

To Smita Kurrumchand and Jordan Reiser, my best friends IRL, and my slew of adult-romance-writer friends with whom I text regularly. Thank you for inspiring me to be the best version of myself I can possibly be.

To my hubs, who supports, loves, and encourages me when I need it the most. I don't know what I did to deserve someone like you, but karma has truly blessed me in my lifetime because of your presence in it.

And thanks to the gods that I've grown to understand and to appreciate over the course of writing this book. I am doing what I love because of the opportunities I've been afforded in this life, and I feel eternally blessed. If you could all do me a solid and watch out for my grandma and grandpa for me, in whatever life they're living now, that would be great. Especially my grandmother, Mohani Punj. The grief from losing her is so fresh in my heart, and her encouragement has helped shape me into who I am today.

ABOUT THE AUTHOR

Photo © 2022 Marco Calerdon

Nisha Sharma is the author of critically acclaimed YA and adult contemporary romances including *My So-Called Bollywood Life*, *Radha & Jai's Recipe for Romance*, the Singh Family Trilogy, and *Dating Dr. Dil* in the If Shakespeare Was an Auntie series. Her writing has been praised by the *New York Times*, NPR, *Cosmopolitan*, *Teen Vogue*, *BuzzFeed*, *Entertainment Weekly*, and more. She lives in Pennsylvania with her Alaskan husband; her cat, Lizzie Bennett; and her dogs, Nancey Drew and Madeline. For more information, visit www.nisha-sharma.com.